it's already the m⬤rning ⬤f the last day

drago jančar ⬤ veronika simoniti ⬤
eva markun ⬤ boris kolar ⬤ maja novak
⬤ mirana likar ⬤ miha mazzini ⬤ jani
virk ⬤ andrej blatnik ⬤ suzana tratnik
⬤ mojca kumerdej ⬤ tomaž kosmač ⬤
tadej golob ⬤ desa muck ⬤ andrej e.
skubic ⬤ dušan čater ⬤ dušan šarotar
⬤ sebastijan pregelj ⬤ arjan pregl ⬤
polona glavan ⬤ agata tomažič ⬤ jedrt
maležič ⬤ sergej curanović ⬤ goran
vojnović ⬤ vesna lemaić ⬤ andraž
rožman ⬤ anja mugerli ⬤ nejc gazvoda
ana schnabl ⬤ vinko möderndorfer

COPYRIGHT © 2023 the respective authors
TRANSLATION COPYRIGHT © 2023
the respective translators
DESIGN & LAYOUT Nikša Eršek
PUBLISHED BY Sandorf Passage
South Portland, Maine, United States
IMPRINT OF Sandorf
Severinska 30, Zagreb, Croatia
sandorfpassage.org
PRINTED BY Znanje, Zagreb

Sandorf Passage books are available to the
trade through Independent Publishers Group:
ipgbook.com | (800) 888-4741.

Library of Congress Control Number:
2023941711

ISBN: 978-9-53351-470-3

Funded by the European Union. Views
and opinions expressed are however
those of the author(s) only and do not
necessarily reflect those of the European
Union or the European Education and
Culture Executive Agency (EACEA).
Neither the European Union nor EACEA
can be held responsible for them.

This book is published with financial
support by the Slovenian Book Agency.

Co-funded by
the European Union

SLOVENIAN
BOOK
AGENCY

it's already the morning of the last day

SAN-
DORF
PAS-
SAGE

SOUTH PORTLAND | MAINE

Contents

Drago Jančar

ULTIMA CREATURA

IF FRANC RUTAR hadn't stared into the enormous letters in the book the woman next to him was holding over her knees one hot, humid, long-ago afternoon, everything would have worked out much better for him. He would not have suffered those horrible things that, years later, when he thought back on them with a blend of agonizing discomfort and fear, seemed like they were in truth images from some terrible dream. From those moments between sleeping and waking. But he knew it wasn't a dream, even though it had all happened in a massive, faraway city, and even today its dreamlike images enter his life through television screens. In the midst of a humid, long-ago afternoon, he was dashing into the underworld, and the god he met there was dark and frightful.

Trade representative Franc Rutar was a voracious reader. Although he forever had numbers and letters dancing before his tired eyes, he couldn't help but devour every other word and letter that appeared in his field of vision. He was one of those people who, in a waiting room or on a bus, wherever, read from newspapers and books that did not belong to him. Those people can't help but peruse the back of a newspaper that's in someone else's hands. Many do this out of laziness and miserliness, some also out of conniving inclinations; reading over a shoulder because they know very well that it bothers the holder of the book, they always look away at just the right moment, and just when they're about to be caught in the act, they're already looking out the window or into their shoes. Some of these readers don't even realize that their eyes are actually feasting on someone else's property, letter by letter, like on parts of a woman's body, like on bread from a table. Though Franc Rutar could not complain of a lack of reading material beyond his work and regular reading, reading newspapers and books that were in the hands of others became his compulsive passion. As he read, he'd test the sharpness of his intellect, for Franc Rutar was a man of precise mind and impeccable memory. He'd instantly connect the dancing newspaper headlines and fragments he read on the bus into meaningful wholes. Sports coverage never got confused with political coverage — whoever has order in his head also understands the order of the world, of that there is no doubt. His greatest satisfaction arose whenever a crossword puzzle flashed before his eyes, for then the fleeting challenge and the risk gave him goose bumps. Here he was able to test the swift workings of his brain, which had expressed itself so effectively in risky publishing deals: swift considerations, swift decisions. His hasty calculations and word shuffling enabled him to solve a crossword puzzle before he reached the next station. By his own conviction, Franc Rutar was among the highest achievements of creation.

DRAGO JANČAR

He proved this already on his first day in New York, having traveled there with a work colleague. After a few hours in the big city, he'd mastered the mathematical intricacies of Manhattan's streets, no trickier than the average crossword. It was thanks to Franc that they swiftly concluded intricate foreign rights deals. On the third day, he felt right at home in this corporate anthill, and he basked in his friend's praise. That's how notable Franc Rutar's mental agility and drive were, and he had reasons aplenty to feel satisfied. Not even after the afternoon on the third day — it was a humid, ocean-moist afternoon — after he'd dined on cheap fried chicken at a fast-food restaurant. He'd sat contentedly on the subway as he traveled in the direction of Battery Park. He was in New York, business was concluded, his stomach was full; the world was at its peak and life was good. But when the world is at its peak, the deepest precipice looms nearest.

He glanced around to see if anyone had unfurled a newspaper. He would test his impeccable English in that risky game of connecting fragments into meaningful wholes by the time he reached the next station. Just as he was about to stand behind a man who was holding a folded newspaper in one hand and a dangling strap in the other, a better opportunity, one more suited to this opportune moment, presented itself. A beautiful Black girl sat down next to him, actually a woman, a girl and a woman at the same time. She opened a book over her knees and immersed herself in it. There was no need to crane his neck, no need to step behind anyone and look over his shoulder, here there was sumptuous reading fixed and spread out over her round dark knees. The letters were enormous and he could easily follow the book's plain English. It was almost too easy. But he'd just come from lunch, and his body was agreeably and idly awash with the greasy warmth of Kentucky Fried Chicken. So he gave himself up to the big letters, to the rocking train that was dashing into the dark underworld.

He suddenly felt excited and wholly alert. The text that rested on her bare knees, blithely chilled here in the subway in the midst of a steamy day up above, surprised him. Franc Rutar had never read anything like this, at least not on the subway: a young woman had just lain, on the book's verso page, in bed with an older man, a truly old man, as it soon turned out. The book was written in the first person. The narrator was a woman. She locked her apartment door behind them, undid the buttons on the old man's shirt, and by the top of the recto page she was leaning against his neck, feverishly and pleasurably inhaling his aged skin.

Franc Rutar was a stranger to frivolity, and the order of his reason resisted bodily temptations and contact with strangers. He avoided all those things some of his colleagues actively sought out on business trips. In Hamburg, he'd once eyed the women in the window, but he'd never dreamed of spending his hard-earned cash on them. Yet now, before he could come to his senses, a shivering fever that he had never known before swept over him. Was it the humidity, or was it merely the incomprehensible fact that a young woman, who was not yet a woman, was sitting next to him and reading such words? Even the sudden conclusion that he would not exit and his logical mind would not finish off the text, that he would read the thing above those knees, came automatically, not from his mind, but

DRAGO JANČAR

from some unfamiliar region of his brain and body. He raced to the next page where the irrational erotic event continued and where he could ascertain only that the girl in the book was either dazed, crazy, or cryptically in love. He waited impatiently for this slow reader to turn the page. He now had a few long moments to look at her. He watched her lips move. Moist red lips. He had missed his stop and still she hadn't turned the page. She was moving her knees. A naïve girl, he thought, sweetening her life with cheap, large-print novels. She probably works in one of those department stores, her fingers clumsily folding clothes all day long. He figured he'd get off now anyway. Then the round knees moved, she draped one leg over the other, turning the page at the same time. And at the same time, everything was happening simultaneously, her hot thigh pressed against his for so long and with such vigour that something stemming from his brain and sex struck him in the chest, shot into his heart, and something hollow collected above his stomach and refused to dissolve. The letters danced before his eyes.

He didn't get off. He heard the thundering of a train that was dashing somewhere underground. She raised the book and through veiled, dazed eyes he saw the fluorescent red cover with its expanse of cleavage, above it a broken necklace, crystal droplets of sweat or water. The book's title, which he read in a hundredth of second, was: *The World Is Full of Married Men*. Whatever was weighing on his heart gave way and whatever lay hollow above his stomach dissolved. He winced, and his brain circuits began working at computer speed; grating emerged from under his cranial vault from the sudden effort. This here, he realized, this here is a setup. This girl, continued his precise mind, is sitting on the subway solely for this purpose. The letters are so big that anyone can read them, there are bare, decadent knees under the book. And yet, the effort made his rasping brain ask: For what purpose? When it's done for money, it's done differently. Because, his quick brain answered, because this is exactly what the girl wants to experience. She's Black. Discrimination, frustrations. Where else could she find herself a businessman, an older man, actually an old man, if not on the subway? She might become his lover, for it is known that such a man, in most secret dreams, invites upon himself unpredictable events, young Black women. This reasonable explication made him once again pleased with himself, though no less excited; if a few minutes ago he'd been merely excited, and before that merely satisfied, now he was both excited and satisfied. An excited body, a satisfied mind. She'd sat down right next to him, him alone. True, he was already a little soft in the belly, and a monk's tonsure topped his head, but neither was all that obvious. Surely he was infinitely more interesting than that old man so alluringly described in the peculiar pages of the book on her knees. I'll get off, he decided, where she gets off, come what may. After all, he could travel back here in no time. He himself was surprised at his swift decision. If she asks for money, he thought, extending the thought into a consideration, we'll decide about that on the spot. He was satisfied with himself, this decision also stemmed from reason and from satisfaction, and a little bit from excitement.

Now the train was charging toward Brooklyn. We're traveling underwater, he thought, what an adventure, above, there's the huge dark mass of bridge we know from the movies, and he,

DRAGO JANČAR

Franc Rutar, is driving under it, and the Black girl is driving him crazy. He was looking at her knees, the hem of her skirt, his elbow was touching her ribs under her light blouse, his gaze now fixed on the dark skin traveling into her. Derma, his brain quickly offered, a five-letter crossword puzzle word for skin. What's wrong with me? he thought, where am I going?

She stood up and tidied her skirt. He followed right behind her to the doors. He tidied his tie and thought it would soon be undone, like in the pages of that book she was now clutching under a moist armpit. On the platform, she looked straight into his eyes, he felt it deeply. No, he was not mistaken. His heart was pounding. Now it's just a matter of working up the courage to talk to her. Without talk there'd be nothing. His mind was swiftly selecting the words. He would speak voraciously, slightly nasally, so as not to betray his Slavic accent. Her hips undulated before his eyes as they approached the light from the street, the ragged-fronted houses aboveground. He would speak loudly so the beating of his heart couldn't be heard. Before they reached the top, he found the right words. *Interesting book, no?* he said. *What?* she laughed with pearly white teeth. *What? The book,* he said, in a low and nasal voice. *Oh, the book,* she said, laughing loudly. He bounded youthfully up a few steps and now they were on the street. Again, he searched for the right words. He found them. *Can I buy you a coffee?* he said in an even lower voice. *Maybe I can buy you one,* she said, and he didn't know whether this was an invitation or a casually sneering rejection. If you've come this far, said his now-determined brain, then go all the way. Or it didn't say anything at all. Trade representative Franc Rutar was, on account of all the things that had now so unexpectedly come to pass in his life, perhaps without that brain that had so reliably aided him in closing deals and solving crossword puzzles. But he was definitely without eyes. Because if he had eyes, he would have seen himself stalking a young girl down some desperately desolate New York street, jumping over piles of trash and sidestepping bodies lying on the sidewalk. Between the people who were sitting on some stairs, between their faces, he rushed after her, constantly after her alone, through a door into a dark hallway. From here, new stairs led somewhere far up, narrowing wooden walls on either side. Through the narrow corridor, up the steep stairs, he walked right behind her, eyeless with the scent of her tawny derma in his nostrils, sweat pouring down from his tonsure, dripping from his forehead and crawling under his shirt, the smell of decaying wood covered in parts with peeling wallpaper.

At the top she opened a door, then another one. They now found themselves in a small room. From the street they heard children's cries and the drawn-out calls of residents from balconies and windows, also a wild musical cacophony from various directions. In the corner, in the semidarkness, there was a tattered couch with a metal spring sticking out of it. He loosened his tie, though he was still expecting that she would do that for him, before unbuttoning his shirt, just like in the book. Sweat poured down his face, his heart was now pounding madly, also from racing up the steep stairs. From the corner of his brain, not the one where his swift and precise thoughts sprang, but from the one where the hunch rested, something spoke. He couldn't make out what, it did not flow around the corner, it did not emerge. Even if that had happened, if he had discerned what it was that had said something and what it had said, it would have been too late.

The girl sat on the couch in a darkened part of the room, stared vacantly off into the wall, opened her mouth, and screamed. He looked in amazement at the contorted face of that creature sitting there, and could not understand why, why she was seated and why she was screaming, he thought that he should somehow plug the open mouth cavity the high, monotonous scream was coming from. *Sorry*, he said, *there's been a mistake*, he said, *sorry*. I'll hit her, he thought, why is she screaming, I didn't do anything to her, I'll hit her, he thought.

She didn't scream for long, and actually it wasn't even all that loud. The door opened immediately. A young man entered, a thick gold chain around his neck. Nonchalantly he chewed. *What's going on here?* he said, mumbling the sentence rather indistinctly. This surely meant what Franc Rutar had already understood: this is her protector. *He tried to rape me*, the girl said, as if she were saying, *it's four in the afternoon*. The chewing man looked at him accusingly and astonished. *Who?* he asked. She pointed her finger at Franc Rutar.

Now Franc's brain finally understood what was emerging from that impenetrable hallucinatory region. He'd been trapped. He realized he was a stupid, satisfied man, whose brain does stupid things to him and according to stupid instincts, and in fact all of a sudden he couldn't understand how it was he ended up here. *I just happened to be...*, he said. It didn't sound convincing. A cold sweat poured over him and he felt a sort of emptiness spreading over his head, something completely indeterminate, something blank. *Sorry*, he said, *Sorry*, and took a step toward the door. The young man leaned against it. Of course he couldn't just leave. If you get stopped by hooligans on the street, his memory whispered, have ten dollars ready in your pocket. Hand it over immediately, don't say a word. He reached into the breast pocket of his jacket and, relieved, felt the bill was there. Franc Rutar was a fastidious man, he was prepared for anything, including being stopped by hooligans on the street. But this was no street. This was some out-of-the-way apartment, in some out-of-the-way part of the city, the way out of this dismal dump was blocked by the young man who chewed and who jingled the chain on his neck. He didn't even look at the banknote, he opened the door and called someone. In an instant, two others, who were obviously waiting right there, entered. One of them now took up a position at the door, the other, a tall and trim middle-aged man, strolled around the room. He was wearing a white linen jacket, and he exchanged a few sentences with the girl who was still sitting next to the protruding spring, speaking Spanish. Then he turned to Franc Rutar, who was following the man's movements and speech with hopeful eyes. He said they were going to call the police. *Yes*, gulped the trade representative, *yes, the police*. They fell silent, the young man and the tall man exchanged a long look. *No*, said Franc Rutar, *there's no need to do that. Mister*, said the young man with the chain, *Mister, your tie's undone*. The young man lifted Franc Rutar's chin and tied his tie so hard he choked. This makes no sense, Franc Rutar thought, no sense at all. The tall one offered him a seat next to the girl. He collapsed and looked fixedly at the floor. The tall man walked around the room and asked the girl something, she answered with shrieking, argumentative screams, the

DRAGO JANČAR

loathsome screams of the imagined girl with the chocolate derma. Even the mumbling young man joined in the conversation, and only the third one, the one standing by the door, remained silent. Geez, thought the trade representative, they're fighting over the prey. He had to stand against the wall and raise his arms so they could search him. Because there was no table, he had to empty his pockets onto the floor. The young man with the chain suddenly became very upset. There was no wallet among the surrendered items. He shouted something indistinct, twirled around as if he were dancing and slapped Franc on the neck with a half-open palm. Franc collapsed to the floor and immediately handed over his wallet. The man in the white jacket asked him something. He didn't understand, he didn't know how to respond. He grabbed Franc by the hair and shook his bent head, breathing his sweet breath into him. He wasn't able to, he couldn't, he didn't know what all this was. *My dear mother*, he murmured to himself, *oh Mother, what is happening to little Franc?* The girl opened his briefcase and dumped the contents on the couch. With clawlike movements she scratched among his papers, and put his calculator and glasses between the covers of that red book, the tall man took the briefcase. This is fearsome, he thought, fearsome, if his wife only knew what was happening to little Franc, so far from home, and he thought of everyone he loved who was so far away. But what had happened so far was nothing compared to the horror that was to come.

He had to strip. He lay his clothes on the couch. The third man, the one who'd been standing silently by the door the whole time, pulled a switchblade from his pocket, sprung it, and placed the blade against Franc's neck. Then he moved down to his sex. He's going to cut it off, thought Franc Rutar, and put it in my mouth. The girl groped frantically at his clothes. They pushed him around the room and shouted something to each other. Her screams went through his ears, through his eardrums, and pierced the soft tissue of the brain. Someone was turning up the volume on a big transistor radio, someone was drinking from a can and pouring beer over him. The noise was unbearable. Then it was quiet in the room for a moment, and through the misty veil he saw the tall dark man in the jacket approaching. He came very close and breathed very quietly in his ear, making Franc's head ring hollowly from the breath and the words. *I am your god,* he said, *do you understand?* Little Franc nodded. *Repeat after me,* he said. *What am I? God,* Franc Rutar said, *my god. Your great god,* said the tall man, his head almost touched the ceiling when he straightened up. Little Franc was lying on the floor, the small head of the great god was high above. *My great god,* he said as loudly as he could. He heard his voice lost in the empty space, echoing back as if he were speaking in a great hall.

He had to lie on the floor and put his hands over the back of his neck. They were walking around and again they were speaking loudly. They stumbled over him, someone sat on him for a moment. Now he will. . . he thought. . . a knife. Or. . . a blow to the head. He pictured his body floating under the Brooklyn Bridge, the shadow of the giant bridge above him, below him, water, the thundering subway. He remembered a prayer he once knew and began to move his quivering lips that were pressed against the dirty wooden floor. *Our Father, who art in heaven. . .* The infernal noise was far away, all sorts of different music was coming from the courtyards and balconies. Darkness fell over his eyes, sounds and words, screams and slamming doors, all mixed together. The body became numb and dark shadows danced around him. He shrank into a boy being put into a cauldron, then bandied about. Now they're going to cut me open, thought the boy in bed dreaming all this, and they're going to put me in that cauldron, that big pot Mother used for making jam. Then he knew that he was asleep and that he could see his white body floating under the bridge, in its great shadow. His belly was a little bloated, the distant noise of the city engulfed him. The noise changed into a sharp, hissing sound. Steam hissed from a pipe. Now he again heard Spanish words from off in the distance and, then, was that Latin the big dark guy in the white jacket was speaking? Two words he could understand, could make out quite distinctly; from a crossword puzzle, said his brain, which was obviously still at work, from a difficult crossword puzzle. *Ultima creatura*, he said. Ultima creatura. He hurriedly wrote the letters in the squares, his inner gaze saw the boxes and the words written in them. Do these dark gods speak Latin? he thought in amazement. There is some logic to this, he thought, the gods speak Latin, is that what the dark god is telling me?

Then for a long time he heard only the hissing of steam, which came to his awakening consciousness at the same time as distant calls from the street, perhaps from the balconies of neighboring buildings. He opened his eyes. It was dark in the room, a beam from a streetlight fell askew over his pale body. Only now did he see that there were no panes in the window in this empty apartment that stank of dampness, peeling wallpaper, decaying wood. All his senses were working: smell, sight, hearing, even the ailing body. There were holes in the floor, his suit was lying crumpled on the floor, in the corner a white, squalid pile, a shirt, his shirt. His tie was dangling from the spring that was sticking out of the ruptured couch. He got dressed. Through the darkness he groped his way down the steep stairs of the empty house.

He got back to the hotel near morning. He didn't tell anyone what had happened to little Franc. When his friend knocked on the door, he told him he'd been mugged in the park. He didn't think he'd have to explain that. As his friend stared in amazement at him through the open door, at the deep scar stretching from ear to mouth, Franc closed himself into his room and lay down on the bed. Nothing to explain. Nothing to be said. There was no need to think either. He didn't leave the hotel room until it was time to go home. He was lying on the bed and looking longingly at the plane ticket and passport, which, in accordance with the advice from his homeland, remained locked in the hotel safe. Trade representative Franc Rutar was a caring and reasonable man. At least some cause for satisfaction remained.

Many years later, he dreamed of how they'd put him in that big cauldron Mother used for making jam. He swam in the shadow of the great bridge, his belly white and bloated. In the empty space, a great dark god was bending over him and breathing terrible, unfamiliar words into his ear. Whenever the outline of an enormous city or bridge appeared on the television screen, he'd turn off the television and that would start a quarrel with his wife, who couldn't understand him. And he'd always have his way, for he could not bear any humiliation. He avoided young Black

DRAGO JANČAR

women from department stores. Fortunately, there weren't many in his homeland. He never read over anyone's shoulder again, never picked up a crossword puzzle.

One winter's night a few years after that trip to New York, outside the fence of his suburban house, he punched and dropped a drunken bum who'd asked him for some change. *Creatura*, he shrieked, *Creatura*, and kicked at the rasping lump on the ground. He found himself in the crime section of the local newspaper, where, considerately, only his initials were written: F. R. That was all, nothing else happened to him, except for those things that happen to all of us.

Translated by JASON BLAKE

Originally published in the short stories collection
Pogled angela (*Mihelač*, 1992)
First English translation appeared in
The Day Tito Died: Contemporary Slovenian Short Stories;
translated by LILI POTPARA, ANNE ČEH, TAMARA SOBAN, and
KRIŠTOF KOZAK (*Forest Books*, 1993)

Desa Muck

TEENAGERS

NEVER AGAIN

NEVER AGAIN DO I wish to be younger than sixty-five. Ever. And I especially never want to be younger than thirty, or even twenty, god forbid, fifteen. Anything under sixty or seventy is nothing but a mess, an entanglement of euphoria, unfounded confidence or baseless complexes, hormones, obsession, illusions, and all the other shit.

Thus, more or less at peace with myself, soon after my sixty-fifth birthday, which seemed a little like a competition with the other guests in bingeing spritzer and champagne, followed by severe alcohol poisoning, I moved to a small house in the rolling hills of the remotest part of the country where I wished to spend the rest of my life in peace and quiet, occasionally joined by an old friend, simply so I wouldn't become entirely asocial or lose my communication skills, for, truth be told, I would not particularly miss anyone at all. I am fed up with everybody. Fed up with human voices, faces, their needs, and all the energies they bring along with them. You see, soon after my birthday, I retired from my job as a TV executive producer. It's a position in which you have to deal with a million people a day, and crush just as many. They eat you alive. I swear. But from now on... I imagined how I would wake up in the morning and go out onto the terrace with my dog Sunshine. Take my time to drink coffee in peace, looking across the gentle landscape, slightly misty, as in romantic paintings. I look forward to how beautiful it will be in the autumn, and lighting the woodstove when the snow starts falling outside. The pleasure of solitude in such moments is indescribable. But then that all fell through. Enter into my life one of the most selfish and cruel beings in the world. A teenager.

Although I had made sure the house was secluded and the nearest neighbor lived about half a kilometer away, she appeared under my terrace on the very first day I finally moved in and began realizing my retirement dream of zen coffee drinking. She came with a dog. An untrained, huge dog without its leash, which came galloping, just like that, onto the terrace, jumping all over Sunshine, my small, shy, old schnauzer, trying to convince him to play. It was the last Sunday in May. Her name was Mina.

HOW TO CREATE THE IMPRESSION YOU ARE ROLLING IN MONEY

I tried very hard to let her know that I wanted nothing to do with her or her dog, staring at the newspaper without saying anything or even so much as glancing at her. This doesn't bother her, of course. She picks up a magazine, starts flicking through it.

"Wow!" she says. "Look at this ad for the new iPhone. It can do anything. It probably even makes you lunch. I'd love one. No chance, though. My parents don't buy me anything. I have to spend a thousand hours tidying my room and taking out the garbage, just to get the tiniest of things. This chewed pencil, for example." She sighs.

"Do you have any kids?" she asks. I know I shouldn't open my mouth but almost automatically I shake my head. Unfortunately, because she takes this as an invitation for relentless chat.

"Sensible. I'm not planning to have any either. They are annoying. But, if I ever happened to have any," she says, leaning toward me confidentially, "apparently it can sometimes happen by accident. . . I will certainly buy them anything they ask for! Parents just don't realize what emotional stress they cause their children by not providing the essential conditions for survival!"

I glance at her. Secretly. She looks well-fed, suitably attired, has a dog, the latest mobile phone sticking out of her pocket, has a modern haircut and, sure enough, too much makeup.

"My parents want to totally crush and dishearten me," she goes on. "At school we talk about where we will all go for the holidays. Some will go to the Caribbean, others to the Seychelles, some on an English language course in London or New York. I'm the only one who stays silent or quietly admits that we don't know yet. What can I say? Tell them that we will go, as we do every year, to stay in that stupid caravan down on the island of Pag?"

I finally open my mouth. "Why don't you lie too?"

"But they aren't lying! I have seen with these very eyes! We're talking about people where every member of the family has their own computer, and their own TV in their own room, and don't wear smelly trainers that are cheaper than one hundred and fifty euros! Now you tell me how I am supposed to grow up into a self-confident person, someone with a sense of self-worth?"

At the tip of my tongue I have a sermon about children who won't even go to Pag, about children whose parents can't afford to buy them a bike, a doll, not even schoolbooks and food, who spend their entire childhood walking around in secondhand charity clothes, and these children live very close by. Then I remembered how, as a child, I had been told about poor kids in Africa dying of hunger, but it all seemed unreal or as if they were living on another planet. And if I happened to be shown pictures of skeletal children with bloated tummies, I was really shocked and full of philanthropy for a day or so, trying not to put a ton of salami onto my slice of bread but just three or four slices instead. The following day I already felt sorry for myself, upset that someone had a pair of Italian jeans on their bum whereas mine were from the local department store.

"And then people wonder," Mina purrs along, "why so many young people turn to drugs and alcohol, why there are so many suicides, so much crime. They say kids these days are despondent, without values or goals. Of course we are without goals, when they make them impossible. Do you know of any better goal than the Seychelles?"

This time I have to say something. I even manage a short lecture about how life isn't that simple and how the worthiest goals are those you fight for, not those that are given to you. Then you know how to appreciate them.

"So you think I'm not fighting for the Seychelles? I whine about it every day, sulk, pester my parents till I drop. Do you know how much effort this takes, how much nerve? If I ever succeed, this will be a bloody victory and you certainly don't have to worry about me not appreciating it. But it all falls on deaf ears! They keep saying we don't have the money. They could at least think of something a little more original."

I suggest that perhaps they might really not have it; it is not easy to support a family these days. And that there is no greater pain for parents who struggle making a living than not being able to satisfy their children's wishes, and that, after all, they too might have preferred to go to the Seychelles rather than spend their holiday in the trade union caravan. So she should come to terms with this.

"I don't even know why they exist in this world if they cope so badly, and then even decide to have some wretched children. I won't have mine until I am as rich as Bill Gates!" She sighs in disappointment. "Okay, perhaps I will go to that island, after all. But it's the last time!"

I didn't have to lecture her on how money isn't everything and how soon she indeed will not be going to Pag with her parents, not because they will suddenly become infinitely rich but because a period called childhood was coming to an end. She wouldn't know what I was talking about anyhow. Even now she seems to believe she is the only person in the world, besides a few pop stars.

The following day I was out walking Sunshine and I met an old lady carrying a basket full of clover for her rabbits. "Good morning," she said and lingered as if there was something else she wanted to tell me. "I saw that girl at your place, Mina Koprivc. Did you know, she told me they were going on a holiday to Nicaragua. Goodness me, where on earth is Nicaragua?"

To be honest, I wasn't quite sure myself either. So I told her not to worry about the geography. Next year they will have a holiday in space. With Bill Gates.

HOW TO SURVIVE TO THE END OF THE SCHOOL YEAR AND STAY SANE

Let me make one thing clear straightaway. That during the process of schooling it is not only the child who suffers but everyone participating. Including the teachers, the parents, and sometimes other relatives who think they need to interfere. What they have in common is one thing: each of them thinks that they are the ones who bear the brunt of this suffering.

Mina didn't appear for about ten days, then all of a sudden, without even knocking, of course, she turned up in my kitchen and sat herself down across two chairs — in those ten days she had grown about eight centimeters — sighed loudly and fired away.

"Can I move in with you?"

It was as if the question was being uttered by a skunk, an anaconda, and a swarm of mosquitoes all in one.

"There is no way I can stay at home. Not even a minute! My life is in serious danger. I got an F in chemistry and they are subjecting me to ethnic cleansing. I cannot go anywhere until I improve my marks, I am not allowed to watch TV, I can only speak on the phone for an hour…My food portions are smaller than they were before. It is as if I am some circus animal from the last century!"

I am certain that the part about the food wasn't true, for it would have shown.

"All your parents are trying to do is make sure you don't have to sit a retake," I explain.

"What has my retake got to do with *you*? It's my retake. Mine! This is *my* life and *I* decide whether I will have a retake or not. In fact, I *want* to have a retake, I have never had one before, and I think that it will be an important and precious experience for me. They have no right to deny me that."

She speaks with determination while Sunshine hypocritically licks her hand instead of biting off a piece of her finger. I carefully explain that she cannot live with me. I lie that I am having a friend and her family come to stay for the summer. Let her parents explain how life can be just as rich and interesting without the experience of an exam retake.

"The worst thing is that they are deliberately working on making me grow up with a sense of guilt. Mother walks around droopy shouldered, sighing sadly, looking at me like a caged bear whose cub has been locked up at the far end of the zoo. Her face says: although you have ruined my life and your grade in chemistry will cause me to fall ill and die thirty years early, you are still my child, such is my fate. Father, too, holds the paper in a more accusing way, turning the pages as if to say: So I will have to give up on the idea of a new car, clearly I will have to go on paying for your schooling until I am seventy. When he comes home from work and takes off his shoes, his demeanor clearly tells me: We've all gotten used to the idea that we will have our summer ruined by your retake. And do you know what the worst thing is? That they are bringing me up as a typical Slovene example of a guilty conscience that anyone can push around." Mina stands up and hits her head on the kitchen light. "I won't have this! I will make sure I have that retake on purpose!"

And she rushes off.

Sunshine observes me with eyes full of love and loyalty.

"Darling, you won't ever have a retake in chemistry, will you?"

He wags his tail. I stroke him, telling him, "Here boy... you'll never make me have a guilty conscience, will you? That spoiled brat won't lecture us adults on guilt. It's not as if we don't have one, but at least we don't brag about it."

Friends who have kids tell me that at this time of year when they are trying to improve their bad marks, it all reaches proportions beyond the boundaries of reason. God knows how often her mother remembers these days that in her tiredness she watched some soap on the telly instead of checking whether Mina knows her periodic table and how often she allowed her to go out instead of making her study, just to have the chance of some peace to chat with her friend. And her father is probably prepared to eat the ton of newspapers he read through during the year and recycle it in his own body for not being more demanding when there was still a chance. Later, in the shop, I meet an acquaintance of mine who is a math teacher. She looks very gloomy.

"I have no choice but to fail two of my pupils this year," she tells me on the verge of tears. "I don't know what I've done wrong. Perhaps it would be better if I went to work in a bank."

She is an excellent teacher. Only in these most difficult days just before the end of the school year, she has forgotten life's rule number one: All shall pass. Apart from guilt. Guilt you have to kick out of your system yourself.

To my horror, the other day Mina brought along a friend. Cvetka. Even Sunshine sensed my reaction and began barking, which he very rarely does.

"Basically, I think you're quite clever, for an oldie," Mina began. It did occur to me that this was probably because I mostly stay silent during her lectures, hoping she will get bored and leave.

"We've come for some advice," she said. "Cvetka's boyfriend is cheating on her, publicly, for all the school to see."

"Well, he might not be... had Mina not told me about it," Cvetka chirped.

"Hush. We all saw them talking on the playground stands, I saw them with my very own eyes, exchanging phone numbers," Mina growled. "Had it been Milenca from our class who looks like a forgotten sack of sprouting potatoes and who flogs herself with a willow cane every time she gets an A minus, I wouldn't have batted an eye, but Mici going after your Marjan is an alarm of the highest level."

I found out all about how Mici is the most dangerous vixen in the entire school, walking around in jeans and tops so tight she probably needs to chisel them off when she gets undressed. Might I comment that I have never seen jeans as tight as the ones Mina wears, ever, on anyone! Then Cvetka confessed how she and Marjan have been going out together for three months, which is for eighth grade almost like reaching your silver wedding anniversary — and that they also have couple status on Facebook. This makes them practically married. When she gave me the same look that Sunshine gives me as he waits by my feet during lunch, I finally spoke.

"I think you need to trust your partner and that this is the basis for every good relationship. You could, of course, talk to him and tell him your fears." I told her what I had read in manuals. Were I to share with her my personal experiences, the girl would stay single all her life, as I have done. Not that anything is wrong with that.

"Are you nuts? We could have got this kind of stupid advice from my mother!" Mina is upset. "Every girl knows from the time we go to kindergarten that you cannot trust a man. No man! Can you trust a bird on a branch not to fly away, or a dog not to bark? It's their instinct and they can't help it. Every normal woman comes to realize this very early on. If Cvetka were to talk to him about Mici, it would be like alerting him to her as a woman, if she hasn't already done so herself. He might even feel sorry for her! You know how men can turn all compassionate and protective with women in tight tops."

"Dressing provocatively doesn't mean she has any insidious intentions," I blurted without thinking.

"Sure! And she exposes her navel so it can collect pollen that she selflessly donates to the exhausted bees, and her cleavage encourages ignorant Slovene mothers to breastfeed. No thank you! We can do without your advice. Come along, Cvetka, let's attack. Plan A!"

Two days later, when she once again dragged Cvetka along, this time with a scratched nose, I found out what Plan A was and how it had turned out.

They waited for Mici in the school corridor.

"She was wearing a miniskirt up to her chin. I said to her, I didn't know you could get such bad cellulitis at the age of thirteen," said Mina proudly. "Then I asked her whether she isn't ashamed of going for guys who are taken. She said that wasn't true, that she had a serious relationship. As if that's an obstacle for chicks like her. Then she said we were jealous of her and that we should mind our own business. Imagine!"

"And then?"

"I told Cvetka to stand up for herself and hit her."

All that I could find out about the fight that ensued was Cvetka made it very clear that she would not give in that easily. Then they informed me it was now time for Plan B, which included a few strategic moves. Cvetka would walk past Marjan, arm in arm with Mina's cousin, whom they had bribed with a video game. She would totally ignore Marjan, pretend not to know him. Then she will have a bunch of flowers sent to herself, receive them in Marjan's presence, and Mina will spread the rumor that her cousin was very serious about Cvetka, even having mentioned marriage.

"It worked," they excitedly came to tell me the following day. "Marjan was livid!"

"He said he would kill me if he saw me with that guy again! That means he's a hundred percent in love with me," Cvetka said proudly.

"See what guys are like! They can be jealous but we're not allowed to be," Mina huffed.

"Jealousy is a natural emotion." I launched my knowledge gained from the endless relationship manuals I have read at various phases of my frequent unhappy loves. "Nature has programmed us this way so that we reserve for ourselves the male or female partner that our genes consider suitable for breeding. As civilized beings, we are capable and also have to control emotions that lead to aggression."

"You go off to control your emotions and go stick them into your herbarium. I am now going straight to the playground where Marjan and my guy have a match. And if Mici will be there, I will — Plan C — attack her with a lawn mower!"

And off they went. Just as well that Marjan doesn't know anything about these plans.

HOW TO TRICK FAT CELLS

The other day I went as low as offering Mina a piece of freshly baked cherry pie and hiding the rest of it from her, because I was certain that she would not leave before she had polished off the entire tray. But she refused it.

"No thanks. I'm on a diet," she groaned.

It was supposed to sound determined but her eyes were glued to the shiny glaze on the crust like the eyes of a pilgrim upon the image of Holy Mary at Brezje. Sitting beside her was Sunshine with exactly the same gaze. I took a critical look at her healthy teenage body, which had already begun sprouting interesting curves where one would expect it to, but this was all that differentiated it from the body of a young athlete.

I thought to myself, Great, look what we've come to — even kids go on diets. I was about to begin a "when-we-were-young" lecture that was to be followed by one about the pressures and psychological tricks of the media and consumer society, going so far as to force a stereotypical skinny image upon children, but then I remembered this kind of hysteria had also existed when I was young, and that it is clearly some kind of historical ploy. Even in my days, school friends with a slightly more padded out backside were subject to at least mockery, not to mention other cruelty, and the first time we gave in to the concept of dieting was in the sixth or seventh grade. I recall a summer holiday when I was thirteen, during which I spent time on the beach sweating in my grandmother's thick bathrobe that I didn't take off even with the threat of the most terrible of deaths. All of this because, based on fashion trends of the day, I believed myself to be fat, which at that age I wasn't, yet. And these trends don't seem to have changed at all today.

"But you're not fat. Quite the opposite," I said.

"What do you mean?" Mina squawked and started pinching herself around her waist and thighs. "What is this then?"

"Skin."

"What skin? These are sneaky fat cells. In this last week I have been dieting I have realized that these are no ordinary cells, that they have a mind of their own, and that they are as cunning as the devil himself. They will do anything to attract food into the body. They will send your brain images of piles of delicious ice cream, for example, and you look at apples and yogurt as if they are some foul lubricant for door hinges and, just when you think you have figured out all their tricks, you realize they are even capable of converting water into fat. I don't know how it is possible, but in this entire week I haven't lost a single gram! How can you fight such an enemy?" She looked really desperate.

"Perhaps one idea is to attack them with their own weapon," I suggested. "Your fat cells must never catch you dieting. You just mustn't think about it at all. You need to keep telling yourself that this doesn't concern you at all and that dieting is only for neurotic people obsessed with their appearance. Of course you need to eat healthily because that's essential for your body, for you, and, especially in puberty, for your skin. Your fat cells, unsuspecting, will give up their fight, thinking they have won, and you will end up being the weight that is just right for you, and also maintain it."

"Oh, right, look who's talking. What about writing a manual on dieting and putting yourself on the cover," she sputtered with contempt. Her gaze was saying without doubt that she has counted all my 80,000,000 fat cells and calculated my precise fat index, knowing very well that I am 34.18 kilos overweight.

"I'd rather go running till I drop dead of exertion and starvation," she said and rushed off.

"How clever," I shouted after her.

It was the first time I felt sorry for her. This was how it had started with me. A roller coaster of dieting and overindulgence. With this, childhood comes to an irrevocable end.

HOW TO TURN PARENTS INTO DEADBEATS

"Lucky Lili, her parents are never at home, and when they are, they don't have time for her," Mina said with a sigh, standing idly behind my back as I was sweating like a Turkish baklava, madly fighting the weeds in my garden while Sunshine chased after a fly.

"The girl really is lucky," she continued despite my persistent silence.

Whenever I am tackling weeds, I need complete peace and concentration.

"Imagine — total freedom. She can do what she wants, nobody controls her, she is left alone, nobody bothers her, and, on top of all this, her parents spend the time they are not at home earning money, so they can buy her absolutely anything she wants. That's really the primary and only duty of any parent, ensuring their child has all they need. That's the life! Every week some new clothes, shoes, concert tickets, a new bike every year, and at least fifty euros in your pocket every day, so you can buy stuff when you need it."

"Perhaps her parents are simply trying to redeem themselves for not having the time for her and have a guilty conscience," I finally utter, instantly knowing I shouldn't have opened my mouth.

"Bullshit. How can you have a guilty conscience if you buy your child a two-thousand-euro dress for the prom? If my parents did that for me they could kick me with hobnailed boots for the rest of their lives without any guilty conscience whatsoever. And, if on top of this they would be away from home most of the time, I would go and build them a shrine right now. Talking about guilty conscience, my parents must have so much of it they could stack it in the cellar and in the attic. Why else would they bother with me all the time, control me, and keep asking me whether everything was all right, insisting on the hassle called a parent-to-child heart-to-heart talk? If they were confident about themselves and their methods of raising me, they would peek into my room once a week, check that I was still living there, and ask me how much money I needed. That is what modern and effective parents are. Not mine though, they're sentimental fossils. As if that's not enough, they also constantly impose their guilty conscience on me. They keep telling me how much they love me, that they care for me, and that they stand by me. It's emotional blackmail one finds hard to resist, and for a teenager, the only natural response is rebellion. The way you feel when you pull off something stupid is at my age as natural as breathing. I am afraid I might be growing up into a nervous wreck."

There is absolutely no way Mina reminds me of a nervous wreck. She calmly nibbles on my baby carrots, without any guilty conscience whatsoever, and ponders on without a care in the world. She pulls herself out one of my young kohlrabi and continues with excitement.

"On top of all that, lucky Lili can afford everything we, the oppressed slaves, cannot even think about. She drinks, smokes, organizes parties, keeps changing boyfriends, apparently she already takes contraceptives, in eighth grade. Her parents don't have a clue about all this, but it is what all modern, enlightened, democratic parents should be like. Did you not want your parents to be like that?" she asks me.

In fact, that was indeed what I had wanted them to be like, but there is no way I would ever admit to that now because I am today very happy indeed that there had been people in my childhood who gave me a sense of security by showing me that they were not indifferent. Also by occasionally not allowing me a few things. I could trust them because when they threatened me with something, they also followed it up.

Before she leaves, Mina says, "Only yesterday this idiot Lili said to me when I told her I couldn't come to a party because I was going on an outing with my parents: Lucky you! Some people don't realize just how lucky they are. I think all those new shoes must have gotten to her."

She pulls out another carrot, wipes it against her jeans, and bites into it with her healthy teeth. She breaks off a piece and throws it to Sunshine, who eats everything he is given. As a result of this habit of his, all the local vets know us well and are always happy to see us. "So what has Sunshine eaten this time? Surely not another miniature ballerina figurine?"

"Well, I'll be off then," says Mina. "I won't be back for a month because we are going off to the seaside and then I will spend a couple of weeks with my grandmother in Ljubljana. I am really looking forward to it."

And I am sure Ljubljana is looking forward to Mina.

As she disappears, a deep silence falls across the hills and it seems as if dozens of rainbows appear in the sky. I am happy. This is bliss. A month of peace and quiet awaits. . . . And then a slight unease. What will I do now? Perhaps I should even switch on the telly? And what, pray, is this thing I can feel creeping around my heart? Surely I can't be missing her? No, no, no way, it must be something to do with my digestion again.

Translated by GREGOR TIMOTHY ČEH

Vinko Möderndorfer

THE LAST MOVIE SHOW

AS YOU ARE DYING, *life, your life, flashes before your eyes like a film.*
Where have I heard that before? I think my grandmother told
me, a long, long time ago. I spent my childhood with her. She
was the one who raised me. She was kind. Spiteful sometimes.
It depended. She drank. If she was just drunk enough, she was
kind, if she had had too much, I hid under the bed and she would
poke around in the dark with a long wooden broom handle to
try and winkle me out. I would squeeze against the wall at the
far side of the bed, watching the rounded stick prodding almost
right up to my face. Then she usually lay there on the carpet,
groaning. From under the bed I could see her lace petticoat,
sometimes also her thick long knickers that reached down to
her knees. I recall the neighbors calling the doctor a number of
times. Especially when she collapsed halfway up the stairs, or
on the doorstep, or even in the yard. She appeared to be dead.
She wasn't. She had merely fainted. A drunken stupor. She was
taken to the hospital. When she returned, she would say, *I saw a*

film. My film. From the beginning. When I was still a child, and right up until now. It was in color. The entire film. And then they woke me up, dammit! "Dammit" was her worst swear word. She might have been a drunk but she was still a lady. Descended from an old bourgeois family. A family that used to own a button factory and a large apartment in the center of town, and a house in the countryside. Even when she was flat out on the pavement, her legs sticking out into the road, her head leaning against the wall of the house, she always lay there with a certain dignity, hat on her head, leather handbag under her arm. And although you could smell from afar the egg liqueur on her breath, washed down with beer and then red wine, she, despite the signs of extreme inebriation, quietly groaned, clutching her chest, *My heart! My heart! Help me, I have a weak heart!* The neighbors of course didn't believe her but they helped her to her feet and sometimes, if things were really bad, also called an ambulance. As the medics were getting her into their van, quietly laughing at the old drunk with an aristocratic posture, the neighbors, either out of respect to the family or simply because they felt sorry for me, standing there as a six-year-old, eyes filled with tears, would defend her, *No, no, you're wrong, the lady really does have a weak heart!*

My mother wasn't there. She had left. She sometimes returned. Occasionally. She studied. Sometimes she brought along one of her male classmates and they would go to her room and study together. Grandma would walk nervously up and down the large living room, clutching her chest. Whenever Mother came to visit, she always left with a piece of the furnishings, an ancient rug, pieces of old and precious cutlery. Sometimes Mother stayed home for a whole week, even a month. This was usually when she broke up with one of her student friends. When she did, she would argue with Grandma all the time, they shouted at each other, pulling me each to their side, until they became hoarse, and despite losing their voices they continued to wheeze at each other. When this happened, Mother would usually grab me by the hand and take me to the local cinema: Cine Home.

We would sit on the creaky wooden chairs in the half-empty theater that smelled of wood polish and a strange, rancid smell of army uniforms. The cinema was frequented mostly by soldiers from the nearby barracks and the smell that wafted from their uniforms was heavy, greasy, the scent of an unknown machine, mixed with the smell of their young bodies. All this mixed with the stench of saliva and roasted pumpkin seeds that the boys spat out onto the floor under the dark, worm-ridden seats. And sometimes, if Mother had the money, the auditorium also smelled of fruit jellies of different colors and different tastes.

So we watched films. A man with a black hat, a man with a white hat, a gringo with a golden pistol and a black stud, wide rivers they waded through on horseback, a duel at twelve noon precisely, Indians attacking the mail coach, the friendship between the Indian chief and the white cowboy, sacrifices, friendships, unrequited love, sunsets, good defeating evil. All of this shimmered on the big screen at the far end of the theater in the middle of the day. Two hours of shiny landscapes, two hours of hope and hiding from noisy life. Mother always experienced the films we watched at the afternoon showing with great intensity. It was an escape from Grandma and her constant nagging into the safety of the dark theater. Almost always we also talked about the film. Well, in fact, she would do most of the talking. She would go over the story, sympathize with the characters, laugh again at certain scenes, and she often retold the story in a very different way to what we had just seen, in a way that suited her. After the show we would frequently sit on a bench behind the cinema, me a first grader, she a young mother, just over twenty, and we would *continue* the story where it ended. We would create our own film or thoroughly *correct* the story we had seen. We did this with great seriousness and zeal. I was known to later tell my school friends entirely made-up contents of the film because I found *our film*, the one Mother and I made up, far more interesting.

Then she vanished. She started anew. She simply no longer came. Grandma said she had a new family and that I should forget about her. And I did. Today, a few moments before my death, feeling my intestines pushing out of my feeble body, slowly being drained of blood, I can no longer recall her face. Did she look like Gloria Swanson or Marlene Dietrich, was she more like Ginger Rogers or Jane Fonda? She simply no longer was. What stayed with me were the films we watched together.

When I was released from jail the first time, I looked her up. A kind social worker had given me her address although, so she said, she shouldn't. I boarded a bus and rode off. It was a four-hour journey. When I got to the village it was raining and already dark. I asked at the local pub. They told me where the house was. I stood at the large iron gate. There was no bell I could see. On the inside of the fence a large Alsatian kept barking and snapping at me. I kept telling the dog, *Hey! Hey! Anyone at home?* A light came on. It was still raining. A young boy of around eight

called from the door, *Who is it? What do you want?* I told him I
would like to talk to Mother. *There's someone who wants to talk
to you,* the boy shouted into the house. He thought I meant *his
mother,* but I had meant mine. A woman holding an umbrella
came out of the house. She closed the door and opened the umbrella. Behind her, in the window next to the door, the shadow
of the boy watching us appeared. She slowly walked across the
yard. She called the dog to her side. It stopped barking, ran up to
her, and tamely rubbed against her feet. She bent over, stroked
it gently on its head, *Good boy. Good boy, Rex, good!* She straightened herself, wiped her hand on the pinafore she was wearing,
and stepped to the gate. *Yes? What do you want?*

It was her. She was much older. Her face was bony and tired,
her hair thin. She had a bruise under her left eye. I said, *It's me.*
She stared at me for a while. Then she said, *I don't know you.* I
think she really did not recognize me. The youth detention center had changed me. I too had lost weight. My hair was thinner.
I probably looked really bad. I was wet and exhausted. *I am. . .*
I stuttered. . . *I. . . your son. . . they gave me your address. . . .* She
interrupted me. *I don't want to know you! I have a family! Leave
me alone!* She turned around and left. The dog started barking
at me again. In the middle of the yard she stopped and looked
at me to say, *If you continue to loiter around the house, I will call
the police.* Then she went inside and closed the door. The light
in the hallway went off. The boy, probably my brother, was still
leaning against the window, watching me. I could see her step
up to him, grab his shoulder, and pull him away, then draw the
curtain. It was still raining. The dog was jumping madly at the
gate. I don't know how long I stood there. Then I crossed the

road, finding shelter under a large tree. There was no bus before morning, but I didn't care. I didn't think about anything. I just stood there, staring at the house opposite.

Time trickled away like the water in the ditch along the road. In the middle of the night a car drew up to the house. Out of it stepped a rather large man. He staggered along drunk, talking to himself, swearing, and somehow he managed to open the gate and drive the car into the yard. The dog was afraid of him. It squealed and moved out of his way. After a while, when all the lights had gone out in the house, I walked up the road and approached the house from the other side where there was a large barn. Parked inside was a tractor and other farm machinery. I pulled a metal rod off the thresher. The dog began to bark. *Good boy, Rex! Good boy!* I said. The dog stopped barking, squealing instead, and I extended my arm. I got closer and it began licking my hand. I hit it with the metal rod. I hit it until my hand was too tired to continue. Then I found a tank of fuel in the barn. I poured it all over the barn and set fire to it. The fire was huge. I turned around and walked down the road. I didn't look back. I hoped the fire would spread to the roof of the house, their home. When day broke I was already on the main road. It had stopped raining. The first car I came across was the police. I didn't care. I was sent back to jail.

The prison screened films. Every month we would have a screening in the dining room. The cinema operator from town would come. I never went to the shows. Everyone else went but I stayed in my cell. I could hear the music coming from the dining room downstairs. That typically cinematic music, announcing the last duel in *High Noon*, or the quiet whistling accompanied by a harmonica from *A Fistful of Dollars*. Nobody could understand why I didn't want to watch the films. When I had struck the match and brought it to the puddle of fuel in the barn, I had sworn to myself, *No more films, no more dreams in my life*! Without dreams, man is a beast.

When I was released from jail the second time, I decided I would start fresh. That I would start a new film. I went straight home but the key I had been keeping on a piece of string round my neck like a sacred object, that to me meant *home, a new beginning*, no longer fit in the lock. I rang the bell. It was still the same bell but the door was opened by strangers.

Grandma had died over a year earlier. Nobody told me. The neighbors, the ones who had always been so kind to us and helped the old aristocratic lady to her feet when she fell on the pavement and protected her from evil gossip, told me everything. Including that they only found her in the apartment two months after her death. The postman raised the alarm when he noticed a suspicious smell. The neighbors had thought she had gone to visit me, her grandson, as she had been talking about it for a while, especially in the days before her death. She was always proud that I had succeeded in making a life for myself abroad, where I had a button factory and a large apartment in the center of town, and a house in the countryside. It was my mother who sold the apartment. A quick sale. She came one morning with the new owners. They only saw her briefly. She didn't even greet them. She probably sold it so she could rebuild the house and the shed. I smiled at the thought.

That night I smashed a window in a food store. I only stole a few bottles of booze, whatever was closest, and walked round the corner and got drunk right there. I then wandered off to the graveyard to find my grandmother's grave. I staggered in amongst the tombstones, threw the empty bottles onto the black marble monuments, kicked over vases, trampled on flowers and candles. I didn't find my grandmother's grave. The first car that drove past in the morning, when, exhausted, dirty, bloody, and disheveled, I collapsed onto one of the graves, was the police. I was sent back to jail.

I remember the film *Cat Ballou* when Lee Marvin, drunk, on his drunken horse, leans against the wall while his buddies are robbing a bank. Both are drunk, horse and cowboy. They drunkenly lean against the wall and I think even the horse has its front legs crossed as if propped up against a bar. That was how I felt over the following years once I was out of jail again. I was drunk. And so was my horse.

In that period my best success was robbing a garage. I pulled a silk stocking over my head, like in *Phantom* with Henry Fonda in the lead role, I had nicked it off a washing line in some yard, and hit the attendant over the head with a short metal rod that I found among the remnants of piping on the building site next door, grabbing quite a wad of banknotes from the till. I was lucky. As in movies. I was surprised when a few days later I was still not arrested. I took the train to the city where I rented a room at some farmer's place on the outskirts. I stole a bike and rode into town every day. I had money. I ate at various canteens, bought myself a new pair of trousers, a shirt. I met Magdalena. She was from my film. No job, her boyfriend had left her, she drank, and wanted to commit suicide. Whenever she was very drunk she cried and went with anyone who hugged her and told her he loved her. It was also how she ended up with me. She had an apartment in an attic in the old part of town. We instantly became a couple. I had money. I told her that my folk had a button factory, a large apartment in the center of town, and a house in the countryside. That they gave me pocket money every so often. That I was the only son and that eventually it would all be mine. I didn't even consider that the money would eventually run out and that all my stories would become lies. And Magdalena fell in love with me. Perhaps merely because of the money. Who knows. I don't want to think about it. When we were together we had a great time. And that was all that mattered. She had big breasts and a nice, smooth belly. She said she loved me because I wasn't using her, because I wasn't like everyone else who did all kinds of things imaginable with her. She also said that until she met me she didn't even know that it could feel good for her as well. She thought she had to accommodate her boyfriends in every way, that she needed to be available for them to satisfy their fantasies. It was a time when I was truly happy. Someone had praised me, someone was happy with me. That was my only film that could have a happy ending. But it didn't. As I hurried to the shop one morning to prepare breakfast for Magdalena, a car drew up slowly alongside me. It was the police.

I didn't even say goodbye. I sat in the police car as they overturned her place, which I had only moved into a day or so earlier. I thought I could hear her voice, her cries. The next time I saw her was at court. She didn't look at me. She said she didn't know, that she had nothing to do with me, that she never had had anything to do with me. I understood why she was saying that. I wrote to her from jail. She never replied and never came to visit. I felt sorry for her. She would once more be used, once more merely be satisfying the desires of others.

In prison we drank turpentine, aftershave, lacquer cleaning agent, diluted petrol, sometimes also pure alcohol. In order to be sent to the medical center where I tried to steal a bottle of medical alcohol, I deliberately cut my hands, and when there was no more room on my hands and the wounds didn't heal fast enough, I hit my head against the wall. Sometimes I didn't manage to steal any alcohol but I would snatch the bottle out of the doctor's hand and drink it right there. I would drink until the security guards hit me and knocked it out of my hands. I was sent to rehab a number of times. I didn't want to go. All I wanted was to forget. To sink into those white dreams, that white shimmering that always appeared on-screen whenever the film being projected tore and the cactus landscape through which the four avenging horsemen rode in *Gunfight at the O.K. Corral* turned into whiteness.

I got liver disease. My stomach, legs, and arms swelled. From jail I returned to my hometown. I walked from the bus stop and stood outside the house for a long time, looking up at the third floor where I used to live with my grandmother as a child. A beautiful young girl was leaning against the window, gazing out into the distance. She looked thoughtful. Then she closed the window and disappeared inside her home.

I was given an address. A homeless shelter. I couldn't believe my eyes when I found myself outside the long low building of Cine Home. They told me that since last summer it was no longer used as a theater and that the building was going to be demolished. Temporarily it was being used as a shelter for local homeless people. There were still remnants of the sign above the door. They had tried to erase it from the wall. The red paint was gone but the words "Cine Home" were still discernible on the scratched plaster. I entered the building. Everything was the same but so very different. The theater was emptied of its seats. Now it was filled with decommissioned white hospital beds. The tags with the row numbers were still attached to the floor. And the place still smelled of wood polish. Instead of the white canvas, there was now a food distribution point on the stage. Where once stood the snow-white screen onto which they projected the faces of Greta Garbo, John Wayne, Clint Eastwood, were now plastic tables with plastic tablecloths and benches, and a long galvanized counter to which they would bring a large pot of bean stew. In the corner a sink and a box for leftovers.

There weren't many of us at the shelter. Sometimes five, sometimes six, only three of us were permanent. None of them knew that this used to be a cinema. A cinema that was the home of my childhood. They just stared at me when I talked about all the films I had watched in this very space where we were now lying on hospital beds, some of them more than once: *The Great Escape* with Steve McQueen, *Once Upon a Time in the West* with Charles Bronson, *The Hell with Heroes* with Claudia Cardinale — my mother's favorite actress. I saw some films three times in the same day, the four, six, and eight o'clock screenings. I left the theatre at the exit, walked around the building, bought a ticket, and sat in the same seat. I told them where I used to sit, usually in row eight, right in the middle. That was also where I found a bed. I now lay in the very spot I used to sit and watch the big screen.

When the lights went out, meaning it was time to go to sleep, just as they used to switch off the lights and this meant the film was about to begin, I began talking about the films I had seen. I couldn't stop myself. I stared into the darkness and talked and talked and talked. One night, as I was talking about *Spartacus*, the gladiator played by Kirk Douglas, his fighting skills, how he wielded his sword left and right, how he killed all his enemies, I was attacked in the dark. They beat me up without words, from all sides. They knocked my teeth out. *So you'll shut up about your dumb films!* they said in the end as they left me on the bed, sticky with blood, my mouth full of smashed teeth. From then on I no longer talked about films. I lay in the dark, staring toward where the screen used to be. The films were now being played in my head. Just for me.

Once I wanted to remember the last film I had seen in this theater. Was I with Mother? Was I alone? Perhaps we had even gone to the cinema with Grandma? No, I doubt that. Grandma didn't like the movies. I only managed to take her to the cinema a few times and only because the film being shown was R-rated, so an accompanying parent or guardian was required for young viewers. But which film was the last? I kept asking myself as I waited for the drugs at the town hospital that would slow down the disintegration of my liver. I didn't care about the liver. All I wanted was to remember the last film I had seen there, the film that was the end of my Cine Home.

Returning to the shelter in the evening, I suddenly remembered that it had been a terribly boring film about a man who was betrayed, then tortured, and eventually killed at the top of a mountain. Mother didn't like the film. And all I remembered was that the man, as he was dying on the mountain, saw before him his entire life, and that he then returned to the living. Yes, that was the last film.

Now I am lying in a pool of my own blood. Next to the bed in row eight. My cheek against the floor. I can smell the wood polish. And something else, it seems, is reaching my nostrils, a strange, rancid smell of army uniforms, heavy, greasy, the scent of an unknown machine, mixed with the smell of young bodies, the stench of saliva and roasted pumpkin seeds that the soldiers from the nearby barracks once long ago spat out onto the floor under the dark, worm-ridden seats.

It all happened so quickly. In a flash. Just like in the movies.

Only two of us were left in the shelter over winter. Me and a giant with a moustache who kept hiding his bottle of liquor in all corners of the hall. I saw where he hid it. When he went to the toilet I reached under his mattress and took a swig. When I turned around, he was standing behind me and hit me in the stomach with all his strength. I thought that would be it, a few bruises, punishment for theft, I was used to such things. But he was clenching a knife. He stabbed me with it as he punched me. I don't know how many times. It didn't hurt. First I collapsed, then I slowly spread out on the floor next to my bed in row eight. The giant with the moustache grabbed his bottle from my hand, drank from it until it was empty.

In between my fingers with which I tried to stop the warm thick sticky liquid from flowing out of my body, I could feel my intestines, spreading like soft jelly across the floor. The man with the moustache lay down in his bed in the corner and pulled the blankets over his head.

After a while the lights went out.

The on-duty guard didn't check the hall. Out in the corridor where the booth with the lady selling tickets used to be, he merely turned the switch and the light vanished. There were only the two of us staying at the shelter this winter. He didn't have to worry. Fine by me. In this position, slightly bent like a fetus in the womb — this too I had seen in some film — I felt good. Safe, warm, pleasant as I had not felt for a long time. All was fine. The man with the moustache began snoring. The lights were out. The film can begin.

As you are dying, life, your life, flashes before your eyes like a film. Where have I heard that before? I think my grandmother told me, a long, long time ago. I spent my childhood with her. She was the one who brought me up. She was kind. Spiteful sometimes. It depended. She drank.

… My film won't be long. Had I waited until summer, I would have been twenty-three. I don't regret it. I am happy, just like the hero in *Man with No Name*, when he finally realizes that there never was a place for him in this town, that everyone merely feigned love but nobody truly loved him, so he mounts his white horse and rides off into the endless plain, scorched relentlessly by the sun.

If the on-duty guard at the shelter looks carefully enough at my face in the morning when he finds me, he will still be able to see this very image.

Translated by GREGOR TIMOTHY ČEH

Originally published in the short stories collection
Kino Dom (*Cankarjeva založba, 2008*)

VINKO MÖDERNDORFER

Boris Kolar

PHARAOH ANTS

ANTS ARE TINY, six-legged animals with big eyes, determined to find some part of you they can bite. If one fine morning you happen to find an army of ants in your kitchen, aquarium, toilet, fridge, or anywhere else, don't jump out of the window. When what you are dealing with in your apartment are pharaoh ants, the only solution is the appropriate natural control of their population. So what is the ant's deadliest enemy?

Toads, we know from experience, simply love ants. So we can rush off and bring toads into our apartment, bearing in mind the ratio of 9,000 toads to 1 million ants. In developed countries, Crimean toads are most popular. Locals call them Feropol turds, after the town of Feropol, which is the largest trading hub for these animals on the old continent. No worries, prices aren't too high. In Moscow, for example, you can purchase an almost fully grown male for seven rubles. The advantage of Feropol turds over our own homegrown toads is in their size — they are no bigger than a box of matches.

At this point our mechanism of ecological pest control passes into the next phase. In damp apartments and bathrooms, or under kitchen sinks, toads can proliferate, their population becoming excessive for our needs. Following nature's example, we find the toad's natural predator. Into a home with central heating, we can introduce the Aesculapian snake. The ratio should be between 30 to 38 snakes to 900 toads. We recommend the Aesculapian snake because of its human-friendly nature and its calm, quiet disposition. We need, however, to make sure that we don't spoil the snakes too much. They become especially attached to children. A case is known when eco-friendly control of pharaoh ants failed for the simple reason that the children of the house fed the snakes at lunchtime, coddling them into losing all interest in the toads.

In the third phase of eco-control, we need to keep down the number of snakes with their natural predators. Another warning, do not get too fond of these benevolent snakes. The death of a house pet that keeps them company all day might break the heart of any housekeeper. Mexican and Bavarian experts recommend the steppe buzzard as a predator for Aesculapian snakes, namely at a ratio of four buzzards to 32 snakes, the Kyrgyz little eagle at a rate of three eagles to 35 snakes, or the African secretarybird at a rate of a pair of birds for 38 snakes. The latter is especially popular due to its colorful plumage. These birds are a little larger in size and can be relatively noisy in the early hours of the morning. If we decide on the Kyrgyz little eagle, we need to mask any fish tanks in our home with black or dark brown paint to hide the fish from the bird of prey — apparently this species is particularly fond of freshwater angelfish.

We have now established all the links in the food chain in our home. Of course, the pharaoh ants will not entirely disappear with this method, but their numbers will be rigidly controlled and their population will not have a chance for further expansion. It will also give a warm ambiance to our home, as we have brought into it a small part of nature with all its natural laws.

And finally, what is nicer than a Sunday morning with a view of a majestic bird gliding with its wings open right under the ceiling of your living room?

Translated by GREGOR TIMOTHY ČEH

Originally published in the short stories collection
Trinajst (*Goga,* 2020)

Maja Novak

CONSPIRACY

OUR TOWN IS small but kindly. The cottages know their manners and demurely stay close to the ground, barely ever rising to the fourth story. When our town saves up enough pocket money, which is counted into its palm by mum and dad or a visiting godmother or a delegation of the Swedish Royal Academy, it buys a new traffic light. We have three already. Our town scrimps and saves like a hamster. All three traffic lights endlessly flash the yellow light. Here's still another proof of our town's kindliness: if there were red lights stopping the traffic, it would take that single car per day more than a minute to drive through.

Since our town is — as I said — small, it's obvious that we all know each other. Everybody knows *me*. That is to say, when the gossip comes to me, everybody knows who my parents are, when we had our kitchen whitewashed for the last time, to what school I used to go, and why I don't go there any longer. That doesn't mean, though, that they notice me walking down the street. I won't claim that they ignore me on purpose or that they don't return my greetings, of course they do if I tug at their sleeves eagerly enough; the fact is that they simply don't notice me. I'm difficult to notice. Neither fat nor thin, neither short nor tall, neither stupid nor smart, neither clumsy nor nimble, each hair has a different color and all together have none, my complexion is pallid but I'm not an albino, I don't dress in the latest fashion (I ought to check if I dress at all), and I do nothing either praiseworthy or blasphemous. See me then, if you can.

Now you'll tell me: praise the Lord, who's given you a quiet and safe life, you're as snug as a bug in a rug, and who else can boast of such grace these days? But I'm more and more convinced there's a conspiracy afoot. No, no, don't be afraid, I haven't had a relapse, I'm not paranoia ridden, just the opposite: I daresay that it's a kind, benevolent, almost parentally affectionate intrigue; I staunchly believe and want to believe that my fellow townsmen are preparing a lovely surprise for me. This soothing insight flashed into my mind together with the first voices.

They are just pretending not to see me, when they are in fact all too acutely aware of me walking among them, and they are proud of me. What was so long hidden from me lies open to all: that I was chosen for higher purposes — sooner or later I'll achieve something not just important but celebrated — that I'll make history and, in doing so, spread the glory of my fatherland far beyond the northern and southern traffic lights. I'll make good yet, make good, make good. In fact, I suspect they even know where I'm to excel and shine among and above my fellow men, but they won't tell me, just as my voices are still stubbornly silent on the details. But there is no malice or envy in this

MAJA NOVAK

secrecy, don't even think about it. Our townspeople are small but good: they play dumb and heartily grin into their hands behind my back simply in order not to spoil my joy — to give me a more pleasant surprise when my inspiration comes, my revelation, when I flash forth in full glory.

After all, there are obvious comparisons that bear out my idea! Look at birthdays. What would they be like if the birthday boy knew weeks in advance that the others would remember him and congratulate him and gift him, and what with? Well? Granted, these days (these 1,500 odd days!) my birthdays have more and more often tiptoed by, I don't think that even Mum and Dad congratulated me on my thirty-third birthday, but I'm comforted by the awareness that this is simply part of their scheme. While I was still a child and my singularity was not so difficult to hide from me, it was different, of course. They always surprised me in the way I'd expected: pleasantly and completely.

For my tenth birthday, for instance, I got marbles, an electricity-powered martian which walked, hummed, and flashed the lights on its antennae, a fish tank with fat koi carp in white and orange — like semicooked eggs cut in half, in short — a white kitten, which somehow defies description, and a guinea pig in a cage of its own. Quite a luxurious set of presents, wasn't it, and the best thing about it was that it hit me like a hammer because I hadn't known about any of its ingredients to the last — just as they would manage to keep from me for weeks that the martian, its rubber tail forgotten in the electric socket, toppled into the fish tank, electrocuted the carp, and knocked the tank down on the carpet, along came the white kitten and wolfed down the fish unharmed — depend on cats! — but then, raking a bristling and blue-sparking paw through the cage of the guinea pig, which she fancied for pudding, she electrocuted the cage, the guinea pig inside came to no harm either — the Faraday cage, you see? — but smelling the cat and the paw, it panicked and frantically darted in circles among the bars that had saved its life, our housemaid wondered what had possessed it, wanting to help she reached for the cage door, clutching a wet rag in the other hand, and — bang. Exit housemaid. The guinea pig scurried out onto the carpet, into deceptive freedom, but the kitten was still lying in wait, exit guinea pig, and choked on a marble in the pig's tummy. How did the marble get there? Oh well, I'm perfectly willing to shoulder my negligible share of the guilt.

While the housemaid was too bulky to sweep under the carpet, they managed to keep from me for a long, long time that I'd been at the same swoop deprived of the martian, fish tank, kitten, and guinea pig, not to mention the marble, which nobody troubled to rummage after. You'll certainly agree that their white lies ("We've lent the kitty to the neighbors because they have mice, darling") were meant well and only for my benefit.

However, after the accident they started to observe me closely, as if I'd made all that mess on purpose. I swear I didn't! But I did have on my conscience a number of other, minor tricks. I'd always been particularly handy with foodstuffs and wine. The housemaid (still alive at the time), her red fists akimbo, stood over the dripping parcel that she'd brought from the fishmonger's and unfolded on the kitchen table, shaking her head in confusion: she was positive that she'd bought five trout but now they were six, no, seven, wait a minute — she'd check again if there weren't... twenty? Good heavens, she couldn't count anymore! And Dad grumbled: I'm fed up with this loaf, won't it ever end, we're eating bread that's three days old, who's ever seen a thing like this; but Mum was adamant, we're not going to throw bread away, we'll keep eating it until it runs out. And so we did, for a whole week after. But what really got them moving was the housemaid's death. Only then did it dawn on them, as I see now, what extraordinary powers I was clearly endowed with, and they waited for the next miracle with bated breath. A pity — if I'd realized that in time, I would have been happy to oblige. But as it was, all the attention soon began to be jarring to me. My voices are whispering that it was just that which drove me to take refuge behind the ramparts of invisibility; after all, I was a beautiful child, fair-haired, with a gentle blue-eyed gaze, and healthy. Whenever I had a screaming spell, the whole town flocked together; not that this gathering deserved special notice, given the density of the local population, but one has to be creative with whatever's at hand. Later, however, I grew more ordinary from day to day, as if I were camouflaged somehow, I faded and turned gray and pasty-faced, and I no longer screamed except in my belly. Twenty-three years of silent screaming, what a drag, I was getting tired of secretively listening to my own frozen shrieks, but then they were luckily drowned by the voices.

It was about that time they stopped staring at me and started pretending I was off my rocker, that I didn't belong with them, that I was giving myself airs, that I wasn't there — or, better yet, they started pretending to pretend I wasn't there, and my voices revealed to me why.

They're expecting a miracle and want me to be pleasantly surprised when I pull it off by pure accident.

I think it will soon be finished. The town is staging an amateur theatre performance but I haven't been invited to join in, and I'd have every reason to find this cruel if I didn't know that the moment of my glory was at hand, which is driving my fellow townsmen to desperate measures in their pretended ignorance.

On a hill behind the town, beyond the three traffic lights, they're setting up the stage props, three crosses, and whenever I sneak closer, they look away to prevent me from reading in their eyes the delight at the surprise they are getting ready for me.

They're keeping something from me. Keeping from me. Keeping from me. Jesus, there isn't another death coming, is there?

— December 1993

Translated by NADA GROŠELJ

Originally published in the short stories collection
Zverjad (*Cankarjeva založba, 1996*)

Mirana Likar

THE MORNING OF THE LAST DAY

WHO AM I? In this night? This day? Otherwise? What am I? A *badante*: a carer. A tool. I'm lying in the hall, not quite sure whether I'm awake or asleep, inspecting myself in the silent empty deaf gray of the night. Is the sheet itchy? Is it still night? Is it already day? What day is it?

I have the eyes of a hawk. I look at myself from a great height. It's five o'clock in the morning. Friday. It tastes like bitter sour coffee. I get into the rusty old Twingo. My neighbor always gives me a lift. The rainy road winds its way from Peroj to the bus station in Pula. I haven't slept. Too agitated. I never sleep the night before I leave. Leaving is painful to me. I feel itchy. Or is that just the sheet? I retrieve my shopping cart from the trunk of the car. Every badante has one. Or a suitcase with wheels. I prefer a cart. It's lighter. I've tied a silk bow to mine, because there's still beauty in this world. I've filled it with everything I'll need for the next fourteen days.

I buy my ticket. It costs me what I earn for one day's work. Ciao, says my neighbor, kissing the air near my cheek. I'll come and pick you up, let me know when. I don't wave goodbye to her. I can't. Just looking at her paralyzes me. She's free. She doesn't have to leave. Today she'll be at home making that potato soup of hers. Today her kitchen will be filled with the smell of thyme. Her own. From the patch beneath her kitchen window.

Good morning, Marija, says Oto, who is both driver and conductor. My name is still my name, though that's the last time I'll hear it for the next fourteen days. The houses that line the road are in darkness. Raindrops fall on the window and form little streams. The speed of the bus, or the sirocco blowing from the south, makes them flow horizontally. The window smells of metal, salt, needles, and something else. Why does everything I look at have a smell? If I didn't have the eyes of a hawk, he could stab me. With a knife, a fork, anything he can find to stab me with when I turn my back. When I really close my eyes. When I'm not looking. Even a shard of pottery?

I'm a badante. I have the lithe body of a snake. I have no limbs. My arms droop pathetically, my legs are cut off. I can slither in the darkness, my forked tongue detecting a presence, his, hers, she isn't dangerous, I can sense where they are without switching on the light. He can become terrible. I don't look him in the eye. I don't let him see anything in mine. Something for him to get hold of. But I have to be able to see in the dark. If I turn on the light unexpectedly, he might spring at me, knock me to the floor, choke me.... He's still big and strong. And mad. A strong madman.

The calendar helps me get through it. Each day I cross off another day gone by. I do my work, cross off a day, and keep going. Work. Cross off a day. Keep going. The first Friday. The last Friday. The last cross on the calendar. And I wait for my replacement. Time drags on and on. At the end of it is another badante. From the karst. We don't talk much. When at last she arrives, it's all I can do to stop myself from running out of there. My cart is light as a feather, its bow fluttering. What would we talk about anyway? We both know how it is. I've done my bit. Now it's her turn. I hand the sadness over to her. It's all hers now. In my pocket, I have 525 euros. Outside there is wind and sun and the smell of the city and the smell of salt. The bus leaves at two. Until then I can look at the shop windows. I sit on a bench. I breathe. Occasionally, I buy myself an ice cream. Even more occasionally, a coffee. Oto will call me by my name. Hello, Marija, he'll say. Ready to go home?

I have the hearing of a bat. I can tell the sigh of the sirocco, which brought me here, from the howl of the bora, which started blowing yesterday. I can hear the tires of David's bicycle, the breath of the asphalt, laughter. He stands with one foot on the saddle, pretending to be a swallow. . . . Give me the strength to overcome the pain, the revulsion, the fear, the sadness. . . . The bus drives past the marina, I hear people of a different kind, the sea splashing against the Molo Audace, the pigeons in Piazza Unità. . . . If I failed to hear the rustle of a sheet, footsteps in the night, I might fail to hear a tragedy, a catastrophe, days that aren't and days that are. . . . He could hurt me any way he liked and she wouldn't make a sound. She barely knows who or where she is, let alone who or where I am.

I have the heart of a lion. The heart of every badante is made up of other memories. Mine is made of the look in David's eyes, his hands that, on my Sundays, dry the dishes, sit me on the sofa, and bring me coffee, he is my strength, my health. It's for his sake that I allow the clammy sirocco to push me into this marble-floored hall, into the dark, the stench, nonexistence. David drives my blood through my veins as I tie on my apron. For his sake I wipe old Italian backsides. For his sake I don't go mad. Bring this, take that away, wipe, wash.... For his sake I let them be my masters for thirty-five euros a day, they who are no longer masters of anything else, not even their own hands. For his sake I walk a million steps with my legs cut off. If it wasn't for him, I would have put an end to this.

I have the iron stomach of a wolf. That's why I don't throw up now. The stench is brutal. I get up from my camp bed. I'm barefoot. In the dark I silently push open the half-closed door. A puddle glistens on the floor in the glow of the streetlight outside. He's pulled out his catheter again. She's sitting on the floor, naked, like a mute Buddha. She's rubbing her head with her nightdress. It doesn't take my keen canine sense of smell to know what she's smearing over her hair.

I put my shoes on. Open the window. Put on my dressing gown.

I turn on the lights, first the one in the hall, then the little lamp in their room, my lupine stomach doing somersaults. I hold my breath. She's taken off her incontinence pad. Her nightdress is full of excrement. She's spread it from her hair to her toes. It's two o'clock in the morning. He's agitated. Cursing. My arms are growing back, so I go to put on my gloves. I tell him everything's all right. *Va tutto bene.* Come with me. She grins stupidly and toothlessly as I lead her to the bathroom. I push her onto the stool under the shower, throw her soiled nightdress into the washing machine, and select the cycle. I dry her hair. Change her pad. Put her into a fresh nightdress and sit her down in front of the television. Now I stink too. Keep going. I take off my dressing gown.

I mop up the puddle from the floor. If I didn't do it, some Moldovan would do it for less. I hope the acid doesn't eat through my wolfish stomach. I certainly earn my money. My bread and milk. Keep going. I'd rather steal for a living, if only I had the opportunity. Keep going. I tense my muscles. Brace myself. I lift him up, sit him in the armchair, and take off his pajamas. I ignore his insults and keep going. I wipe him with a damp towel, tense myself, brace myself, put him into a fresh pair of pajamas, change the sheets on the bed, tense myself, brace myself, move him to the bed, put his catheter back in, *tranquillo, va tutto bene*, keep going, fetch her from her chair, put her into bed next to him, and turn off the light. I close the windows. Have a shower. Put on a clean tracksuit. It's four o'clock. The sky above Trieste is getting lighter. I collapse into my bed in the hall. I'm exhausted. Thank goodness the wind has changed; it'll bring sunshine.

I ask myself how it is possible. What happened? Where did it go wrong? Who is to blame? There are thousands of us. From Moldova, Ukraine, Romania, Croatia, Slovenia. . . Outside, the bora roams the streets, picking up rubbish and sweeping it into the sea. I write to my president, the pope, the social worker, my deceased loved ones, government ministers, God: you're supposed to be socialists — do something for us poor folk. . . . You're humiliating me. I write and then read what I've written. A pension of 200 euros? Are you crazy? And they send the bailiffs round for five hundred? New words occur to me. Ugly words that sting me. Harden me. Still stinging, I try to fall asleep so that I'll have the energy to finish clearing up before I leave. Fold the sheets, serve breakfast, endure insults, feed, iron, clean. The sooner I fall asleep, the sooner I'll be Marija again. I've forgotten to give him his tranquilizer. But he's asleep. I'm not going to wake him.

Sleep refuses to come so I get up, take my calendar, and cross off a new day. Today I am seventy-three years... five months... and eleven days old. A pensioner of the transition. I'm alive. I have David, my grandson, who has no one in the world but me. I lie down. Close my eyes. Listen. Gaze into my night, in which there are still stars in the sky. Let myself go.

In the breath of the wind I hear him, smell him, sense him. He's gotten out of bed. He's going past me. He can see in the dark, just like I can. Urine trickles onto the floor again, every drop scattering into a thousand stinking particles. He's coming back. He's got something in his hands. Something heavy. Dark. The chopping board? It's made of olive wood. Its year rings are almost black. It has a hole in the handle to hang it from. A groove to drain liquid. A cavity for salt that's shaped like half an egg. I left it on the table, forgot to put it away. From the depths of the bedroom she encourages him, toothless and giggling. I can't open my eyes. He's going to smash my face. Shatter my skull. I can't move. Perhaps it isn't the chopping board. He's brandishing something. Is it a knife? A pillow? Any second now it'll bury itself in me, envelop me, suffocate me.... I can't open my eyes. I can't.

Perhaps it's nothing. Perhaps I can keep my eyes closed. Perhaps. Nothing. Perhaps the badante has simply let the bora sweep her into a dream, because it's already the morning of the last day.

Translated by HUGH BROWN

Originally published in the short stories collection
Glasovi (*Modrijan, 2015*)

Miha Mazzini

FLIES

HE WAITED FOR the alarm clock to ring, listening in his sleep to a fly that kept hitting the window. He knew he shouldn't move if it landed on him. I mustn't, I mustn't, he kept repeating to himself, sinking back into deep sleep again until Sabine's hand gently shook him awake. He helped her dress Grete and walked them to the door. He locked it and went to open the windows. The fly was nowhere to be seen. After last night's storm the summer had cooled enough to leave the windows open. Berlin apartments: in none of the previous places he had been moved to was there this much space at such a rent.

He went to the bathroom, shaved, showered, and stared for a long time at the mirror without really looking at himself. Sometimes he got stuck like this, even when Sabine and Grete were at home. It always made him feel embarrassed, though his wife pretended not to have noticed and his daughter never knew him any different.

He kneeled in the right direction for prayers. The wall needs whitewashing. Sabine planned to work on the apartment during her annual leave. The empty shopping trolleys pulled along by old women going to the market clattered hollowly down Zossener Straſse.

On Tuesdays he made beef steaks, but as he waited in the queue at the butcher, gazing at the cuts of meat, some hanging from hooks, some arranged in the display or neatly packed, he recalled the buzzing and unwittingly leaned forward as if he was shortsighted, looking for flies. They should have been sliding across the pink surface, crossing the lines of the muscles, across the strips of trimmed fat, changing direction, flying off, landing again, rubbing their legs as if mocking the onlooker, but there were none.

He preferred to go to the fish market. A vacuum pack of calamari in hand, he waited at the greengrocer for potatoes. They were packed in mesh bags and every one he picked up from the pile weighed exactly five kilos. German orderliness never ceased to astonish him. Back in the Yugoslavia of late socialism where he had grown up, you could never buy just a kilo of anything; whatever appeared in the shops was grabbed up straightaway to stock, for you never knew when you would find it again. Those places were not shops; they were hunting grounds — you stepped through the door guessing what, if anything, you might catch. And here, all these bags, each one the same weight. And no flies anywhere. He could not recall whether there were any flies in Yugoslav shops. There probably had been. For how long would the German state have to be collapsing before they appeared here?

In an attempt to display her independence, the pensioner in front of him counted out her money herself, taking forever and making mistakes. The entire queue, together with the shop assistant, waited in silence. This too would not have happened back home, he thought to himself. The lady's hands were shaking and she eventually pushed the pile of small change toward the cashier. The girl quickly picked out the correct amount but it then took a while for the old lady to collect the rest of the coins scattered on the metal counter and put them back into her purse. "I don't know what it is with me lately," she said.

Well, you can wonder about that one until the day you die, he thought to himself, it will only get worse.

He looked at the reflection of the queue in the shop window. Heads of ash-gray hair. He could instantly pick out his own because it was the only male head and stuck out above the others. Germany is a land of old ladies, at least in the mornings. I mustn't get stuck, I mustn't. Have a good day, the girl at the till said routinely.

At the pedestrian crossing he waited for a procession of nursery school children to cross the road. They were holding a rope, each their own handle, obediently being led by an aging punk such as he had seen many of in this quarter — a red mohawk that would seem threatening on a dark night but was now merely an orientation point for the children. Judging by their faces, at least half of those marching along in the row must be Turks, among them a few girls in headscarves, plus a few Black children, some Asians, a few Caucasians, a couple of unidentifiable origins. He concentrated on the rope. Is there a fly on it? Strange, this is strange. Why today? Had I dreamed the buzzing or had I really heard the fly bothering me?

He spread the potatoes out on the table and pulled the knife out of the wooden block. Next to him he placed a biodegradable green bag for organic waste. How long had scientists worked on developing something that would not decompose? When they finally invented plastic, it took over the world and there was only one complaint: it didn't decompose. So they had to invent one that would still be plastic but would no longer have its properties. He held it in his hand, astonished at how fragments of previous thoughts resurface, falling upon him like dandruff, covering him like snow. He was stuck, didn't know how much time had passed.

He sank his face into his palms. His body hurt from inside, as if it was somehow not put together properly.

A fly sat on his forearm. I shouldn't move. He opened his eyes: darkness, a few pink outlines where the fingers were not pressing firmly against each other. The animal slowly moved up his hand. I shouldn't move. He could feel each of its legs on his oversensitive, irritated skin, his left hand was about to strike, his right hand was twitching to try and get rid of it. Then it stopped. Try not to breathe, breathe as little as possible. He pressed his palm against his nose and the air he was drawing in wheezed. Very slowly, millimeter by millimeter, he moved his palm from his face. The fly was walking up the inside of his arm, then out again, reached the elbow and stopped.

It isn't. . . he said to himself, it isn't. . . I shouldn't move. It was too strong, too strong. He needed to obey. But surely I can look? Just look!

He released the pressure from his palm and then slowly turned his head to the right, his eye moved across the index finger and above the thumb.

He couldn't see the fly. He could feel it returning toward his wrist, but he couldn't see it.

He didn't move until it flew off. Then he put both hands on the table in front of him and looked a thousand times at the path the fly had taken. The normality of the skin bothered him.

Well, doctors would say, just nerves. Whenever they said that, he imagined before him the dense tree with branches that thin out from anatomy textbooks. He went to the bathroom and thoroughly rubbed with soap the skin the fly had trodden on. Nothing like this had happened to him before. What if it happened again? On his way back he held on to the doorframe and once again lost track of time.

Sabine worked late on Tuesdays, so he went to collect Grete from nursery school early. She went straight to her corner and began playing with her Barbie dolls. Little girls are strange, or is it only she who is like that, boys. . . boys.

His boys.

(Sead. . . Safet)

He sat himself at the table with a jolt — it was time for peeling the potatoes. He found the knife and picked up the first tuber, staring at it for a long time. There was not a trace of soil on it, as if it had not even come from the ground. Cutting into it revealed its whiteness.

Grete sneezed and said *gesundheit* to herself. He looked at her. A German, I have produced a German. After all this. . . a German. Blonde-haired, blue-eyed, light complexion, my child without any of me. Pure Sabine, only even more beautiful. Sabine says of herself that she is more of a gray mouse and he had indeed not really noticed her. He would go to report at the agency, respected all the rules for asylum seekers, it was Sabine who had to make all the moves. He was waiting in the queue and noticed that she was gazing at him strangely. This one will cause me problems, he thought to himself. But as he was putting away his passport, there was a piece of paper in it with a phone number jotted down. He didn't want to call but in the afternoon he fell asleep — he shouldn't have, sleeping in the afternoon always ended up with nightmares! — and when he leaped up, sweating and screaming, he simply had to hear a human voice, he had to break through the darkness that had descended upon him, so he dialed the number.

He let himself be led through the relationship and she let him get stuck occasionally. Physically things between them functioned if she spent enough time paying attention to him and if he closed his eyes. And one result is the German girl sitting before him playing with Barbie dolls. At the beginning she reached toward him, especially when she was learning how to walk. He impulsively moved back, then consciously refrained from doing so, waiting for her hands. The delay made him a clumsy keeper, and Grete often fell over. At the age of two, she preferred to crawl toward him and kick him in the groin with all her strength. This lasted quite a few months, then she abandoned that as well.

Now, as soon as they were alone, she devoted all her attention to her dolls and excluded him entirely. He expected Sabine to show him the door one day, but she treated him gently, carefully, like a patient. Perhaps she likes my cooking, he thought to himself without a hint of humor in the thought.

"*Du bist sehr schön*," said Grete to a freshly combed Barbie doll, sighing as she placed it on the tiny pink sofa.

She's German, has nothing of mine, none of my features, none of my history, my past. I have given her nothing, she is nothing to do with me.

She is safe.

The fly landed on the back of his hand.

I mustn't move.

He looked down and couldn't see it, he only felt its trail toward his wrist. When a second fly landed on his neck, he almost twitched. Then a third, a fourth, he stopped counting. He looked straight ahead, at the wall above Grete. Flies were swarming all over it.

I mustn't move.

Slowly he closed his eyes and tried to breathe as inconspicuously as possible.

Light red. It needs to turn to dark red, the evening, the night, then he would be able to creep away.

He just must not move.

Flies, everywhere, on his forehead, across his eyelids, making them twitch — he couldn't control himself, had they seen him? Are they right above him? Just now someone was talking about petrol, he wanted petrol, but now there is nobody around, it's hot, they went for a beer, the excavator broke down or there wasn't one, they were shifting the earth with spades, it went slowly, we should have left enough of them alive to bury their own, he heard them say, someone tried to deal with it all by singing, the others didn't join in, sometimes they were so close he could smell the *rakija* on their breaths, but mostly blood, blood, blood. Excrement, urine, sweat, with every droplet satiated with fear, giving it a very specific smell, blood, blood, blood. The exuberant scent of soil. Black soil, full of roots. He didn't want to smell, didn't want to hear, all he wanted was to live so he kept saying to himself, I shouldn't move, I shouldn't move, flies walked all over him, under his vest, his trousers, swarming everywhere, a hand lay across his face, his mouth, they won't see I am breathing, just not petrol, hope they don't find petrol, night, night is coming, I mustn't move, I mustn't move, blood drips from the hand, flies drinking it from his skin, then the blood stopped, the bodies he is lying on are stiffening. Are Ines, Sead, and Safet somewhere under him? No, he mustn't think, dead, dead, dead, he mustn't think, I mustn't think, I mustn't move, flies, flies, countless tiny feet upon him, all over him, I mustn't move. (That morning the Dutch commander had told them, You're safe, but his gaze was fixed somewhere above their heads. His stomach stiffened, fear oozed out of it in drops. He and Ines looked at each other, "*Babo! Babo!*" Sead called out and tugged his sleeve, Safet was sleeping in Ines's arms. So we can now leave, said the commander, and they left. An eager relief on their faces as they jumped into their transport vehicles, they could not even pretend any longer that they were disciplined. At that moment he comprehended how naïvely he and the other people in their town had believed in Europe, believed in Yugoslavia, and when Yugoslavia started killing them, transferred their faith to Europe. But Europe is little more than a trade association, everything else that is attached to this is an unnecessary embellishment, from culture to the army. They were not a market big enough to fight for, those among them who were good enough buyers had moved away long ago and Europe was glad to take them in. Later, when he was offered asylum in the Netherlands, he rejected it; I spit on them, he thought to himself, and accepted Germany. At the same time he was well aware that even his father's generation spat on Germany because of what they had done in the Second World War). I mustn't move, someone has descended into the pit, they are walking, bodies move like planks of wood, the person is rummaging through them, robbing them, but they had taken all they had from them before, they'd already been made to empty their pockets, it is hot, more and more flies are coming, the thief won't give up, he is foraging, swearing, perhaps he is one of those weekend fighters he had heard about, during the week they work as officials, tradesmen, whatever, back in Serbia, then at the weekends they come to fight in Bosnia with estate cars so they can fill them up with loot, and on Monday morning they are sitting at their desk once again (a new shop, just a shop, only that here they offer knives and Kalashnikovs instead of contracts), someone shouts to the person walking around the pit, he is already really close now, swearing more and more, he hasn't found anything, we cleaned them out, shouts the other man at the top of the pit, the thief swears and climbs out, I mustn't move, heat, sun, is my belly exposed, can I breathe? I cannot feel my legs, I am buried, a throbbing pain in the left hand, flies. Flies. Buzzing, layers, blankets of buzzing. I must not move. He stepped in front of Ines and the children when the men raised their weapons, with his right hand he had grabbed Sead's head, pushing his face against his trouser leg. Close your eyes, son, he said, when they began shooting. When he came to, there were flies, flies, flies everywhere.

I mustn't move.

He opened his eyes and got lost in the whiteness of the wall. Flies crawling all over it.

I mustn't move.

He looked down, the young German was playing with her Barbie dolls. Why am I here? Why am I at all?

He heard someone shouting from the pit, "Kill me!" and then a round of gunfire. Why had he stayed silent?

Grete was combing a doll with black hair. "*Wie groß bist du geworden! Mashallah*," she added and knocked with her index finger knuckle on the wooden floor.

Mashallah? But that is not her word, that is his word, the word of his sons. He never used it, where did she hear it? Kindergarten. There are probably quite a few Turks in her group, it is their word, a remnant they also left in Bosnia. And now here, in the middle of Berlin, it came in a roundabout way to this young German girl, his word, a word he had received from his parents and passed on twice, in vain, and never wanted to pass on again, now came after him...

His skin teeming with flies, he slowly stood up, slowly put down the knife, went across to his daughter, and knelt on the floor in front of her. Wide-eyed, she diverted her attention from the game, pressed the doll against her chest.

Flies swarmed all over his arms when he opened them.

Grete leaned forward, looking at his open palms.

He stared at the parting on the top of her motionless head.

With a swift move she brushed against his skin with Barbie's hair. The flies shied away, disappeared, then gradually, one by one, settled back on his skin.

Grete slowly lifted the doll to his face. He touched it with his right hand. The plastic was covered in the sticky sweetness of children's hands.

MIHA MAZZINI

Grete moved the doll away and instead brought her cheek closer. She pressed it against his palm, the body followed, his hand could no longer resist and Grete curled up into his embrace. To begin with, he felt nothing. When her head pressed against his chest though, the flies stopped moving.

Translated by GREGOR TIMOTHY ČEH

Originally published in the short stories collection
Duhovi (*Goga*, 2010)
First English translation appeared in
Bristol Short Story Prize Anthology, Vol. 4; translated by
URŠKA ZUPANEC and LAURA SNYDER
(*Bristol Review of Books*, 2011)

Jani Virk

DOORS

OF COURSE THEIR reproaches at the time weren't true: that I
had nothing in the world to do. If nothing else, I took the ear-
liest workers' bus at 5:05 AM to Ljubljana twice a week. This
alone was not child's play; today I probably couldn't carry on
any longer. My fellow passengers' faces were vacant and worn,
and their clothes reminded me of rusty cages in the zoo. I felt
no solidarity with them. Even though my clothes often stank of
drink or vomit, though my jeans were torn at the knees, though
the zipper of my burgundy velvet jacket was trashed and my left
sneaker had lost its tongue months ago, I had nothing in common with them. You see, I'm a spiritual person. And that makes
a huge difference. I hated the bus people more than I was willing
to admit to myself. Without my fear of solitude, I couldn't have
been deceived by the sense that we were close to each other.

On such days I arrived in Ljubljana a little before six. I'd
stroll along Miklošič Street down to the Three Bridges, filch a
copy from the pile of freshly delivered newspapers in front of

the tobacconist in the outdoor market, where the vendor never appeared until half past six, and took my morning coffee at an Albanian's bar by the Ljubljanica River. At a quarter past seven I'd roll up the paper, stash it under my arm, and head for the Faculty of Theology.

My attendance at the cosmology lectures jarred my girlfriend. "That word's outlandish for me," she'd say. In fact, she didn't know what it meant at all. "Not just for you, it's outlandish for everyone," I'd counter. What I didn't add was that there are various degrees of ignorance and outlandishness; there are people who even find outlandishness homey. She was becoming dissatisfied with me. Earlier, she hadn't cared if I skipped the lectures at the Faculty of Arts, she herself led me to neglect the lectures and come to her while the children at the kindergarten where she worked had their compulsory rest. I didn't even count the number of times I'd laid her across the plush teddy bears in the toy closet and lifted her work tunic from behind. And now, out of the blue, I should start going to the lectures even though I'd been neglecting them for two months at least. Or at least find a part-time job. Or something else. All of a sudden she was bursting with brilliant ideas about what I might do. Anything would suit me except cosmology. Once, when we were bickering on our way from the cinema, I nevertheless asked her just what cosmology means. She maintained a stubborn silence for some seconds, and then raked her nails over my hand in tangible proof of her fury. On such occasions I was never gentle or considerate, for her own sake as well. With well-aimed insults I ripped off in a single move the buttons of her lace shirt, under which she wore no bra. (For which I'd criticized her before we left her rented flat, but to no effect.) In a jiffy, a dozen stupid, leery men's eyes started ogling her bare breasts. I started away, but in seconds she came running after me, firmly holding her shirt closed. She pressed against me so hard I had to put my arm around her shoulders. We didn't speak all the way to her car. But while we were driving toward her basement flat, she burst into tears and told me, sobbing, that she could hate things even if she didn't know what they meant. Naïve as I was, I felt then for the first time that we might split someday. "Is real love possible between a man who is spiritual and a woman who is not?" I wondered with a sense of great emptiness because I divined the answer.

"Cosmology, cosmology," I sometimes whispered into her ear, panting on top of those plush teddy bears, and on such occasions she usually made love so vigorously that the bears' straw stuffing crackled maddeningly. "Can malice which has a positive goal be a reflection of spirituality?" I often wonder. "Is there such a thing as a positive goal?" I often wonder.

Every Monday and every Wednesday found me at five minutes to half past seven sitting in the lecture hall of the Faculty of Theology. The faces of the people who took their seats around me were hardly ethereal. I'd had a similar sensation among the pale pimply faces of the students at the Faculty of Mechanical Engineering, where I sat through several lectures next to a close friend. By his looks, the lecturer himself might have been a conductor on an intercity bus. He talked about various theories on space — ancient Greek, medieval, and quite recent ones. He spoke about the boundaries of the universe, about atoms and the void inside them, about the disintegration of the universe, about the central point, about billions and billions of years. His words were always strung impassively, with the skillful rhetoric of the expert who is tired of always repeating the same things. Some students were zealously jotting down in their notebooks such sentences as "the universe is considered to have been created so-and-so many million years ago"; "the universe is considered to measure so much in length and so much in width"; "some stars are considered to be gone but go on emitting light"; "measured in millions of years, the universe is considered a very uncertain proposition, and the question is what lies beyond its edge." Others were preparing for the next lecture, and still others were leafing through magazines under their desks. From time to time, the lecturer would yawn. Of course, measured in hours, it was very early still.

For months I sat twice a week, from half past seven to nine, in the lecture room at the Faculty of Theology, floating through the universe with my brain open. Sometimes it happened that I preserved that feeling for days on end, and gradually I settled for hearing the lectures just once a week or even once in a fortnight. My girlfriend often taxed me with being cast out of the world. "You're cast out of the world," she would say, and those words always made me imagine how the parents of the sleeping children in her kindergarten would someday discover the two of us on top of the plush teddy bears and toss me, small and dingy, through the window, but I'd float on the air, soaring ever so light and barely still physical higher and higher above the earth, finally to float away into the universe.

The clashes between us grew worse and worse, and I was already toying with the idea of just giving in, partly for the sake of peace and especially because she wouldn't lend me anymore money or her car, which I, as a kid from the city outskirts, often desperately (as the phrase goes) needed. But then something happened to divert me from my intention.

One day, at half past seven sharp, there appeared in the lecture hall of the Faculty of Theology a woman I'd never seen before. She took her seat at the front desk by the window just after I'd noticed her. The sun, rising over the roof of the next-door building, was casting a beam of light on the very spot where she was sitting. For some moments she seemed to have scattered, to be gone. It was only later that I glimpsed her again, after several seconds during which I'd been motionlessly piercing through the layers of scattered air with all the sharpness of my sight. Now it often happens that I watch a woman I fancy. I know about the pleasure of aesthetics and the pleasure of eroticism. But what was taking place that morning in the lecture hall of the Faculty had nothing to do with pleasure. For an hour and a half my eyes were fixed, with an evocative pain in my breast, at the back and hair of a woman whose name I didn't know, whose very face I hadn't seen at all. "Eternity, universe, black holes, solar flares, comet collisions," the lecturer was droning on, and his words were rebounding from my look to snow on the woman by the window.

When the lecture was over, I elbowed my way among the bored pimply students toward the exit, and caught up with the front-desk woman on the stairs. The view of her face confused me for a moment. She was definitely older than me, but I couldn't gauge her age. Her face, even more beautiful than I'd imagined, carried a kind of oscillation that obliterated the years.

Was she twenty-five, thirty, or thirty-five? I invited her out for a coffee and she accepted. "Come to think of it, we can have it at my place," she said. "I don't like bars and their noise." Walking through the empty streets, she told me about the illness which had kept her away from the lectures for several months. "Why do you go to those lectures?" I asked. She didn't answer. Hadn't she heard me? I repeated my question. She didn't answer.

She lived on the third floor of an old house. We entered a big room full of old stuff and cobwebs. Under the window stood a folding bed and on the wall opposite hung a dusty mirror; next to it was an old oak door with an iron bar, similar to the door at the entrance. I thought it led into the bathroom or toilet, but she fetched water in a coffee pot from the corridor. "The toilet's outside," she said in the doorway.

Later, drinking coffee, we talked about cosmology. She spoke softly and slowly, and the smile on her face was unfathomable. She moved as if she were bodiless, but at the same time aroused in me such a strong desire to touch her body that I barely held myself in check. She noticed my excitement and asked, still smiling, if I hadn't better leave. "Of course," I said, glancing at my watchless wrist, "it's high time." I rose, took my leave, and, a little confused, headed toward the door with the iron bar. "Not there," she said worriedly, and I could see her approaching in the dusty mirror. She took my hand and led me to the entrance door.

Since that day I regularly attended cosmology lectures again. My girlfriend kept threatening to write me off for good. "You've become estranged, you just exploit me and don't even visit me at work anymore," she'd carry on. And I didn't even deny it. I couldn't understand myself why she was sticking with me. If it hadn't been for her car, which made my life easier, there would have been nothing for her truly to give me. All I was interested in was the woman from the lecture hall. Twice a week, after the lecture, I would go to her place for coffee and talk to her about cosmology. We talked and talked, and I couldn't distinguish between psychological and physical attraction. She gave me no hint that *she* could do so. But none that she couldn't, either. And when I started dropping in even on days when no cosmology lectures took place, she accepted it as a matter of course. She was always at home and always seemed to have been expecting me. And before she sent me away, she would always utter a sentence in our talks which meant the most to me and which I didn't fully understand. "Physically, I feel eternity," she would say, giving me a smile that made it hard for me to keep my seat. "Do you know what that means?" she would ask and lean toward me, so that my glance could slide from her lovely face under her shirt, almost to the nipples.

All I remember from that time were my comings to her and goings away from her. The world and my life were transparent and needless when I wasn't with her.

One day, our talk lasted into the evening. When she leaned toward me as I was just about to leave, and when I saw the gentle swings of her breasts, I couldn't hold back any longer. I embraced her and slowly slipped my hand under her shirt. Touched her nipple, which was hard and rough and tickled my finger. She didn't resist: instead she yielded so softly and gently that I wondered if I was touching her in reality or only in my mind. I rose and carried her to the bed. Then I slowly undressed her and laid my face against her cool skin. Stroking my face, she began to undo my buttons. We made love long, late into the night.

"Go now," she said when we were finished. I put on my clothes, she took my hand, and led me to the door. She undid the bar and let go of me. Under my tongue, words gathered for a question. She kissed my cheek, opening the door. As I was stepping through it, I caught her smile in the dusty mirror by the door. Then I walked into the void. And fell. Behind me I heard the soft click of the door. With my back down I was falling into the deep, looking at a sky full of stars. I heard a crack as if a bird's wing had snapped somewhere nearby. And I felt in the air for a moment a sense of eternity. And. . .

— 1989

Translated by NADA GROŠELJ

Originally published in the short stories collection
Vrata in druge zgodbe (*Mladinska knjiga, 1991*)

Andrej Blatnik

THE POWER OF THE WORD

THEY SAY IT'S not the tiger's fault that it devours the antelope. Devouring antelopes is in its nature. It's nice to be a tiger, the world is large, and when you get hungry lots of antelopes await you. Night is descending, you'll fall asleep, sleep deeply, and dream of being a tiger. And now test your power in a different way: explain to another tiger that the antelope is a living being that feels. Tell him: just imagine this, you're no longer a tiger, now you're an antelope that's fleeing from that tiger, you're out of strength, but you run, you run, the tiger is getting closer and closer, you realize you should be running in the other direction, but now it's too late, the tiger's running from that direction. And when your knees buckle and the tiger finally, inevitably, catches up to you, you, the antelope, say to the tiger: "You're not going to eat me, are you? Meat is murder. Your steak had feelings." And the tiger stops. Ponders.

Translated by JASON BLAKE

Originally published in the short stories collection
Saj razumeš? (LUD *Literatura*, 2009)
First English translation appeared in
You Do Understand; translated by TAMARA SOBAN
(*Dalkey Archive Press*, 2010)

Suzana Tratnik

A CASE FOR IRA'S SUQ PHILOSOPHY

ALLOW ME TO make use of this marvelous occasion and shed
light on the fate of my former neighbor and fifth cousin, Miss
Ira. Ira was known to few people, and even those were mere
casual acquaintances. I myself had the honor of dining with
her twice and, after her doubtlessly premature death, of being
the recipient of her diary. This cemented my conviction that,
far from being a drab little loner, Miss Ira was a restless spirit
developing a singular philosophy in the solitude and exile of
her hostile fate.

Ira always loved stealing. She never tired of it. And she never regarded herself as a thief. Because thieves were the same as
criminals. And to that subculture Ira definitely never belonged.
She had formed her own philosophy of stealing, the SUQ philosophy: Small — Useful — Quality.

Stealing small items actually harms nobody. Every single
person in the world can dispense with a bagatelle, let alone

shops or huge discount stores; after all, those have hundreds of small things, and identical ones to boot. If you steal small-time, you are difficult to catch, which is not unimportant. Ira used to shake her head over the gluttons who stole large objects. How could it occur to someone to steal a TV set? Or those megalomaniacs who stole cars, fitness equipment, entire firms, children, or people in general: those were a fine piece of work all right! S, the first part of Ira's philosophy, was the principle: You shall not steal what you cannot tuck in your pocket or handbag or under your shirt.

Ira was no kleptomaniac, it should be noted. Because she only stole things that were useful. And there are so many small and useful things in the world! Lipstick, playing cards, a piece of clothing, books, nails. . . Everything she ever stole was put to use. She never stole jewelry, which could admittedly be small but was useless, really. Those who coveted jewelry were merely pretending to care about aesthetics; in fact, they had no appreciation of prettiness but were after something bigger, and as a rule even less useful — a car, new kitchen equipment, a piano, or an equally covetous woman. Therefore, Ira never lost sight of the S principle: you shall not steal at random, every stolen item shall be of use and a delight to you. If you are caught stealing a useful thing, you can appeal to the S principle — in practice: I just had to steal it, I'm sorry but I desperately needed it.

Particularly elaborate was the Q principle, the last link in the SUQ chain. Q for quality: if you steal, steal high-quality goods. If there are several identical products of different brands at hand, steal the best. After all, when you are shopping, you never tell

SUZANA TRATNIK

the shop assistant, "Give me a shirt that's totally out of fashion," or, "Would you happen to have a liter of milk turning sour?" For example, if you are stealing cigarettes, steal the best, the ones you like to smoke most of all. Never filch the first pack at hand simply because you have the opportunity to do so — it is opportunity that makes a thief! And if you do happen to get caught, there is more dignity in being shamed for stealing the perfume of a prominent brand than for dropping in your pocket a bottle of cheap stinking cologne. People do not realize that what shop assistants resent most is the style of the theft. If they tell you, Why on earth did you have to steal those batteries, they're cheap as dirt and conk out in a trice, then your goose is cooked. In addition to being clumsy, you have insulted the assistants and the shop itself, and have no style worth speaking of. Small wonder if they phone the police. Your name may end up in a police file — because of a few perfectly worthless batteries!

Ira did have a police file, but not because of theft. So far she had been caught stealing only three or four times, but it was known to none but her. Besides, she always got off by pretending it was a misunderstanding rather than theft.

No, Ira's name was in a police file because she had once run over someone: nobody knows exactly who she'd offed, but he was rumored to have been a big fish. It is difficult to say when it happened precisely because she did not talk about it with anyone. What irked her was how some of her closest acquaintances traced her lust for stealing to that unfortunate incident. After all, as I said before, Ira had been stealing long before, from the cradle, so to speak. It is true, however, that she did not steal for a while after the accident and the innumerable hearings; it was too dangerous and she felt she was in a glass house. Apparently, it was unclear for months, or even years, whether she was going to do time or not. But at last she blew her cool and started yelling at the final hearing that what she'd run over, purely by accident and without the least intention, had been large, useless, and low quality anyway! The court found her guilty — you know, the circumstances, witnesses, speed, battered car and all — but Ira was sure it was only because she had dared to tell, loudly and publicly, the state to its face what she really thought. Then she was locked up for three years, I think, and when she came home from jail, she largely isolated herself. Her closest acquaintances claim she never had sexual relations again. But not even this fact, of course, should be mixed with her genuine, practically innate joy in stealing. Ira was jailed because of her suq philosophy.

The consequences of her political persuasion went on haunting her practically to the end of her solitary days. Living under the threat of a conditional sentence of several years, she had to be careful, especially when stealing. And all she had to rely on was her high-minded philosophy.

Translated by NADA GROŠELJ

Originally published in the short stories collection
Česa nisem nikoli razumela na vlaku (*Beletrina,* 2008)

SUZANA TRATNIK

Mojca Kumerdej

KATSA AGENT

I REMEMBER WAKING up in this hotel room. And memory is what I'm dealing with most. I was on the bed, opened my eyes, and saw walls covered in wallpaper. A green background over-laid with a lattice of round white patterns that optically contour the room's sharp corners into an oval. The room has the musty odor of old, never-cleaned wall-to-wall carpet. When I got out of bed I was dressed in a white shirt, a light-gray jacket, and gray trousers. My brown suitcase is standing next to the bed. My clothes and toiletries are inside it. Probably. The suitcase is locked. I have no idea where my telephone and laptop are. After we landed at the airport, I took a cab into the city. . . . Only which airport? Which city?

The scenes in my recent memory are disconnected. I recall only that I was looking at run-down concrete suburban districts through the cab's window. The kind of suburbs that could be anywhere. The driver asked me if this was my first time here. I told him I'd been here before and was familiar with the city.

The next scene is at the hotel reception desk, where the receptionist takes a key from behind a glass lamp refracting an orangish light and places it on the counter for me. And so probably, it seems, I left my passport on the counter for her so she could enter my data into the computer. She is in her midthirties, short reddish hair, white, with a black beauty spot on her right cheek (or is it her left?), and a teardrop-shaped pendant on her chest. . . . Or maybe it wasn't a pendant, but actually a pin on the edge of her open blouse? The time between going to my room and the moment when I opened my eyes on the bed has been erased. And if I say "erased," that could be literal. If I say "erased," there could be reason for concern. If I say "erased," I say it out loud, to hear myself speak, to hear my own voice, which I am trying hard to hold on to. Because it's also possible there is no me. This is a real and constant possibility in my line of work.

I'm afraid I fell asleep on the plane. When there are strangers sitting next to me on my trips, I rarely let myself do this. The woman beside me was in her midfifties, corpulent, black hair done up in a high bun, drenched in sickly sweet perfume, gold jewelry cutting into her large, fat hand. We looked at each other exactly twice: once when she stood up to let me have the window seat, and again when I took the packet of food from the flight attendant. I noticed nothing about her that I needed to pay attention to. And attention is not the same as paranoia; attention is a cautious defense against the slide into paranoia, and I have disciplined myself to preserve that thin line between caution and paranoia. But what if this time my judgment was in error? I glanced at the woman the moment I opened my eyes.

MOJCA KUMERDEJ

She was sitting motionless beside me, her eyes shut, but from the expression on her face I know that she was not really asleep but had only closed her eyes.

Each of my identities has a different way of talking. A different language. Various languages. I speak several languages, some in different accents. Depending on the documents I carry. Each of my identities also has its own body language, which I rehearse in advance, the way actors prepare for a role. And in my line of work one of the biggest mistakes you can make is to be contaminated — contaminated by some movement or tic from one of your other identities, especially from your true identity. Did something go wrong this time? Did I slip up? Maybe not verbally but physically? Made some gesture I shouldn't have, some movement of my own — to the extent that my own movements, my own body language, after so many years of false identities, still exist? But there is sure to be something left, some movement or tic from my most immediate ancestors, in which my late parents come back to life and which others recognize more easily than I do.

Buenos Aires. May 10, 2008. El Mirasol. We've been looking for H. S. for over a year and a half. Three months ago, we received a tip that in all likelihood he was living in Buenos Aires, in the Palermo district. That he had adopted a false identity, changed his appearance, and was circulating among antiquities dealers. Two Argentinian colleagues — *sayanim*, who assist us with our inquiries — gave me the names of three antiquarians: J. P., A. W., and S. D.

I had booked a table for two at El Mirasol. The woman across from me was smiling. My companion, who did not know why we were in this restaurant on this particular evening, had interpreted my invitation as attraction, although I am no longer sure about this. I did find her appealing, but in my life, the assignment takes precedence over emotion. And I can use anything, including emotion, as a tool for carrying out the assignment. I had met her a few weeks earlier while walking around the San Telmo neighborhood. Although I hadn't just been walking around; I was in search of H. S. That Saturday afternoon, an elegant woman, about forty years old, entered A. W.'s antique shop just a few moments after I did. She began haggling with the proprietor over the price of a wooden walking stick with an ivory handle shaped like the head of a rattlesnake. I was standing in front of an old portrait of two children, probably brother and sister, and feigned interest in the painting as I listened in on their conversation. She was not especially beautiful. Her face was rather long; her features, although regular, were sharp, which I don't find especially attractive in women; and her narrow mouth was circled by two deep, sharp creases, such as one sees on people with gastric problems, whose breath is usually acrid and foul. She suddenly came over to me and, in a voice surprisingly soft, given the angularity of her face, asked me what I thought of the walking stick. She did this without warning, spontaneously, or so it seemed to me at the time. But now I have to wonder: Why me? There were three other people in the antique shop, not counting the proprietor: a middle-aged couple, male and female, and an elderly gentleman, probably local. And that's everything I remember from our first encounter. I don't even know what I said to her in response, or how we later became better acquainted.

MOJCA KUMERDEJ

The next scene in which the woman appears is, in fact, that evening at El Mirasol. She was casually chatting about all sorts of things as I, although looking in her direction, monitored the arriving and departing restaurant patrons in the window's reflection; in this way I had a clear view of what was happening in the room. A few minutes after nine, a group of five men, ages thirty-five to sixty, entered the restaurant. One of them was J. P. They sat down at a circular table reserved for six people. One chair remained empty. When the waiter arrived, J. P. leaned toward him, whispered something, and the waiter cleared the extra setting. I made very sure that no one at the table sensed me looking at them. The look — that amorphous thing, that prehistoric human organ, which invisibly grazes another person so they instinctively turn their head — has a power most people aren't aware of and don't know how to use. I, however, in such situations know how to avoid every kind of eye contact, and not just the direct kind, since eyes can also meet on reflective surfaces.

After half an hour of observing what was undoubtedly a table of businessmen in the evening reflection of the window abutting the street, I was convinced that this time, too, I would be leaving empty-handed. But then I froze — for just an instant — and the very next moment my gaze, riveted on the glass surface, seemingly dissolved. Sitting across from J. P. was a man of about sixty. In the window's mirror, I surveyed his nondescript profile, his thick and entirely gray hair, and his full, well-tended beard. His manner of communicating with the others was refined and reserved; he always waited for the person he was conversing with to complete their thought, and even when the most excitable man in the group interrupted him midsentence, he showed no annoyance or offense. But then, suddenly, he put down his eating utensils: the knife in his right hand and the fork in his left he laid against the edge of his plate; then he picked up his glass with his right hand, took a sip, set down the glass again, and with his left hand — not his right, as one would expect of a right-handed man — ran his fingers through his thick hair twice. At this gesture, at the way he twice ran his left hand through his hair and, at the same time, slightly cocked back his head, it suddenly dawned on me (although, to all appearances, I was at that moment attentively chatting with the woman opposite me and even interjecting an occasional joke) that I knew this motion. I recognize and identify people not so much by their faces, which can be altered, as by the way they move. Over the past twenty-three years I have compiled a sizeable archive of body movements characteristic of the individuals with whom I have been professionally connected. I have invested an immense amount of time and knowledge in this endeavor: long hours of reading documents, examining photographs and video recordings, analyzing data and configuring it into diagrams, into my own coded diagrams to which only I know the key — although I am not such a fool as to think they could never be decoded; after all, my colleagues on the opposing sides (and in my line of work you can never be entirely sure who is on your side and who is on the side of your adversaries) have been similarly trained and educated.

There was almost no chance of him recognizing me. We had never met, and I doubt he had even heard of me, which is one of the reasons I was chosen for this mission. In the days that followed, with the help of the Argentinian sayanim, I investigated and confirmed his identity: H. S., of Lebanese descent, who three years ago narrowly escaped capture by Mossad Kidon agents and vanished into thin air (although we had tips that he was in South Africa, we were unable to locate him there), has for the past two years been living in Buenos Aires under the alias L. D., a dealer in antiquities. As a right-handed man with a thick gray beard and refined manners. All I had left to do were the preparations for the final act — to inspect the place where he was living and follow his daily routine — after which I handed my plan for the last part of the operation over to four Kidon agents. Once I complete my part of an assignment — scouting the terrain, collecting information, analyzing it, and then planning the operation — I disappear as inconspicuously as I appeared, always making sure to leave no trace. Two weeks later, while driving home, H. S. was in a car accident. Cardiac arrest, the media reported, citing the forensic findings. Nothing suspicious; death by natural causes. And I, who always wait for the mission to reach its conclusion, was now ready to leave. A flight to Spain, a two-day stopover in Madrid, then home to Tel Aviv. But two hours before I had to leave for the airport, the bell rang. Standing at the door was my Buenos Aires friend with the surprisingly soft voice, who for the last two months had been interpreting my attention to her as attraction — although I doubt this more and more. She glanced at the suitcase in the front hall.

"You're leaving?" she asked.

I told her I was going on an urgent business trip but would be back in four days.

"Where are you going?"

"Not far away," I lied.

She entered the flat, leaving the door slightly ajar.

And after that — well, I don't know exactly what happened after that. The scene that followed is doubled in my memory, and I'm not sure which version is real, which of the two scenes is true.

Is it the first? In which she took a step toward me, looked at me beseechingly as the creases deepened around her mouth, and said, "You can't just. . . Please, Vladimir, I'm asking you . . . At least stay long enough for us to talk. . . . Because what we have together. . . the feelings I have for you. . . Vlado, please. . . don't leave. . . ."

Or the second? Where she stepped toward me and, with a strangely cynical smirk, looked at me and said, "You're not going anywhere, Vladimir. . . . You're not getting away from us this time. . . . We've been looking for you for years. . . and now. . . Yon . . . Katsa Agent Yonatan Reuven. . . we have finally tracked you down. . . ." She called me by my name — by my real name, my birth name, which I never use anywhere but at home.

If the first version is true, then I probably arrived at the airport (only which airport?), went through the necessary formalities after landing, and then, as I remember, got into a cab in front of the terminal and headed to the city (which city?). The interval between the suburban apartment blocks and taking the key from the receptionist with the teardrop pendant is impenetrable darkness. Nor do I remember anything between taking the key and the moment I woke up in this room. My senses tell me that more than a few hours have passed, maybe a day, or even several days, but the intervening time is simply a blank for me. The window and door are locked. When I picked up the receiver of the telephone on the bedside table and tried to call reception, it was my own voice I heard on the other end, as if I'd slipped into some sort of Kafkaesque telecommunication system. On both sides of the long, narrow window hang green curtains yellowed from cigarette smoke. There is a clock on the wall, just above the door. When I woke up, it was showing three o'clock and, since it was light outside, I assumed it must be three in the afternoon. Now the clock shows six, but I'm convinced it has been tampered with and doesn't show the right time. At first, judging by my own senses, it seemed to be running properly; later, however, the hands started moving more slowly. I know this because, when I was lying in bed, I watched the hands move as I counted off the seconds and minutes. When I first went to the window and opened the smoke-stench curtains, outside in the courtyard I saw a brownish-gray cat perched on a dumpster, sniffing at its contents. It swatted at something with its paw and then, with this thing in its mouth, jumped to the ground and set about tormenting its prey. A cook stepped from beneath an awning carrying a yellow trash can filled to the brim, which he emptied into the bin. Meanwhile, as the cat was mauling its prey, a pigeon flew over its head and alighted on the stone ledge of a grated window. I went over to the minibar. Inside were juices, soft drinks, mineral water, two beers, vacuum-packed peanuts, and two small bottles of whiskey. I didn't touch a thing. On my way to the bathroom I glanced at the clock; the minute hand had moved a few minutes ahead. While washing my face, I sipped water from the tap and rinsed out my mouth. Ever since

I woke up, I've had a metallic taste in my mouth. And I've felt a bit dazed. As I washed my face, I noticed that my spittle, mixed with the draining water, was swirling clockwise in the sink. But it should have been moving counterclockwise. In the northern hemisphere water swirls counterclockwise when it goes down a drain, and swirls clockwise in the southern hemisphere.... Or is it the other way round?... So maybe I never left at all?... And the second version of the story is the true one?... And I am still here... in Buenos Aires... somewhere?

Again I go to the window, look out, and again I see the brownish-gray cat swatting at its prey, the cook tipping the trash can into the dumpster, and the pigeon alighting on the stone ledge of the grated window. I sit down on the bed and turn on the television. Most of the channels are dark; the rest are showing documentaries about different cities and places. On one channel I see a woman with dark hair, about fifty-five, wearing gold jewelry. She is sitting on a plane; then she stands up to let someone take their seat — I can't see the person's face since the scene is shot from their perspective, but from the gray suit they are wearing I assume it's a man. After this, the channel switches automatically to a video from a restaurant where a forty-year-old woman with a long, narrow face is sitting at a table; as she talks to the person across from her, the creases around her mouth become more deeply etched. And when the channel switches yet again, I see myself: I'm in a gray suit with a leather bag over my shoulder, walking along Ben Yehuda Street, and when I cross the intersection at Jabotinsky, for a brief moment I seem to sense the breeze off the Tel Aviv marina in my nostrils. Then, right away, there's a new scene: I am in bed asleep,

MOJCA KUMERDEJ

alone in the darkened room of the flat I was renting in Buenos Aires. So who is that woman who came up to me in the antique shop in San Telmo — my Buenos Aires friend with the unusually soft voice — in whose company I more than once happened to fall asleep? What if this time I really did make a mistake and misjudged the woman?

This time I'm in trouble like I've never been before. I go over to the green curtain again, and through the window I see the cook bringing out the plastic yellow trash can and shaking it into the dumpster, and, as the grayish-brown cat mauls its prey, a bird flies over its head and alights on the stone ledge of the grated window. Now I am sure that the window in this room, which appears to look out on a courtyard where dumpsters are lined up against a high wall, is not really a window, and that there is no outside behind the glass surface, but only plasma, on which the same scene is being played on a loop. And that the hotel room I'm in is not actually in a hotel, and that none of the boundaries of this space border on any outside world; they are only the inside edges of the world in which I am imprisoned. And because I feel a bit dazed, I cannot fully rely on my body or my senses, and less and less, too, will I be able to rely on my mind, although I am doing my best to maintain a clear and logical thought process. Where do the videos that I see on the screen come from? Are these memories I experienced or are they implanted memories? I don't know. But I do know what is being done to me. I am very familiar with the technique of erasing a person's memories and introducing artificial ones. They intend to keep me here until they have successfully eroded my last ounce of certainty — until they have successfully degraded my structural integrity to the point where I start hallucinating and my resistance to the selective crushing of data and memories is entirely broken.

I am doing my best not to go mad. Slumped in an armchair, I am talking in order to maintain my concentration. And as I talk, I have my hand placed against my neck so I can feel the vibrations of the words I am speaking, so I can maintain an organic connection between my thoughts and my body, even if what I am speaking is total nonsense. I am talking out loud... completely trivial things.... I am describing the objects in the room .... I dig the fingernails of my right hand into my left hand and I verbalize the pain out loud.... And when from somewhere (but from where, from where?) I hear a woman's voice saying: Yon... Yonatan Reuven... I remind myself that survival means fighting to the death, and I refuse even to flinch.... And I wait... as I talk... and I wait some more....

Translated by RAWLEY GRAU

Originally published in the short stories collection
Temna snov (*Beletrina, 2011*)

Tomaž Kosmač

SCREW THIS

ARMED WITH NEWSPAPERS and a bottle of watered-down wine, I sat on the bench next to the footpath. People walked past but mostly didn't bother me, a few of them slowed down, uttered some polite cliché or even tried to draw me into a chat. I didn't respond to their trite phrases. Stubbornly I stared at the paper and pretended to be deaf to any attempt at conversation. With my unapproachability I routinely kept folks at a distance until a pair of lovers intruded into my oasis. A busty girl and a young man in black thought nothing of edging me to the far end of the bench and, without an ounce of embarrassment, started making out right next to me. With little indication that they intended to end their hanky-panky, and in the hope that they might comprehend that they were not welcome on private property, I nervously took a few loud gulps, but what I achieved had the exact opposite effect. Loud and annoyed slurping didn't drive them away. Even worse.

The guy stopped snogging the girl and said, "Give us a swig!"

Out of sheer habit, I automatically passed him the plastic bottle.

"Can Katja have some too?"

"I am not usually this generous, but since I have quite a lot of reserve in my backpack, go ahead."

Unnecessary honesty. They stuck to me and we guzzled on the watered-down wine until the evening. The lovebirds weren't that bad. Especially not Katja, who became very talkative after a few drinks.

"I have huge problems at home. I don't know who's worse, Father or Mother. They are total idiots. They don't allow me to go to any parties. They just shout, *These places are full of debauchery! Orgies! All they do is fuck! Sooner or later somebody will knock you up, and what, do you expect us to look after your bastard? No chance! Under our roof you will obey our rules!* They have even been known to lock me in my room on the weekends. Sometimes I manage to escape but that's when all hell breaks out. Slapping is no rarity and, caught between four walls as I am — the morons even unplug my computer — I read a lot. Mostly fairy tales. In them I identify with some enchanted princess and dream of a prince who will come to save me. Well, now he has!" She snuggled up to Klemen.

The prince didn't react. He was concentrating on rolling a joint.

"I suggested to my parents that I might get a job, but the assholes don't want to hear about it. They say I would be wasted in a factory. They are trying to make me study, but I'm done with education. I had difficulties even at primary school. What can I do, if I'm not clever? I can't wait to move out. Anywhere. But I am still underage and if I were to run away now, the idiots would have a missing person report issued."

Katja took the joint Klemen was offering her, inhaled deeply, and continued. "With the excuse that I have a poor self-image that she could try and improve, a friend of mine once dragged me to Ljubljana. I half expected that we would visit some dumb psychotherapist, then perhaps find some suitable company, cuddle up to the guys, that kind of stuff, but no, nothing of the sort. Instead of going to some ridiculous séance, the bitch, believe it or not, took me to some lesbian commune where I shouted, 'I only came with you to get a good fuck and you drag me here to these ugly bitches!'"

Katja smiled nervously. "Screw this. I need a piss."

She went off into the bushes and Klemen prodded me. "So, what do you think of her?"

"She's wonderful. When will you break up?"

"Why?"

"I've fallen for her."

He didn't like my style of praise and as soon as Katja finished, he grabbed her hand and dragged her off into the night. I also slowly waddled off into the darkness.

In the very same spot a few months later, I sat trying to catch the soothing rays of the early autumn sun. I quietly longed for a drink, stealthily kept a watch on passersby, browsing through a three-day-old newspaper. I had picked it out of the trash. I had no cash on me and I humbly asked the heavens for any kind of help. My prayer was miraculously answered. Klemen appeared out of nowhere with a plastic bag full of bottles. He plonked himself down next to me.

"What do you want? White or red?"

"White." I quickly took the bottle and rushed over to the stream to mix the wine with water in my plastic bottle. He had his neat. Clearly he was used to this, showing no sign of intoxication even after a liter and a half. Mostly he stayed silent, occasionally, if at all, responding monosyllabically to my questions. In vain I tried to break through his shell. No theme yielded any results. The silence was becoming awkward and at a loss for any further ideas I eventually repeated the question I had asked him at the beginning.

"Do you just like to drink or are you celebrating anything?"

He graciously gave me an answer. "I got an apartment."

"Great! Is Katja living with you?"

"The court order states I am not allowed to come within a hundred meters of her."

"Why's that?"

"Her parents went to the cops and said. . . well, right. . . lots of things."

"Like what?"

"Shit, you're nosy!" he suddenly exploded. He blew his cigarette smoke at my face angrily and growled, "You want to know everything! Do you want to screw Katja?"

I didn't react.

"Tell me!" His face was right in front of mine, and he once again puffed straight at me.

The guy had totally lost it.

"I am married to solitude," I said. "It would resent me being unfaithful."

"You got out of that one well." He stubbed out his cigarette angrily with his studded boots, spat on the ground, and left.

Clearly, he couldn't handle his drink as well as it seemed. But, he forgot his bag. The bottles winked happily at me.

The public works job to which I was sent by the employment service and could not avoid was finally coming to an end. After three months of wasting my life, I could once again breathe freely. The soul-crushing drudgery was over and, relieved of torment, I was dancing playfully along the footpath when Klemen and Katja suddenly appeared in front of me.

"What's the humming for?"

They'd come rushing out of the forest hand in hand. They had probably been smoking a joint in among the trees because they could hardly contain their laughter. Both dressed in black. Goths. Klemen was like that anyway, Katja was merely imitating his style. They had a bottle of whiskey with them and I took a sip, then a few large gulps.

"Woooh, it'll kill you," said Katja.

"She's just worried that she will have to go and get another bottle from the shop. We nicked this one."

"Screw this."

Whenever she found herself in an uneasy situation or lost the thread of the conversation, she came out with the platitude she could not go wrong with. She had problems concentrating. I returned them the booty and revealed the reason for my cheerfulness.

"I won't rot away at the factory forever either," said Klemen. "I will hand in my notice and go off to Ukraine to find a few whores."

He was cut out to be a pimp. Tall, muscular, cunning, tattooed, and wicked. Women stuck to him like honey.

Katja wrapped herself round his neck and chirped, "You won't force me into prostitution, will you?"

"No way," he said, winking at me mischievously.

I regularly saw the lovers around town. As soon as Katja turned eighteen, she left her parents' house and moved in with Klemen. It seemed their souls were linked in a genuine love. They walked around arm in arm, smiling. Probably, to a great extent, due to the weed and booze, but few people knew this.

One day they invited me to their place. Their nest was incredibly clean. Klemen had decorated it in red. The walls, the curtains, the wardrobes — all red. He was probably converting the joint into the brothel of his dreams. Outside the front door I followed their example, removing my shoes. In the kitchen I plonked a few bottles of wine on the counter.

"Don't you have anything stronger?"

"Nope," I said almost apologetically.

They glanced at each other, rolled a joint, and offered it to me. Initially I refused but on the second bottle accepted the weed. It hit me straightaway and I only vaguely caught Katja's words.

"The only good thing on me are my tits."

"Show us, then!" I leaned toward her.

She was about to lift up her T-shirt when Klemen freaked out.

"Are you nuts or are you just pretending to be?"

"I dunno." I burst out laughing.

"You'd better go while there's still time!"

I didn't move and without hesitation he grabbed me by the collar, threw me through the door, and slammed it shut behind me. I was so stoned I didn't even put on my shoes. It was mid-January and I walked through town in my socks.

I was hitchhiking one day toward the end of winter. The car that stopped was Klemen.

"Hey, where have you been? Ukraine?" I teased him.

"Work."

"And Katja?"

"We're no longer together."

"How come?"

"She was too wild for me."

"Where is she?"

"The psychiatric ward. Apparently."

I could not get any further information from him. Not surprising. Someone whose dreams fall through and is stuck at the factory instead of being a pimp is not likely to boast about it to the world.

In the spring I was getting drunk at Janez's place. The doorbell rang. He went to open it and in stepped Katja.

"Aren't you in the nuthouse?" I blurted.

She grinned. "I just wintered there."

"She's currently staying with me," Janez told me when she vanished into the room. "Poor girl, didn't have anywhere to go, so I offered her a roof over her head. No strings attached."

The retired miner had the reputation of a drunkard. Even those who occasionally used his place to get smashed, berated him. They were probably jealous that he was a pensioner. He had retired at fifty and, unlike most of the others, he didn't have to hide the bottles from his bosses or wife. He was his own master, lived as he pleased, and was the only person to help Katja. Some of his visitors publicly condemned drunkards, were disgusted by parasites living off the taxpayers' hard work, went to church on Sundays, and considered themselves to be wonderful people. Along with the herd they trumpeted about ethical principles but as soon as words needed to be turned into action, their magnanimity magically vanished.

"She's really hardworking. The other day she cleaned the entire apartment. It's all messy again today, but. . ."

Katja peeked out of the room. "Do you have any pills?"

"Nope. Sorry."

"Fuck," she said and closed the door.

"She needs them for her nerves," Janez explained.

I glanced at the bowl he had once shown me. Then it was full of baclofens, tramadols, and similar analgesics. Now it was entirely empty.

"I feel really sorry for her, she needs so many drugs," he sighed.

"Right, but it's not because of her nerves."

"What do you mean?"

"Forget about it. Let's drink."

We raised our glasses and the following morning he gave Katja his last pennies for a fresh supply of plonk. We were both too drunk to make it to the shop. The poor girl didn't come back and while waiting I slowly sobered up and made my way home. In the evening Janez called me.

"She has only just come back, and is behaving strangely. She isn't drunk but looks like she is. I don't know what's wrong with her."

"Did she bring you the booze?"

"No."

"And the money?"

"Didn't ask."

"When you get your pension," I advised him, "you'd better hide it from her."

He would go to the bank on the first day of every month and take out his entire pension in cash. At the counter. He didn't trust bank machines. "Don't be so mean! Katja doesn't steal!"

I was about to say something but, knowing that I would be talking to deaf ears, I bit my tongue.

Less than a week later he called me again.

"She took all my money. Vanished into thin air. Do you think I will ever see her again?"

"Hope dies last," was all I could say.

"And how am I supposed to pay the bills? I gave her everything and this is what I get." He was desperate. "I just don't get it."

Janez didn't get many things.

Katja disappeared. There was talk of her wandering around Ljubljana, Koper, Celje, Kranj, here and there. Slowly she slipped out of memory and few people ever mentioned her. In December I had a call from Janez.

"Would you come to the psychiatric hospital with me?"

I was worried I would lose my boozing station and cried out, "Surely you're not going dry?"

"No, no," he reassured me. "I want to visit Katja. She's in the high-risk ward."

I went off to town and on our way to the hospital Janez revealed how Katja had explained the theft to him. She had apparently stolen his cash under the influence of drugs. "She was not aware of her actions," he summed up. "I have forgiven her."

Instead of the usual oranges, we took her some cigarettes. It was as if we had brought her pure gold. She locked the carton in her cupboard. In the asylum patients are always scrounging for a smoke, they have plenty of everything else. Katja seemed happy. She had figured out a system that gave her partying in the summer months and a warm comfortable rest in the winter when it was cold.

"Will you ever return to my place?" Janez asked her.

"Dunno."

The male nurse brought the trolley with the pills and we were forgotten in an instant. She jumped up. "Food time."

As she swallowed the intoxicating treats Janez and I made our way toward the exit. Outside he said, "I hope she's better soon."

"She'll come to as soon as the snow melts," I reassured him.

After the winter holiday at the psychiatric institution, Katja, as expected, got well and moved into Janez's place again. Officially she was also away for a month or two at a time, or at least it seemed so. She wandered round the country, camped wherever she could. Often she became friendly with some guy, wrapped him round her finger and milked the sucker dry until he got fed up. She never contributed a single cent toward her stay. She used up all the money she received from social services for herself. One evening she appeared at my door.

"Can I stay the night?"

Knowing her, I was hesitant.

"Just for tonight. Then I will go back to Janez," she added.

Janez was her base camp. A place where she could rest, cool down, and gather up strength for new adventures.

I didn't want her to pupate at my place, so I reluctantly grunted, "Why don't you go to his place right now?"

"I am dead tired. I barely managed to hitchhike here from Godovič."

I gave her my bed and slept in the sleeping bag. Katja didn't easily spread her legs and I didn't want to push her to justify some stereotypical masculinity. If she wanted more, she would let me know. At dawn I was woken up by sobbing.

"What is it?" I switched on the lights.

"Klemen died."

"When?"

"In the night."

"How do you know?"

"I know!"

"You dreamed it."

"I didn't. He hanged himself!"

Despite the early hour, I checked her premonition — you can never underestimate female intuition. I called Klemen. He was getting ready to go to work and I handed the phone to Katja. She didn't pay any attention to the mobile. She just kept repeating tearfully, "Because of me, he hanged himself, because of me, because of me...."

I could not persuade her that Klemen had not kicked the bucket and that she was delusional. It took me a long time to calm her down and when I managed to bring her to her senses I dragged her straight to town. As soon as we arrived at Janez's place she changed entirely. Her tears were replaced with laughter. She hugged him mockingly and then slipped into the bathroom.

"It wouldn't do her any harm if you get her off to the psychiatric hospital," I suggested.

"What for? I have never seen her this happy."

"She's stunned."

"Don't be ridiculous," he said dismissively.

Refreshed, Katja joined us in emptying a few bottles and I thought that perhaps Janez was right. She laughed like crazy.

Janez was always inebriated but never so much that he lost sight of his horizons. He surpassed all the company that gathered in his den. He would collect food from the old people's home and shared it generously with his flatmate and it seemed Katja had rid herself of her demons. She no longer roamed all around the country but only around our town. She sat in pubs, drank whatever others bought her, on weekends partied till she dropped, but apart from that sat around in her room. Normally whenever she had a good supply of various pharmaceutical products. When we would drink and shout a lot, she sometimes kindly asked for some peace and quiet. We did what we were asked, for a few minutes at least. Often she had no choice but to join us. At first she would spontaneously join in the conversation, over time she became more and more embittered.

"What's the problem?"

"What do you think the problem is?" Brane shouted and rubbed his crotch. "She's got everything, all she needs is the right piece of meat!"

He was mad about her but didn't know how to behave toward her.

"Is something wrong?" I asked.

"My head is throbbing."

"Due to the noise we make?"

"No, it's the same when you are quiet," she said, smiling faintly.

"Have something to drink and your woes will be over."

We poured her a glass. She drank it and moved to her room. Nobody bothered about her state because in ever shorter intervals it fluctuated from deep depression to pure euphoria. Bottles gathered on the table.

Brane and I wandered around various joints and at the last place managed to get three bottles on account. Shaky legged we staggered back to Janez's place and we took the booze out of the bag.

Brane asked, "Where's Katja?"

"She went off somewhere this morning. It was odd because she doesn't normally get up that early. She didn't say where she was off to."

I opened one of the bottles and went to the kitchen to mix our usual watered-down beverage in a plastic bottle. Over the sound of the water I caught the phone ringing.

"Helooo," Janez drawled. "Who is it?"

In his state he was incapable of reading the name on the caller screen. He was truly drunk. I returned just as he was putting the mobile back into his pocket.

He whispered numbly, "Katja killed herself."

I was stunned. "You're kidding me?"

"Threw herself under a train."

"And we were about to get married," Brane uttered. "She was carrying my child."

Janez approached him slowly and punched him in the face with such force that Brane fell off the sofa. His nose smashed, he tripped over onto the wooden floor from where our host literarily kicked him out into the corridor and, covered in blood as he was, threw him down the stairs. I was about to follow the comrade but the brawny Janez uttered, "Please stay. I don't want to be alone. You are someone I can talk to."

I had never seen him violent, even though word spread that he was a tough old nut you didn't want to rub the wrong way.

I agreed to his request and asked him, "Who told you about Katja?"

"Mladen. From the police. An acquaintance."

There were no further doubts. Katja had indeed committed suicide. I didn't feel anything. Her escape from the world did not touch me.

"Let's drink and remember her for the good and fun things," I said.

There weren't many but fortunately Janez had quite a stash of wine, which meant we could extend fleeting impressions *ad infinitum*.

The criminal investigators found no foul play in Katja's death. Her body was handed over to the undertaker and I overheard them talking in the street.

"She died instantly. She didn't suffer."

But what about before? Nobody goes and kills themselves out of the blue. I notice many potential suicides all around me but I don't jump to their aid. I nonchalantly ignore them. If I knew for certain that a person committing suicide fucks up their alleged eternity, I would perhaps make more of an effort, try to convince the defeatist that they ought not to turn their back on life, but... Why procrastinate? Sooner or later we all are pushing up the daisies. Would encouragement really help the miserable person or merely perversely extend their agony, were the thoughts that crossed my mind as I considered whether to attend the funeral. Even though I normally honor the deceased, I could not see myself in the sorry cortege. Katja simply didn't mean enough to me. Many justify not going to a funeral by saying that the dead person doesn't care anyway. Well, even if they do, their relatives certainly don't, I kept saying to myself until I picked up on the news that the ceremony would be close family only. I breathed a sigh of relief and about a week later Janez and I went to the cemetery and lit a candle for Katja. She was buried in the family grave.

"In the end," I muttered, "everyone ends up at home."

Janez was silent. He respectfully placed a bunch of carnations on the marble gravestone and could barely hold back his tears, so I avoided further smart comments. We stood in silence next to the grave, then he gently stroked the headstone, slowly turned round, and we went off to the pub.

Over a bottle of wine he said, "It's only kin that you can rely on."

"How come? I thought all your family had written you off, and weren't Katja's relatives ashamed of her?"

He ignored me and said, "I will get pissed out of my head. You?"

I hesitated, then said, "Screw this," and joined him in his liquid mourning.

Translated by GREGOR TIMOTHY ČEH

Originally published in the short stories collection
Ko jebe (*Beletrina, 2021*)

Tadej Golob

SOMETHING ABOUT MARIBOR

THAT FATEFUL MORNING, in fact it was still night, an inconspicuous car drove into the parking area in front of the Habakuk Hotel under Pohorje. Out of it stepped a man who would have drawn much attention in town but he was spared all that due to the darkness and the almost-empty parking lot. His long, white-lined, scarlet-red cloak sparkled in the light of the lamp. The man's brow was tall, clear, noble, the silver hair above it must once have been black. Older people might have recognized in him a little of Richard Chamberlain as the Count Monte Cristo. He looked around, glanced toward the stairs leading to the hotel, and sighed. We might only be guessing the reason for this reaction, had it not been for his barely audible utterance: "What's this supposed to look like?" Once again looking around, he shrugged his shoulders and made his way to the foyer where, despite the deathly hour, there was still a light glowing.

The receptionist raised his head, glanced in bewilderment at the man's attire, and hesitated for a brief moment, as if deciding what stance to take.

"Good evening, how can I help?" he said obligingly — after all, you never know.

"I would like a coffee," said Count Monte Cristo. "Would that be possible?"

"Of course," said the receptionist, happy that he had approached the matter in the right tone, for he could sense in the arrival's voice that he was a gentleman. The cloak was indeed odd, he initially thought, but perhaps he was some actor after a performance. Though at this time of the night...

"A long shot, and a table near a socket."

Monte Cristo raised the briefcase he had until then almost unnoticeably been holding in his hand and placed it on the counter.

"I am low on power."

"Of course, of course," the receptionist said hurriedly, eagerly moving from behind the counter to lead the guest to a table not far away, pointing to the socket.

"Will this do?"

The Count nodded.

About a kilometer away, on the residential estate on the same bank of the river that split the town in two, the river Drava, Jože Vogrin, a forty-eight-year-old former employee of the Maribor Automobile Factory, was fast asleep. When the company had collapsed a few years ago, he lost the first and last job he had in life and everything went downhill from there. It was only the fact that things were far from good even before this that made the downward path seem not as steep. That night, as he often did, he lay at rest drunk and unwashed, something his indifferent wife, Lidija Vogrin, née Župec, was almost used to after all these years. In such a family, the children — twelve-year-old Marija (named after the Virgin Mary) and eight-year-old Vinko (named after his uncle) — didn't really have many opportunities. In about a year's time Marija would, I guess, finish elementary schooling, the last in her life, and then try to find a job in some factory as unskilled labor, even though there were fewer and fewer such jobs around. The son would be a drunkard, that was clear, as he was even now being given handkerchiefs dipped in brandy to put in his mouth every time something hurt or burnt, sometimes even when he just cried, as children do. Ever since he was in diapers. However, our guessing is in fact pointless, for this evening was to be their last.

Count Monte Cristo took a sip of coffee — Austrian, he thought to himself, not only the curtains and everything else, even the coffee is Austrian. He opened his laptop, plugged it in, waited a few moments for the start-up to finish, and then typed in a few commands. A map of the town appeared on the screen. From his briefcase he produced a pair of earphones with a microphone and placed them into his ears. He tapped the microphone.

"Ay, ay, ay. . ." came from the other end.

He waited a few seconds, and then said, "One two, one two. . . Is that fine now?"

"Better," said the voice of the Godzilla.

Using the mouse, he zoomed into the location and marked a place.

"On site?"

The Count took the mumbling in the earphones as an affirmative.

"Let's go then," he said.

Gently, surprisingly gently for a beast that size, a huge paw descended from the sky and flattened the entire apartment block next to number 47 Proletarian Brigades Road. Including the unfortunate Vogrin family and everyone else. (See, it isn't true that every family has misfortunes of their own).

Some other place, some other town, a long time before this.

Journalist: But how come your literature is not more engaged?

Writer: (thinks) Perhaps because of the workers.

Journalist: The workers?

Writer: Yes, they get on my nerves. Are you surprised?

Journalist: Eeeeh...

Writer: None of them will ever read any of my books. If I would happen to end up in the gutter, nobody would, when they lose their jobs or their homes, they swear at everyone and demand help. They are dull, uneducated, and aggressive. (And they stink, he adds to himself.)

Some other place, Maribor, thirty years ago. Count Monte Cristo, then still a student at the secondary school in town, is walking one evening behind the Ljudski Vrt Stadium with two of his schoolmates. Four people approach and attack them. The schoolmates run away, two of the aggressors run after them, Count Monte Cristo finds himself being restrained by one of the others who breaks the Count's two front teeth with a knock of his head. Jože Vogrin.

At the bus stop in Lenart, the morning bus taking factory workers to Maribor. Count Monte Cristo manages to squeeze himself onto it, squashed against the door with his face pressing the front windshield. The stench is unbearable. The Count can't wait to get off the bus in Maribor and take a deep breath of the purple air filled with the smog and dust from all the factories that were still operating at the time. He later traveled a great deal around the world but nowhere did he find such filthy air and the purple sky he remembered from the bus station in Maribor in the 1980s. Thinking about it now, sipping his coffee at the Hotel Habakuk, he feels a pang of nostalgia.

"What now?" asks the Godzilla.

"The bus station," says the Count.

The enormous animal invisibly makes its way across town. It stops at the bus station, next to some monument squeezed into a corner and an old steam engine that is on display there. It looks around.

"There is nobody here."

The Count checks his laptop.

"Sorry. You went to the old bus stop, which is now used for urban transport only. Go back down the road you came on, Partisan Street, and find the new one."

The Godzilla grumbles. The Count is used to this; it always groans but mostly does what he tells it.

"Right, and?"

"Find the sign for the Murska Sobota and Lendava buses."

The bus stop in Maribor (the old one), a long time ago.

"Do you have a reservation for Mürska?"

Count Monte Cristo tries to get on the bus.

"No, well, sod off then! You guys from Lenart have your own bus."

"Found it," says the Godzilla.

"Go right ahead," says the Count. "Bust it."

Through the earphones he hears the earsplitting cries of vowels that cannot decide whether they are an a, an e, or a u, or all of those at once. The Count even thinks he can smell the stench of burning flesh.

"Oops," says the Godzilla. "Perhaps I overdid it a little. All gone. The entire bus stop."

The Count wonders whether he should be angry with the Godzilla or not. He decides not. He cannot imagine how the bus drivers from Bistrica could possibly be any better than the ones from Prekmurje, even though he never had much contact with them. And anyway, schoolmates from Bistrica also teased him, just because he was from Prlekija.

"Oh, well, shit happens," he says.

"What now?" asks the Godzilla.

The Count thinks. Creeping across his motionless face was the slightest, almost unperceivable sliver, or hint, or whatever you might call it, of clarity. Gleefulness.

"That's it, it's over." And for a moment he feels like Jesus. "It is complete." A touch of suaveness. Four years of Maribor and he cannot recall any further grudges.

"Can I go for a walk?" asks the Godzilla. "The night is young, so I thought...."

"Go ahead," says the Count.

TADEJ GOLOB

He thinks, Is this really everything? Nothing stronger? Is this all that is left, a bunch of banalities that I can't even be bothered to write about? He becomes aware of his ridiculous attire and blushes. Count Monte Cristo, as if! The receptionist gives him an expectant glance from behind his counter.

"The premiere dragged on," the Count stutters apologetically. "I didn't have time to. . ."

The receptionist doesn't understand and the Count dismissively waves his hand.

"Could I get another coffee?"

The Godzilla stands on the old bridge across the River Drava, singing to itself: *"Across the Cobblers' Bridge, across the Cobblers' Bridge, left to Town Square, right to Old Square, collecting memories, recalling youth. . ."*

This is Maribor, silly, the Count thinks out loud. The Godzilla is embarrassed and briefly falls silent. It scratches its head and then starts again.

"He promised he would marry me, and start to build a bridge, a bridge to freedom, solid as the Drava Bridge. . . ."

The Godzilla sings along, and through its eyes the Count gazes at the dark deep water, thinking about how, when he used to walk across the bridge, he would have the feeling someone was calling him from below the bridge, but when he leaned over the railing, all he saw was a fuzzy image of himself down on the surface of the water. As if a hand was rising from a whirlpool, ready to pull him down into the depths.

"It's cold at the bottom," the Godzilla is now reciting. *"Dead ferrymen. Disappointed brides. Drunken fishermen. Drivers that*

fell from the road. Dancing. Waiting. Waiting with the wild Turks, hiding in the black mud. The missing youth with a colorful tie. Next to him a troop of German soldiers having lost their Fatherland. They call out to me like church bells from the cold water."

"How come you know the lyrics?" the Count asks.

"Nice words," says the three-hundred-ton beast as a two-hundred liter tear rolls down its cheek, which sizzles when it falls into the Drava, and the following morning, down on the banks of the river at Melje, a member of the Pesnica Fishing Club, Slavko Pirtovšek, fishes whole piles of bloated carp out of the water.

The Godzilla is outside the Ljudski Vrt Stadium. Here the Count used to play football, in the youth section of the Maribor Branik Club. In the generation of Marko Simeunović, who later became the national team's goalie and whose father was at the time the national team coach. And the one and only time that he came to see the youth section's training session to spot any potential talents, the Count scored a goal. His only goal in his entire life. Okay, it wasn't as if he suffered greatly because of this, he was too slow for any notable football career anyway.

The Godzilla circumvents the refurbished stadium and goes to the playing fields behind it with a view of Kalvarija, a hill the Count was made to run up during their PE classes. When they reached the top, they had to line up on the wall in front of the church so the teacher could count them from the valley below. In fact, he should also find the PE teacher, but not for this reason. He liked running.

"Do you want me to get him?" asks the Godzilla.

"Forget it, I can't be bothered," says the Count.

The Godzilla reaches the cathedral. The Count is indifferent. No particular memories connect him to this end of town, no bar that he would hang around in with his schoolmates. There is the theater where he had seen a few plays: Tone Partljič's comedy *My Father, a Socialist Kulak*; Partljič's translation of Ivo Brešan's work about the villagers in a remote village deciding to stage a performance of *Hamlet*, interpreting and adapting it in their own way; and laughed at Janez Klasinc in *Woe to the Clever Ones*. Beyond it is a small park with a monument in it. This wasn't here before. The Godzilla bends over and takes a look. Drago Jančar, Slovene writer.

"How predictable," sighs the Count. "How very predictable."

As he utters this he realizes the incongruity of his thoughts. If it is predictable, why does it annoy him, not to say upset him? How can something upset you when you expect it? Though — the Count bites his lips not to utter any obscenities — do these people have no imagination? In Mostar they erected a monument to Bruce Lee. He rolls his eyes and returns to his laptop. He notices the Godzilla. . .

". . .surely not!"

. . .lifting its right hind leg, releasing a burbling stream of urine right over the bronze cast of the famous Maribor writer.

"Are you nuts?" he shouts. "What was that about?"

The Godzilla looks down at him, well, it would look down anyway, of course, but this was a haughty look.

"You know very well what that was about. Don't feign ignorance."

The Count holds his head. Partly because he knows what will happen. "Look at him, *pissing on Jančar*," when he can barely play second fiddle to the man. Partly this and partly because he really had no ill feelings about him. *Northern Lights*, for example, is. . .

"Is a load of shit!" the Godzilla shouts and pisses on the statue a second time. "Not to mention *The Galley Slave*, now that's shit if there ever was any!"

The only thing that annoyed him about Jančar and his entire generation was a kind of mystical self-assuredness, the conviction that anything they happen to produce is art by default. *An sich*. Beyond doubt. Because when he, Count Monte Cristo, signs a piece of writing and sends it off into the world, all he can do is hope that some of the water will stay in the palm of his hand, to put it metaphorically, and he has to constantly try and catch his balance for it not to spill over or evaporate. Surely it could have been better written, and the darkness could be less banal, more engaged, less vulgar, and all those unfortunate swear words. . .

At a literary reading in Metlika. An elderly lady, a professor of Slovene (reproachfully), "And would it not be possible without the swearing?"

And an hour later, the Count standing there with a piece of cake in one hand and a glass of juice in the other, the professor utters as she leaves, "Well, I hope you write a better book next time."

Did Jančar ever get this? He doubted it. Whenever he opens his mouth his charmed female readers gaze upon him, and the literary journalists such as Alenka Zor Simonitti mutter, "A new literary treat. . ." — oh, no, that's what she says about Vlado Žabot — with Jančar it is "a new literary masterpiece!"

Jančar's words (at presentations) are slow, thoughtful, just as in his books, and his subjects cogent, for example the protagonist fighting totalitarianism, and things like that, dark scenes, swamps, rare birds, stench and mud. . . while he pathetically mumbles along about housing and employment problems and stuff like that. And when this generation of writers. . .

"Old farts," the Godzilla howls. "Moldy fossils. . ."

. . .uses quotes, they are references to the great classics of world literature, philosophy, and such, while he talks of Godzilla and Count Monte Cristo. All that's missing are Piggeldy und Frederick.

Should he too write about something similar? What does he know about Slovenia's quest for independence or even about the Second World War?

"War?" shouts the Godzilla. "How does Jančar know what it was like during the Second World War? I don't believe a word he says. He was born three years after the war ended. And why the Second World War? What's wrong with the First?"

"Calm down," the Count tells the Godzilla. "Things aren't that simple."

The Godzilla snorts and shudders. It turns around — thank goodness, says the Count to himself, it is leaving, we're done with this, it won't get us anywhere — and then suddenly from somewhere comes a high-pitched voice.

"You primitive beast!"

The Count holds his head. Not this.

He shouts a warning. "Godzilla!"

Too late. The thirty-meter beast slowly turns round and bends over. Down below stands the retired professor of Slovene,

Slavica Podbevšek, from the secondary school across the river Drava, who happened to have some stuff to do in this neighborhood. She is shaking with disgust.

"What did you say?"

"You damned animal, that is what I said! How dare you attack our laureate this way!"

She is running out of words. Holding a basket with bread, milk, and some chicory lettuce (doesn't matter that it is bitter, as long as it is soft, the dentures don't fit quite properly) in one hand, with the other she waves about a copy of the *Večer* newspaper with the headline *Ex-PM gets five years for the arms deal and five for other shit* (just to make it a little engaging).

"You are obviously a total blockhead," she says, hopping about. "Boorish, uncouth buffoon..."

"I see," says the Godzilla. "I see!"

Miss Podbevšek falls silent, as if she only now realized that this could be rather dangerous for her.

"Buffoon, you say?"

The Godzilla looks up at the sky. When it returns its gaze to the ever-more-worried professor in front of it, its eyes are glowing. The Count knows very well where this is going. He feels sorry for the old lady, but tough luck, it's her own fault.

The Godzilla looks left and right. From its height it has a great view of the entire town. Maribor. On its northern outskirts the Pyramid Hills that used to be grassy, and which the Count with a few schoolmates once volunteered to empty of a few larger rocks as a way of missing a few lessons at school; below these hills the town's villas and a few newer buildings belonging to the town's high-class residents, then his school and

Lenin Square, which has now apparently been renamed Maister Square with its monument to General Maister, then there are the hotels Orel and Astoria. It's where you used to be able to get the best Bienenstich cake in town, the Count smacks his lips, although he never liked going there because it was a joint for uptown ponces. Then a pub, farther down the Main Square, and the bridge, across to the Pohorje Hills where he was now sitting, observing the Godzilla.

"If you are a stranger, a newcomer, a displaced person," says the monster, "you only feel at home in your memory..."

"...in your head," Miss Podbevšek finishes off the sentence. "Lojze Kovačič."

The Godzilla nods.

"Who also says that a woman who loves is not a measure of your power, as you might think, but shows the measure of her own pain."

Now it is the old lady's turn to nod.

"And," the Godzilla continues, "that the coitus is the only noble remnant of genuine trance. Did you know that?"

The old lady blushes.

"Although that footage of the mummy in the final years of his life, toothlessly explaining to his faithful followers..."

The Count holds his head and blocks his ears. He does not want to be part of this.

"...doesn't really strike me as fuckish. What do you think?"

The retired connoisseur of literature and linguistics raises her hand before her eyes and screams. It is the last thing she manages to do in her life. The Godzilla belches and from its mouth comes a glowing ray of light. When the brightness dies down, all that is left in front of it is a pile of ash and a little melted plastic.

"There is no worthier being in the damned theater of this world," the Godzilla roars, cracking all the windows between Kamenica and Podbrežje, "than one who is full of love, like God, and who thus needs a person to love."

The scene turns epic. The Count raises his head from the laptop and gazes out of the window toward Maribor in the distance. Regular circles of light seem to be spreading from the center of town, accompanied by the smell of burning.

"Oh, damn it," the beast rages out of control, spitting fire and brimstone all across the awakening Styrian metropolis. "Why do you always get to know a person at the end, when it is too late!"

It roars, spits fire, and howls, "*Ali boma ye, Ali boma ye, A-li bo-ma ye!*"

"I didn't know you read Kovačič," says the Count.

The Godzilla blushes. "Everyone has their own guilty pleasure."

"Pleasure?"

The Godzilla shrugs its shoulders. "You listen to Bon Jovi."

"Only in the car," mutters the Count. "If they happen to be on the radio."

They look upon the fiery dance that the wind is blowing toward Pohorje.

"You know, it's harder and harder to keep you under control," says Monte Cristo.

The Godzilla shrugs its shoulders again. And they piggeldied off home.

Translated by GREGOR TIMOTHY ČEH

Originally published in the short stories collection
Monte Cristo, kolesa, kurent (*Litera,* 2012)

Veronika Simoniti

CRETE

SHE INSPECTS THE bicycle's split tire, straightens up, and swipes her forearm across her sweaty brow. Even with the strong muscle relaxing, her skin is pulled taut. Sometimes all it takes to get things moving is a gesture, a movement, in our case a handshake.

Her fingers deftly reach under the tire, which she has removed from the front rim, pulling out the inner tube at once; its replacement is in the bag attached to the basket. Cicadas are droning and the air around us is a concentrate of herbal scents wafting on the wind. Here, the colors are the essence of life.

We've been biking for three days now and are not yet exhausted; our gear is good and there are no blisters. Before departure I'd meticulously planned our route myself: we would leave out nothing but the most frequented spots, we'd circle the island, and make two detours inland. *Women are best off traveling with women*, she said back at home, and I couldn't agree more.

In the evening we're sitting at the guesthouse, the only guests there but for an elderly German couple, with whom, every now and again, we exchange affable smiles and converse in low voices. The landlady brings the two of us a small wedge of cheese, olives, cucumber salad, bread, and red wine, setting it all before us with particular attention.

The last time I served him food so neatly, he swept it all off the table, says Nina. Rather than give her a compassionate look, I gaze past her into the dark distance, knowing there's more to tell, knowing she has much to tell me yet — there's a gap to be filled because one day, years ago, she'd simply cut all her ties to me and shut herself up in her shell. We should make up now for all of that.

The night song has been seamlessly taken over from the day's cicadas by crickets, all is quiet, too quiet. The German couple has already retired, and we are staring each into her own distance.

~

I do so want to go cycling all over Greece once in my life... will you come with me? she said long ago, when we were still thicker than thieves, and we shook hands at once, squeezing harder than normal, almost to the point of pain. We never wondered when we'd go or what would become of our children and partners in our absence, things would sort themselves out, women are best off traveling with women: no rebellious children or sudden diseases, no wasp stings to cause allergic reactions, no men nagging that we should go for a beer and hang out all afternoon with the locals. When women travel, their route is clearly outlined and they see much, with nobody to curtail their time if they want to take a peek at a nearby clothing or shoe store; and if something goes wrong or malfunctions, for instance a car or, in our case, a bike, women can resort to the helpless act, allowing some local he-man to help them.

There's nobody curtailing our time now, we can stay on this solitary beach all day and even overnight if we feel like it. Our bikes are in the shade and we have food and drink enough. *If Gregor were here, the sun would drive him crazy, and if there were other men on the beach, they'd certainly pester me if I was topless*, Nina tells me humorously. Like in a children's game we tread the silt, like little girls we build a sand fortress with a moat, and run across the yielding surface, our tracks blurred by wind and sea.

~

Right now things are looking up, says the email message. I open it on my phone in the morning, alone on the terrace. *Watch this space. Best, Saša.*

Turning off my phone, I gaze over the railing. We are in one of the loveliest island places, a hamlet with a quaint name, which almost seems to have more inns than ordinary houses, practically all of them sporting a terrace above the sea. Off the hamlet is a small islet, to which the village boatman will ferry you for a trifle; there you can stroll among the ruins of an ancient villa and then pull on a thick rope in the chapel belfry next to the ruins, summoning the helmsman to fetch you and bring you back across the channel with its powerful current.

A drowsy Nina joins me at the table, the terrace still steeped in gentle shade, and pours for herself some watery coffee, complaining about the lack of espresso because she's a poor sleeper. She needn't have explained it because I know it very well. She keeps waking up and wandering around, or she screams in her sleep — and tonight was no exception.

I had a dream about Gregor again, she says, *and about Pia.* She's afraid of the ideas he might put into Pia's head while she was on this trip; she would have preferred to bring along her daughter but couldn't do so as Pia had to spend two summer weeks with her father by court decree.

Spread on the nets that are hung on poles and marking out the terraces, the morning catch is drying: Gorgon-like octopuses meant to lure the few tourists into the eateries, but the effect is just the opposite; we're almost nauseated, and they are only eyed covetously from the beach by seagulls.

~

Nina leaps into the sea and begins to swim toward the islet with the ruins of the ancient villa and chapel. I notice the current has started carrying her to the left; it's running strong. *Nina!* I start up, *come back!* She can't hear me. Once Gregor had persuaded her to go swimming in the Soča River, claiming to have found a safe spot on the internet, but she was almost sucked under by the whirling water and barely rescued by rafters, while Gregor

VERONIKA SIMONITI

stayed on the strand and maintained afterward that it was her own fault because she was not strong enough.

I don't understand how she can have kept falling for his tricks, or why she didn't stand up to him sooner; if she'd stayed in touch with me throughout these years, I'd have tried to dissuade her, I'd have opened her eyes and helped her gain independence — as it was, though, she distanced herself from me instead, as if she was afraid I might try to bring her to her senses. She evaded my pestering reproaches. Friendship — just what does it mean to her? When she began to break up with me, why couldn't I believe that she no longer wanted to see me or hear from me? Why did she say on the phone a little later, *If I want to know how you are, I can hear about it from others or from Saša?*

~

We set aside a whole day for the archaeological museum at Heraklion, but in fact we were finished by early afternoon. Statuettes of buxom fertility goddesses, reconstructed frescoes, and stone bull's heads, especially one which appealed to Nina so much that all the postcards she bought to send bore his image: a black head with golden horns and white lining around the nostrils — like the coalesced foam of fury. Minotaur of Knossos.

Signing Nina's postcards, I see that one is addressed to Gregor: *I love you* are the only words written in the white space, like in a cheap novel — and after all he'd done to her, and their complicated divorce too. I'm definitely not signing this. If I'm not clear about what friendship means for Nina, I'm just as unclear about her notion of love.

~

Surprisingly the day is cloudy and not so hot, which makes cycling less arduous. The road, lined with brambles, rocks, and olive trees winds uphill; every now and then a goat or sheep peeps from behind the brush. Then the road begins to descend toward the bay; at the end, just by the sea, where it turns sharply, there is an old cottage. We stop and drink from our water bottles. A long-haired and toothless Poseidon comes out of the house, smiling, and says *kalimera* and points to his courtyard, but we don't understand what he means. Then he starts bringing glasses, *retsina*, he says, and pretends he wants to drink. We exchange glances and nod to him. Two glasses of wine fill our hands and his gibberish our ears. We can't wait to get a move on, especially Nina, who feels uncomfortable — after what has happened to her, she has a distrust of men.

The first time Gregor hit Nina was before her marriage. They were drinking together and when she teased him that he was slow understanding jokes, he hit her with a glass of wine, it splashed into her hair and trickled down to her forehead, where a bump sprouted from the redness. I could imagine him, a bull with nostrils rimmed white with fury, snorting, himself surprised at the impulsiveness of his reaction.

~

Matala is the only place on our route where we have to resign ourselves to crowds of tourists. There are huge booming breakers rolling onto the beach, depositing light gray silt as well as water.

VERONIKA SIMONITI

People, in foam up to their knees, are standing next to each other and waiting for the next wave to spray them, knock them off their feet, maybe dash them against the ground, or drag them a few meters closer to the open sea. According to legend, it was here that Zeus brought his mistress when he changed into a bull to seduce Europe.

On the right side of the bay loom rock faces with Neolithic caves, which were first used as tombs and then, in the early 1970s, discovered by hippies, who moved there almost like cave dwellers, making a tourist attraction of the fishing village across the bay, which at first resisted the onslaught of Westerners and their provocative exhibition of free love.

Your adored Cat Stevens was here too back then, I tell her, having read about it in my guidebook, and Nina seems to grimace a little. She dislikes having her former tastes dragged into the open. Slipping from her T-shirt and shorts, she runs down to the sea. She has a lovely figure, petite and thus well-nigh calling for protection, but also muscular, which makes her so independent.

Once, when I presented her with a buff-colored toilet bag, which she'd admired some weeks earlier in the window of a city center store, she merely thanked me coolly, as if she didn't like it anymore. *If you don't like something, you just replace it*, she said on another occasion, and later I often thought of that sentence. At the first opportunity I'll ask her whether she'd replaced me with another confidante after she broke up with me. And if so, why hadn't she shaken off Gregor too and replaced him with other men? But I know the answer: she wouldn't have wanted to stay alone even for a split second. Strong and at the same time helpless, she had always needed a retinue, a sympathetic public, a witness to her side of the story.

~

Madame Amalía's house, the highest in the village, is walled in by mighty opuntias and looks unapproachable from a distance. In the corridor, where no one can see me, I pull my phone from my pocket and look at my email: *Things are looking up today too*, Saša reports, *the blood and urine values are settling back to normal*.

I step out of the house, and there is Madame Amalía, stocky, with her arm in a cast; her husband is sitting under the trellis, morosely staring straight ahead. *I bet he broke her arm*, comments Nina, who comes after me, smilingly nodding to Madame Amalía, her angelic curls slightly stirring. With the fingers of her left hand she encircles her right wrist, which had been twisted by Gregor years ago. Soon afterward she became ill, she tells me in front of Madame Amalía's house, because of his presence, his words, his gestures, their home was charged to the point of crackling and little Pia was growing up into a problem child — that makes you ill, supposedly we can become physically ill because of our psyche, because of the people nearest to us, or because of our thoughts.

Nina's kidney stones worsened into sepsis, and Gregor paced up and down the hospital corridor, clutching his head — they were already in the divorce process. What if the mother of his child should die, that was what worried him. Nina pauses; she knows that I'm bursting with curiosity, that I'm eager to fill in the picture from the period when I wasn't there. When she was discharged some weeks later, Gregor took her in and hired a hospital attendant so that he could go his own ways, but he paid for the nurse's attendance with Nina's money, and as soon as he completely emptied her account, he sent the nurse away and suggested that Nina should move to a place of her own, even though she hadn't fully recovered yet.

Well, in my imperfect picture of Nina one area at least has been filled in, though it's been garishly colored. I'm moved by genuine pity. With her beauty, cleverness, and sociability she'd had an exceptional starting point, she could have chosen anything and anyone, which makes it the more tragic that she should have opted for a way of no return.

~

Madame Amalía dozes off in the morning shade, her head drooping down on her shoulder, while her husband, sitting beside her, is still silently looking across the courtyard.

When I was my old self again, more or less, I moved in with my mother. The sequel you know: the last stage of the complicated divorce process, we even changed our minds at some point, but at last we did break up officially.

As if divining what I would have liked to ask, she explains that she wanted to be alone in her situation, and later, when she might have called me, she believed that I must have been offended by her silence — at the time still short — and that it was too late.

How lucky we were to run into each other in the street. Everything became so simple again. . . . How lucky that you reminded me of our handshake, of our resolution to go cycling all over Greece, she says.

I keep quiet, waiting for her to say more, but she no longer knows what I know or don't know. . . .

~

When Nina had withdrawn from me, I ran into Gregor several times in town. We exchanged some superficial chitchat. More eloquent was what was left unsaid. He didn't know how much I knew or how much he could disclose; he was never really sure about my degree of intimacy with his — then already ex — wife.

He didn't know that I knew — knew from before, from Nina, because I wasn't getting regular reports from Saša back then — how he had thrust her against the wall not long ago and threatened suicide if she attended her high school reunion, raging because she'd only announced it the day before. He didn't know that I knew how he'd charged her several times with not dressing properly, though she looked good in just about everything she put on; he didn't know that I knew about his secret liaisons with women from his painters' circle. He didn't know that I knew how unhappy he was because he couldn't eke out

a living with his pictures and his own artistic voice, and therefore always had plenty of bull's heads in baked clay in stock at
his studio; he didn't know that I knew how they grated on his
nerves but he couldn't do without them because they were
commercially successful, as the phrase goes, and sold like hot-
cakes in art galleries — whatever it was that people saw in them,
perhaps strength, lust, virility. He didn't know that I knew his
studio contained as many jars of paint as bottles of wine, and
he didn't know that, except for the blind spot when Nina had
cut me off completely, I knew a great deal about them, even
about their first meeting at a party in the hippie days of long
hair, tight jeans, and Cat Stevens's songs.

Incredibly, Nina's face doesn't show all she's been through;
she has maintained an innocent yet self-confident grace, not in
the least stained by embarrassment, a genuine wonder open to
the stories of others... and how admiringly they looked at her,
those others, like her daughter Pia.

~

I thought we were going to see the labyrinth, complains a disappointed Nina, and in my guidebook I trace the explanation that
the Minotaur labyrinth of Knossos, where we are now, is a mere
myth. In dusty sandals we walk among dark-red Mycenaean
columns, among stunning rectangular palaces, which were reconstructed over a century ago by Evans the archaeologist in
concrete without the slightest compunction. We walk under
entrances marked with scratchings of the doubl- axe symbol

to avert killings, among walls painted with frescoes in earthy colors, along overpasses, lodges, stairs. *From here,* I read from the guidebook, *hails the inscription in Mycenaean Greek found on a honeypot, da-pu-ri-to-jo po-ti-ni-ja, which means "Lady of the Labyrinth," from here came the philosopher and seer Epimenides, author of the celebrated paradox that all Cretans are liars.*

Looks like nothing's going to come of your labyrinth after all, I finally tell her, heading for the exit.

~

It's true what they say, says Nina in the evening. *I mean, that myths never happened but have been here forever.*

That night I dream about her swimming across the channel and being carried away by the current, the helmsman trying to pull her into the boat but she slips away.

~

The following morning I hear from Saša again: *With any luck at all he'll be transferred today from the* ICU *to the regular floor.*

A load is lifted off my mind. The waiter in Chania has been eyeing me askance the whole evening; he must find me strange, a foreign woman traveling all alone. He brings me light Greek coffee and I thank him. I have been traveling in silence for a whole week, wrapped in my thoughts and imaginings, so the words fall clumsily from my disused tongue; on my solitary trip I have been communicating with few locals, and even then only about the most pressing matters.

After the waiter leaves, I turn on my phone and tap on the email icon: *They've done some analyses and it seems the cause was a plant chopped up into particles, it has almost no taste but the effects are the worst, with some sort of epileptic seizures.*

The waiter brings me a small carafe of wine and the corner of his mouth twitches mockingly — a woman, alone, alcohol, I read in his expression. He asks me the places I've been to on the island.

Mochlos, Heraklion, Matala, Knossos. . .

And all that by yourself, he asks with his pitying glance.

I'd seen a lot and I knew what she could be like, but I never imagined she'd go that far. She has to see the investigating judge tomorrow, continues Saša.

I notice that I'm also being ogled by a group of locals sitting at a corner table.

   I'm sorry if this message comes out disjointed, but that's how I feel myself: Saša, Nina's brother, the good Saša, who helped me unravel so many events over these months. In April I met him at the opening of Gregor's exhibition, where I showed up un-invited, I simply saw the announcement on Facebook and went, partly in the hopes of meeting Nina. But she wasn't there. There was no bull's head on the exhibition, just the most original of Gregor's latest paintings and sculptures.

Saša, the good and cruelly truthful Saša, who came up to me as I was standing alone in front of a painting with a glass of wine in hand. We started chatting and exchanged email addresses, and ever since he's been keeping me informed, explaining the past events, trying to understand them together with me. . . how she had staged an accident in the Soča, how she had been found to have transferred all her money from hers to her husband's account so as to accuse him of embezzlement, how she had twisted her wrist slipping on the wet floor of a department store and then laid the blame on Gregor, as she'd done so often, claiming that he had twisted it at home, how she told tales about his drinking, jealousy, and other women. . . . He managed to get a divorce but she did everything in her power to complicate the process, and started coming back when it was agreed upon, intruding in his studio unannounced, showing up at a bar where he used to meet his friends, at the school where he taught. . . . at last she and Pia had all but moved back in with him, having heaped up at his place their belongings, clothes, objects. . . . He allowed himself to be persuaded, for who wouldn't have believed her?

And now this poison plant, it seems she's long been dosing it into his food.

~

VERONIKA SIMONITI

Indeed, who wouldn't have believed her. . . . Her or her quon-
dam handshake before she broke up our friendship, whatever
it had meant to her. . . I had believed, firmly believed that for
all that, someday she would be in touch again and say as if we'd
last seen each other just the day before: *Remember that plan to
go cycling all over Greece? Well, when do we start?*

Translated by NADA GROŠELJ

Originally published in the short stories collection
Fugato (*Litera, 2019*)

Andrej E. Skubic

"UN CHIEN ANDALUSIA"

"EVERYONE'S WAITING, SOON we will see," bellows Boštjan B., one meter up in the air, oh my god, riding a seesaw on the dark playground next to the club K4, in a monumental pose. "Stella Maris fruits of the sea!"

Trojka vodka in front of K4; a classic winter night, 1989. There was a TV warning this evening about increased concentrations of sulfur dioxide in the air. Cold fumes, and residual fog on the ground that sloshes about when you walk on it. People with weak respiratory systems should stay at home.

No problem. I breathe like a horse.

Primož P., half-seated on the seesaw, pats his thigh, looking around anxiously. Where's this heading? Such an aimless night, an aimless nocturnal existence. That's not cool, that's not cool. Where the fuck is this heading?

"We gotta do something," he says and pats, says and pats. "How about we go beat up someone?"

"Who do you want to beat up now?" says Samo G., holding the Trojka and running in place on the asphalt to keep warm.

"Some New Romantic. Some little Albanian. Whatever. Fuck, I don't know. What it is you want from me. You want philosophy?"

"Where you gonna find a New Romantic around here?"

The cold, though actually it's not even below zero, is so fucking damp it creeps through my leather jacket.

"Remember that fight we got into up on Rožnik?" says Primož P.

"The fuck it was a fight. You stretched out your arm once and they kicked your yellow ass."

Samo G. can be mean.

"Yeah, I remember," says Primož P. "Just so you know. I won't forget how you just ditched me."

"What won't you forget?"

"Five of them jumped me," says Primož P., "and you and Gogi stood there like two idiots. You shit yourselves like. . ."

"What do you mean five, dickhead? There were fifteen of them, at least. How can you kick a guy's ass when you know he has fifteen others covering it?"

"There were more than fifteen of us," says Primož P.

"Yeah, there were, but scattered all over the hill from Lenin Park to that Cankar pub. There's no one around, dickhead, and there you are picking on that guy in front of the church door where there's no one around, and there's fifteen of them."

Primož P. is still patting. "If you'd yelled, we'd all come running."

"Like shit you'd all come running. From where? You're the dickweed who should have had his own ass kicked."

It's time for us to head to к4. к4 beckons.

K4 isn't always there, sometimes it's not. That came out stupid. Sometimes K4's closed. Sometimes they're fixing it. Sometimes it's at Building Four in the student village, before that there was FV in Šiška. That place was a dump. From the filthy floor, from the peeling paint and the dampness you always ended up with blue shoes. We used to call it Šiška blue.

"Have you heard the new Slayer?" Damir C. asks Samo G.

"Slayer? They have another album?"

"*Reign in Blood*. Man, they're so good."

"Are they good?" says Primož P.

"Dude, they're so fucking good."

"Hey, did you know Tom Araya was punk back in the day?" says Damir C.

"Which one's Tom Araya?"

"The vocalist. Did you know he used to be punk?"

"I don't give a shit if he was punk. He wasn't New Romantic, that much I'm sure of. Where did you hear that?"

"I read it somewhere. I don't know, maybe in *Stop*."

Primož P. leans over toward Vladimir S., who is sitting on the bench, head resting in his hands, all in one clump.

"Do you want a kiss from Auntie Klava?" he says. Vladimir S. doesn't move at all, just sits there, not giving a shit.

"Don't dick around," he mumbles, eventually.

There's no helping him, it seems.

"Maybe you'd rather be drinking bitch offal?" Primož P. chirps.

Fuck, he's annoying. He's annoying, but he keeps chirping. He always has to shoot his mouth off. He pushes on ad nauseum. Moscow-Petushki. It was me who brought this book to the scene. Those Russian cocktails, with cologne and red wine and stuff. A guy is taking a train to see his chick. He doesn't have any cash, so each time he has to tell the conductor stories. Kind of like Scheherazade. What's the big deal? You need stories? It's December 1989 here, there are no fucking stories here. I'm not a story guy. Fuck, I don't wanna be in any story. I want to choose my story.

Hmm. Well, all right, here's Zaphod Beeblebrox, he rules. He shows up in a crazy good story. One that makes sense. Or this one: there was a guy in *The Master and Margarita*, some Woland or something like that. That's the kind of story I'd choose. Yeah, that's who I'd be. He took care of everyone else, he screwed the KGB, he got that guy out, the Master, who got screwed over by the Commies because he wrote, like, a real story about Christ. I mean, what a joke, I don't give a fuck about this Christian bullshit. That one was basically a weird prank, God and that Woland were friends, even though he was like some devil or something. Just a guy. But a cool story.

Well, good, so stories can be cool. If they are, I mean, if they're good.

"Hey, have you met Boris?" Primož P. asks Boštjan B. Boštjan B., who has now climbed down from the seesaw, is slapping warmth into his hands.

"Which Boris?"

"The Bosnian, from Fojnica or wherever it is he's from."

"I was with you," says Samo G.

"Who was he?"

"Just some dude, fuck, a proper Bosnian, a farm boy," says Primož P. "Down there he was supposedly some sort of village hippie, and he came to Ljubljana, because it's less lame here in the big city."

"At least it's better than Fojnica."

"He walked right up to us when we were standing around drinking in front of the shop on Puhar. He asked if he could buy us all a bottle."

"What happened then?" asks Boštjan B.

"I don't know. He bought drink after drink. I guess he'd just got his first paycheck and wanted somebody to hang out with."

"Do you know what kind of company he was looking for? He told me in Palma later," Samo G. says. "He was still buying round after round in Palma. He must have wasted half his check there. But the guy was all right."

"Yeah, but then he starts asking me if I know any girls here," says Samo G.

"Ooh, hoo. So that's our Boris."

"I thought to myself, poor guy, who around here is gonna like you? A Bosnian simpleton."

"Simpleton? Do you know what those Bosnians think?" asks Primož P. "He wanted to pick up a Slovene chick. Down there they think Slovene women are all sluts. The ones who come up here to work say that when they go back home."

"What do you mean, Slovene women are sluts?"

"Well, they're more liberal than down there in those villages. Sex before marriage and all that."

"What the fuck do you mean, *sluts*? Can you imagine what it would be like if all Slovene women were sluts?" says Boštjan B. "That would be crazy, eh?"

"Fuck, that would be nice. I'm all for it, with immediate effect!"

"Only your mother wouldn't be one."

"I don't care about my mother. Let Mamma have a good time too, at least then she'd leave me in peace."

Poor Boris. I know that all he wanted was some loving. Love always seemed like a cool thing to me. *Poison running through my veins.* I look at my forearms. *I will always love you.* But chicks, hey, chicks ain't worth shit. I mean, all those faggots, they've found the *easy way out.*

But what can chicks do? They want tenderness. Then they want a tough guy who won't run away off to Rožnik when things get rough. But a clean, washed one. No druggie types who raise hell. A real well-mannered guy, a shining knight, fragrant shit and raised right.

A real man knows what to do when he runs out of vodka, a real man...

...knows when it's time for K4.

I don't know how we ended up down here. Past the mad-ass bouncers, guardians of the passage, dogs with a thousand eyes, eyes like saucers, and muscles like strings of steel, and with many other problems. I don't get it. It's just a fact: we ran out of vodka, and now we're no longer on the cold asphalt, but inside, on the staircase at K4. I don't get it. But it doesn't fucking matter, the main thing is we're here.

When I turn and look back, Primož P., Samo G., and Boštjan B. are nowhere to be found. They've disappeared. Gone to better places. It's okay, we'll meet up again later. From the staircase, I go through the door to the inner hallway — the dance floor is on the left. Not that way, at least not yet, I'd say, anyway. Through some haze and strobing I see Vladimir S., parked on a bench and continuing to enjoy the rhythm of the music. And the contents of his stomach. The fact that he has managed to hang on to them, I mean. And now a little something for my solitary pleasure — a beer. Vodka drains a man. Like a true wise man, I hid the rest of my cash from my friends. Enough for two beers. That's no joking matter, it's a necessity.

The bar's crowded. My heart is an olive. I'm not just saying that. My heart is a reddish-black ripe olive.

I am thinking of the olive rubbing up against the ice cubes in the glass that a girl my age at the bar is sipping from. Actually it's a green olive, but no matter. I once saw a movie where a monster or something rips out a guy's beating heart and the black and red reminded me of the color of ripe olives. . . . Basically, I'm out of it over here. Whole avalanches of frizzy, pale flax are forcing themselves over the shoulders of this princess. She's talking to some slick-looking guy. You can tell she's in rough shape. What's with her? Something's wrong. But she doesn't mind because the guy is so slick. She is saying something but her look is total horrible misfortune that's bringing her down to the ground. Her eyes are completely muddy, she's blinking.

Then she smiles for a moment. And it's unbelievable! The way this girl smiles! All the music goes silent, replaced by gentle, ambient keyboards. It gets very bright in here. The way she smiles. Fuck, what a smile.

But then she's not smiling — she looks crazy unhappy. She probably won't be able to finish her martini. Why, why aren't I standing there, next to her?

I'm holding a beer. I'm holding a beer and I'm standing there like an idiot, even though the flaxen-haired princess is talking to a guy, a guy whose hair is parted, not a flattened mop like mine. She is drinking a martini, she's on a different poison than me. Too many poisons. She can hardly open her mouth. She will make someone happy tonight, for sure it'll be that guy who's pouring all those martinis into her.

I should split.

On the dance floor, everything is fused and diffused. The benches are full. Everything's waving, up there on the platform, on the stairs, and all the dancers. The stage itself is still pretty empty. Don't stick out. Lean against the wall, that's the best thing. I lean against the wall. This music is earsplitting.

Got me a movie, I want you to know. This music goes straight to the veins. *Slicing up eyeballs, I want you to know.* The Pixies are masters, of monstrous proportions, ah, they're crazy good. Maybe I should go hardcore. Thank God long hair is compatible with that. *Girlie so groovy, I want you to know.* But it's still too early to go crazy on the dance floor, and tonight's probably not the time for it. Just listening. Don't know about you, says the guy, but I am *un chien Andalusia*. This rules. I think I just came.

I need a cigarette. I see some space on a bench, and immediately my ass is on it. Vladimir S. is gone. My ears are buzzing. Now it's Patti Smith: "Gloria." This also rules.

If I really think about it, this is all going too fast for me. So fast it's hard to focus. That scene on the dance floor. It's hard to get in there. How do you blend in if everything's moving so fast? That can be a huge problem. You're watching and watching, but everything around you is happening crazy fast. It can

ANDREJ E. SKUBIC

be. . . I mean, it can drive you nuts. But actually, do you have any intention of going somewhere? I mean, actually, if a person really looks at it. Is that your intention? The fuck it is, buddy. You just wanna be left in peace. At least nobody wants anything. Sit here and listen to music in peace. If someone wants to mess with you, they have to make an effort. Let them figure out how they're gonna do it. Let them try it.

For example, like this: my flaxen-haired princess slowly emerges from among the shapes by the dancers and meanders toward the benches. Basically heading right for me. Then things sort themselves out all at once, all on their own. I don't have to do anything really. When she gets to the bench, when she gets to me, she looks like she's gonna collapse. Like she doesn't even see me. She just kind of slips down, I sort of intercept her, and everything's cool. In an instant things are totally different, it's shocking, unexpected, absolutely good, totally different. Her head's in my lap. I can feel her hair in my hands. Her curls brush over my warm skin. Her hair's insanely strong.

Man, she's really wasted.

I'm sitting on a bench, to the right, a bottle with two swigs, to the left, the princess resting against my lap. Slowly, a little awkwardly, she turns her head and looks up at me. Smiling. Turquoise eyes.

"My name's Tadeja," she says.

I don't know exactly why right at that moment a story by Slavko Grum comes to mind. Slavko Grum is as out there as The Pixies. The name just isn't right for her. No, not a chance. Slavko Grum was cool.

"You're shitting me," I say, brushing her hair from her forehead. "Your name's not Tadeja. It's something light, Lana, or something even lighter. Yeah, Lana, that's your name."

The sounds of darkness whirl above us. The dance floor is less full. At the other end of the room Boštjan B. is moving in slow motion. Lana sleeps. Is she sucking my thumb in her sleep? I wish. Princess. I would like her to suck my thumb but that's unlikely. Fuck, she's beautiful. Oh, Lana, my object of adoration. She's sleeping like the dead, motionless. Look, Snow White. The ideal woman. Flaxen, frozen Lana lolling in my lap.

Faith No More's "Epic" is blasting now. Through my head. The night's already in its second half. They keep changing the tunes, the faces change with them. Folded images of beer-wielding shapes shift about, like they're behind tinted windows. I whisper, Lana listens, even if she's sleeping. I know her whole being has transformed into an ear, for sure, and if she transforms more she'll be a Ferengi from *Star Trek* and then I won't like her. She's listening to my stories. I tell her something about winter, about what winter should be basically like, not as it is, wet and smelly, but really, all snow and that smell of ice — actually, I mean what does the cold smell like when it's real? But what do I know about all the crap that's running through my brain. Lana agrees with everything I say.

And here we roll along like stars in the universe: absolutely as it should be. Everything's in harmony. Bursting from the nuclear reactions that warm us, we pour beer and some even heavier elements into ourselves. We are gradually cooling down. But what am I dicking about for? Never mind: just watch.

ANDREJ E. SKUBIC

Boštjan B. plops himself down next to me. Ogles my sleeping beauty. Ogles and grins. I'm gonna go ballistic. What's this bullshitter doing here? But he's better than I expected — not actually bullshitting. He's talking about something else.

"The bouncers beat the shit out of someone again," he says. "He wouldn't leave when they woke him up after he passed out on the floor."

"And rightly so! Sleep should be eradicated," I mumble, looking at my bottle, from which the last drops of beer are disappearing into Boštjan B.'s face. This is admirably shameless.

Admiration makes me forget I should be pissed off. I calmly look past him. Methanol in my eyes. Do I have menthol? What do I know, what it is. A sort of a glassy feeling. Last year in Spain a disco burned down. People were choking on carbon monoxide.

I try to imagine the faces around me, but it doesn't work. All these people. Blue faces, blue lips. Blackened eyes. Grasping at their throats. They squeeze in one last hug. I can't do it, I'm faking it.

It's boring without beer. Boštjan B. is reeling ecstatically next to me. Lana is peacefully, trustingly comatose. How could I leave her? But perhaps Boštjan B. could watch over her for a moment? I search my pockets for the last of my cash. Seventeen dinars, exactly. Man, did I calculate things precisely.

"Keep an eye on her, will you?" I say, looking at Boštjan B.

He nods and looks down at Lana. It's all good. She'll be safe. He really is a bud.

It's a totally different scene at the bar. Bunch of yappers. I watch the crowd. It'll be an uphill battle. I sense Belinda P. beside me. She has a ponytail and is wearing a silk blouse and black, rose-patterned nylons.

"First shluck's mine!" she demands loudly and rubs up against me.

Well, who could resist? A bottle appears out of nowhere, I don't know how it happened. Behind me I feel Belinda P. She's good to look at, tipping the bottle. But she's no Lana. God, no, she's no Lana.

I cross the dance floor again. Everything's pushing into me. My white flannel shirt's almost blue under the neon lights. Then I'm at the bench where I was sitting. No Lana. And Boštjan B. is also nowhere to be seen. What's all this about? We were sitting right here. I told him to keep an eye on her. Boštjan B. is a serious man. Responsible.

I look around. Just happy dancing faces. Now they're playing Miladojka Youneed. Everything changes. Lana. Lana? My eyes are kind of glassy again now, that's what's bothering me. The bodies are clouded in a murky darkness, I can't see. Fine. Let's think a bit. They were sitting right here. Lana was out of it, so she can't have gone anywhere. Did he carry her off? No way. He'd have to carry her over that spinning mass of bodies, no chance. They'd be trampled by the dancing maniacs. Were they abducted?

Well, you'll have to go find them. Maybe something was wrong with Lana. I don't recognize a face in the crowd. Now there's nobody I know. Slowly, with a meek courage, I make my way through the crowd.

Miladojka brings you down. What's wrong with me today? I usually like them, but now it's like their trumpets and saxophones are stomping on my neck and bashing my brain. It's annoying.

ANDREJ E. SKUBIC

"Lana? Lana," I call.

Speak up! What's wrong with you? A person loses sight of you for a moment. . . .

Cowboy types are standing in the hallway behind the dance floor. They're sucking down whiskey and smoking cigars. They don't look twice at me. I'm tempted to ask them about Lana, but they look so untouchable and lofty that it's hopeless. They would bust me, pop me like a soap bubble, no joke.

Something's not right here. And it was such a beautiful evening. Lana! Fuck, Lana, speak up! Speak up, I haven't gone anywhere. Do you remember that time we hitchhiked along the coast of Greece together? We had salami, cheese, and olives, and drank Heineken by the side of the road. In Seville we drank tequila and rolled joints, and at Paris-Austerlitz we drank wine and ate brie — you said you didn't like it because it tasted like penicillin — Lana, remember! Stop screwing with me, I don't like it, like that time in Lisbon when you just pissed off and left a note — don't just forget, Lana, it's not funny, Lana. . . .

I watch the swirling faces, swirling brown bottles, and tall green glasses. No, nobody I know. I march toward the pisser. Get away from the crowd. For sure Lana's there. She went to get some air, that's it. Why am I so afraid? I'm in Ljubljana, close to home. This is my home.

The entrance area is much less crowded. I even see Samo G. at the stairs, leaning against the corner and talking to some punk girl. At least somebody I know! I join them.

". . . it sucks, I'm telling you, Malcolm McDowell was basically the king until he sold out to those American whores."

Oh yeah, Samo G. is crazy smart. I grin at him and whack him on the shoulder. He immediately grabs my beer and takes a swig.

"What are you dawdling around out here for? I don't know anyone in there," I tell him. Samo G. nods at me and keeps on talking to the girl. I take a deep breath and look at the faces around me. There's a lot more light here, and the colors converge; everything is a bit deader, and the clothes are mostly black. But Lana's not here either.

Samo G. is eyeing me carefully now. I see him, his eyes are poisonous. Inquiringly, I turn to him. We gawk at each other for a while, then he nods.

"Let's go," he says.

I'm a little surprised, but I obey — he turns on the stairs and marches toward the pisser. I follow. There's always a crowd around the entrance, always shooting their mouths off. This is K4's speakers' corner.

In the toilet, the screaming whiteness once again blinds me, cuts into my eyes. We pass the sinks. Samo G. opens the door to a stall. Behind it, darkness. Stairs. He walks through the door and beckons. Marching into darkness. I stand for a while, then follow him and close the door behind me. Total darkness all around us. What the fuck is this?

Oh shit. What's up with these stairs? I've been to the pisser here tons of times but never seen anything like this. Judging by feel, they must be pretty new, not worn down, but also not very dirty — they are dry and rough. I hear the echo of Samo G.'s footsteps ahead of me. I follow him. When I clear my throat, the only response is an echo from the empty space. Dark as a sphincter.

ANDREJ E. SKUBIC

"Hey, Samo," I say quietly, my voice echoing in the darkness, the music from the club no longer audible.

Samo G. mumbles.

"Have you been down here lots?"

Silence, footsteps. Samo G. grinning in the dark feels like a mild warmth breathing somewhere in front of me. "Well of course I have...."

I'd like to stop for a bit to get my thoughts in order, but I'm afraid he'll ditch me here in the dark. That would suck. It's all kind of spooky. So we push on. It's pitch-black and maybe a little bluish here in the dark, and I can't hear anything but the stomping of two pairs of feet and breathing. A strange anxiety grips me. Where the fuck is he leading me? I'm still reeling from all the vodka and beer, and things can't be any better for Samo G. And Lana? A painful memory strikes me again. What the hell happened to Lana? I'm trying to make sense of it. Well, I can't. Where the hell are we going? Shit, we've been walking for ages. We must be crazy deep by now. I'm starting to worry.

"Hey, are we almost there?" I ask.

It's downright stifling. Samo G. clears his throat ahead of me. "Ummm..."

I hear footsteps.

But then he says, "Almost there."

Darkness rubs out my thoughts. It's getting suffocating, maybe a bit warmer though. That's good. Looks like we'll end up somewhere after all. Somewhere warm, maybe they'll have beer there. For free. That would only be fair, after all these crazy steps. Deafness strokes my hands. I almost trip. What's with Lana? I can feel her bristly hair on my hands. I can feel her warmth on my knees. The taste of cheese and olives in my mouth. The tequila running down my throat.

Samo G. stops and I almost crash into him. The footsteps fall silent, I can feel the handle on the door. Creaking.

"We're here," says Samo G.

The door opens, light washes over us, blinding at least me for a moment. I blink with a shrunken face and slowly open my watery eyes. Yeah, looks like we're here.

No more stairs. A lighted, warm room opens before us. My eyes are teary and I can barely make out the huge piles of junk. It's like we've landed in the middle of Dürer's *Melencolia I* the room is full of instruments, strange devices, bicycles, mathematical drawings, and tools, and everything is totally dusty. It is impossible to tell where the light's coming from; definitely no lights around here, no candles or anything like that, though a soft glow blankets everything. Only now in the midst of all this gear do I spy a mighty seat, luxuriously transparent and bright, and it reminds me of a decorated toilet seat. And one sits on the throne. And he that sat was to look upon like a jasper and sardine stone: and there was a rainbow round about the throne, in sight like unto an emerald. The picture completely arrests me: the majesty and decadent luxury emanating from the one is so great that even those thick layers of dust cannot take the edge off. I'm completely blown away. I would never have imagined such a thing, not somewhere in the basement under к4 — that's never been mentioned anywhere. Samo G. takes a few steps forward, then quietly, respectfully kneels. He presses his forehead down.

"Thou art worthy," he whispers, "to receive glory and honor and power...."

Hey, dude, unbelievable.

The room is silent. Samo G. is kneeling on the floor. The one on the throne doesn't move. His head leans to the side, like he's sleeping. It looks like dust covers him too, just as it covers the things in the room, although his radiance pierces through it and warms our eyes. He wears a loose robe of glittering, luxurious red fabric; from under the lower edge of the robe you can see his protruding, hairy, bony legs ending in gigantic hooves, shod with massive horseshoes. Great is this lordly beast, this lord.

Samo G. slowly raises his head.

Now I too am mustering some courage. I step forward and kneel next to Samo G. I respectfully press my forehead to the floor.

I whisper quietly, pleadingly, "Lord, do you know where Lana is?"

The silence in the room continues. Samo G. slowly, cautiously, gets up. Nothing happens. He slowly approaches the stationary one in the warm, radiant throne. He stops in front of him, right before his hooves. He holds out his hand. He takes the one by the wrist.

For a few seconds there is complete silence in the room. Samo G. feels for the pulse of the sitting one. The one doesn't move. Samo G. slowly, disappointedly, lets go of his hand.

"Oh shit," he says, "he's dead."

Translated by JASON BLAKE

Originally published in the short stories collection
Norišnica (*Beletrina, 2004*)

Dušan Čater

SUN, WHAT?

ENTERING AND LOCKING the door, he double-checked if he'd done it right. Then, he turned on the light. Careful not to make too much noise. His leg was broken, causing him fits.

In the kitchen he whipped up a sandwich. Ham and cheese. He'd taken just one bite when she showed up.

"Third time this week," she said.

"What?"

"You coming home drunk!"

"The sun and stuff," he explained.

"The sun, the sun..."

"Listen," he told her.

"What?"

"What?"

"Yeah, what?" she asked one more time.

Shaking his head, he took another bite.

"Listen, you," she said, leading this time around. "It's the third time this week. Where were you all night? And who with? And, does the sun shine there as well?"

So many questions, all at once. Mr. Arnelly, that was his name, shrugged his shoulders. His head wasn't particularly clear to be honest.

"Do you have any idea the things I go through waiting for you? Something could have happened and I'd never even know," she continued.

He tried apologizing.

"The sun and all that," he said.

"The sun, the sun, yeah. . . You've been saying it for three weeks."

He nodded. But he couldn't resist asking, "And you, for how long?"

"Me, what?" Now she was surprised.

"How long have you been saying it?"

She stared at him, announcing, "You know what? Sun or no sun, enough is enough!"

"But the sun!" clamoring in his defense.

"Listen, Mr. Arnelly. What you're seeing isn't the sun. It's just you. Why'd you run off on your wife and kid if the sun's to blame for everything? You even took off on a rainy day! Is that the sun's fault?"

"The sun?"

She waved her hand around. He did the same.

"You were lucky this time, but remember," she said, wagging her finger.

Taking another bite, he wondered, "We're going or not?"

"What?"

"I'm asking, are we going?"

"Going where?"

DUŠAN ČATER

"To bed, where else," he mumbled.

"Oh, just like that, to bed!" she said, shaking her head.

He couldn't hear her anymore. Mouth full of sandwich, he was asleep.

"Didn't even take off his shoes," she sighed, looking out the window.

It was daytime — the sun was high up in the sky.

Translated by JEREMI SLAK

Originally published in the short stories collection
Flash Royal (*Karantanija, 1994*)

Dušan Šarotar

THE HAUSTOR

1

I REMEMBER HOW the man in the worn black suit would sit at the top of the stairs day after day. He would smoke his pipe and his cigarettes, alternating from one to the other. His fingers were yellow from the smoke and his right thumb hard as leather from tapping and packing the glowing tobacco in the bowl of his well-gnawed pipe. He was never without that smelly smoking utensil. He used to carry it in his suit jacket or in the deep, baggy pockets of his trousers. He usually wore warm, high-top slippers, even in hot weather. He walked slowly, with short steps, like an old man — always shuffling, never lifting his feet or bending his knees. He had been like that forever, even when he was still in his middle years, as if one day he had suddenly turned old. He was like that most of his life. He died in his eighty-fourth year. Slowly, the way he had lived.

Today I ask myself, just as I did then, when I would see him sitting at the top of the stairs smacking his lips on the stem of his pipe, what he could be thinking about. I don't remember him ever saying anything or telling any stories. He spoke entirely in clouds, in thick, gray clouds of cheap tobacco smoke, which tumbled down the old staircase in circles and ribbons.

I see his bony head slipping slowly onto his chest. When the stub of a cigarette or the smoldering tobacco burns his dry lips, it startles him, as if he's had a thought or a flashing dream. And his eyes, usually so bleary and empty, are glistening.

Was it only the smoke that brought a tear to his eye, I ask myself, or was this merely a trace leading to the world inside him, a world he had long ago stopped letting anyone into?

Now I, too, am a smoker. I don't know if I learned it from that silent man, who more and more often comes to sit by my side, just as I once knelt at his feet, but I sense that the smoke is the same smoke I used to smell. I can't help but remember the clouds I would watch in my boredom through the staircase window as the days passed in stillness and silence, days that will perhaps not return again, even in my dreams.

But that boy who sat on the stairs gazing through the staircase window, which looked out on a large courtyard, possessed a secret power that would still frighten him many years later, when the staircase and even the courtyard were gone and the tobacco smoke had long since dispersed. Only the feeling would remain that somewhere, perhaps, there still existed that thought by which he could make objects move or lift them into the air. For he still remembered, could almost hear, the clatter and crash of breaking glass in the courtyard, which had been triggered by his gaze.

It was one of those numberless days when he and the man in the black suit were sitting in their usual spot on the staircase.

DUŠAN ŠAROTAR

The old man sat silently, gazing into the distance, through the smoke, to somewhere far away, somewhere only he could go. The boy was trying to follow him. He was looking through the window, trying to catch the old man's thoughts as they slipped away without a trace, like time. Then all at once a truck fully loaded with crates of beer drove through the passageway. The beer was for Maček's, the ground-floor shop that had its storeroom in the courtyard. The man on the stairs didn't bat an eye; he calmly smoked his pipe as if he was somewhere else entirely, but the boy was annoyed by the truck. And he sensed he had the power within him to move things. So he thought: *Turn over, break everything!*

The very next moment, for no apparent reason, the truck backed up and collided full force into the overhang of the roof, which sent the first row of crates crashing to the ground. The driver, who was totally confused, then shifted into first and went forward, thinking he could still avoid the worst. But now the crates were falling like dominoes. The racket and rumble of crates falling and falling, almost to the last one, disturbed even the man with the pipe. He said nothing but only looked at the boy, who was watching the scene in the courtyard half-smiling and half-afraid, since he did not yet understand what had really happened. But the gaze that settled on his shoulder made him think. That is when he first sensed somewhere that there was someplace bigger than himself and deeper than everything.

But if the boy knew anything at all, he knew that when he became a man he must never abuse this power. So whenever he saw a plane flying high in the sky, he would think, and maybe say out loud: *Keep flying, don't you dare fall!*

Just as those clouds were scattered by the wind, or simply melted away, and again formed somewhere into thick, gray yarn, so the tobacco is again glowing inside me and smoke is spreading that was never lost. Nothing ever really changes; the dead still tell their tales in silence, and we the living think up our own stories, by which we try to name and call forth the memory of which we are made.

The only thing that actually changed was the long street on which our house, as I still call it, used to stand; to the right, in my memory, stood the squat houses of tradesmen, which the road was consuming as if a river was flooding them. For whenever the pavement was widened and modernized, which simply meant pouring gravel and sand over the rutted, potholed surface, the road would rise, until eventually it was almost as high as the windows of those old houses. I remember when I walked down this street — it was too narrow for any sidewalk — I was able to look through the curtained windows directly into the houses, even though I was still only a child.

Usually it was the kitchen that faced the street — low-ceilinged and narrow, with a large wood-burning stove and, against the wall beneath the window, a table with a plastic tablecloth and a bench on which people would be sitting in silence. Today, I am sure, if I could lean my head against those windows, it would touch the upper edge of the frame; then, however, it reached only to the handle. I still remember those motionless eyes, heavy and weary, watching as bony fingers crumbled bread and felt for dry bits of crackling. Through the windowpanes, which were misted and greasy from cooking, the bent heads and shoulders of those people looked like pieces of fresh-chopped gnarled wood, while their

DUŠAN ŠAROTAR

skin, which almost never saw the sun, since they spent their entire days in some cramped cabinetmaker's or tailor's workshop, at the whetstone or cobbler's anvil, or in a laundry, was thin and translucent. At night I used to dream that this thin skin would one day wear out, would tear like an old shirt, and only then would real human flesh peep through, covered in true skin.

Nothing ever came of this, I realize now, as I recall to memory all that human passing. But those tiny, diligent fingers must somewhere remain, digging even today through bread and greasy crackling, if only to feed those insatiable dead eyes.

Streets are like people: if they didn't have names, it would be hard, if not impossible, to recognize them years later. Faces and façades change quickly. This one is more crooked, that one is now gray or bald or toothless, a house has been enlarged or renovated, or a whole row of houses is gone and in their place stands an apartment building, or supermarket, or maybe a playground. Luckily, the street had kept its name, which I read with relief and with a feeling I had not known before. I was standing in front of a not particularly successful apartment block; I'd sooner say it was shabbily built, maybe even ugly. No. 8 Lendava Street. This is definitely where our house had stood, I was deeply sure of it, despite there being no visible trace left.

Nothing but a translucent shadow, the warm earth that in memory never grows cold — the thought comes to me again — this feeling in the hands of that boy does not go away. Sometimes I close my eyes and stretch out my hands as if I am standing by a fire, and again I feel the warmth of that long-ago home; I touch the embossed design on the wallpaper, as I used to do in the darkness of my room, sliding my fingers across the golden tendrils of the vine, the Parisian-blue grapes, the nectar trickling down rocks and running in streams and basins, a pair of young lovers kneeling by the fountain with a pitcher in their hands, drinking long draughts, and still drinking, although the wallpaper is torn and has separated from the wall, but behind it is another, blue and without patterns; I dig at it with my finger and tear it slightly in the darkness — I can't sleep, after all — and beneath the dark vinyl wallpaper I feel at least two more layers, as if the house is glued together from layers of yellowed paper, behind which lie only emptiness and the smell of mildew.

Now, as I write this, I see again in front of me empty, white, unwritten sheets of paper, crying out like a lonely man in the wilderness, calling for the word from which that vanished house will one day be recreated.

I need to open the window above the bed; veiled moonlight is resting in the courtyard, and a breeze is swaying the branches of the weeping willow that grows just beneath my window in front of the apartment block next door. Its long, thin fingers are scratching at the tin ledge as if trying to say something, as if they are whispering in a language no one wants to comprehend. Beneath the willow tree, which still exists — I see it again as I stand in front of our house — I used to play sometimes with the children from the Jewish Block, as people still call the building today. There were a lot of these children. When the old, abandoned rabbi's house at the end of our courtyard was still standing, we would often hide in its decrepit, mysterious skeleton. Anyone brave enough to climb up the crumbling stairs to the attic would never be found. At times in my dreams, I catch myself still waiting in that attic, hidden behind broken beams with the caved-in roof around me, and I'm sailing on clouds.

From here I would usually run in the evening with the milk can through the passageway to the road. This high, dark space, the *haustor* we called it, led out from our big, walled courtyard. Now, as I stood in front of it with my black briefcase in my arms, just as I had once held the milk can, I could again, unmistakably, smell the distinctive odor that used to come from it. There the air was always somewhat damp and cold, and pungent with cat urine. It would be hard for me to say if this was, perhaps, the hour, the same time of day, when I would go for milk. Even the light has changed here. As if that thick evening light, which once oozed from the low, radiant clouds, had somehow been thinned out. Now everything was somehow too obvious, too prosaic, lacking that characteristic depth and magical perspective, which could be delineated only by the lines of the sloping rooftops vanishing in the distance. Maybe this light had been hiding in the houses, or even in the people who just then, at dusk, would sit down at their tables, and all that vast invisible silence, that concentration, would begin to relax, to shine in the darkening sky.

Another step and I would be engulfed by the old haustor — it was so close — and would find myself again in the world I had left behind. I now know that my childhood dreams were not empty, and that my thin and translucent childish skin had itself been somewhere painlessly torn, had frayed apart and scattered like fog. What now is standing and walking through the narrowest of passageways through time — this is something real, but the haustor is gone, or rather, it is only memory, which is stronger and more lasting than skin.

It is not in the nature of adults to still be capable of surprise; we merely remember. I know those silent people in their tranquility have long ago moved on, to God knows where, and soon so will I. There comes a time when we all stop worrying about our ever-thinning, disappearing shirt, and resign ourselves to the thought that one day we will have to strip naked.

The only question is what will be left.

2

When I stepped off the train, time stopped. I was back at the beginning, at the place where long before I had boarded a train. I knew the day would come when I would return and again want to share with someone things that never can be fully shared. Now, as I stand at my last stop, here, in this forgotten railway station, with no one who might be waiting for me, I know there is nothing I can give to the past or take away from it. Only memory remains, and the feeling that the world I each day leave behind is perhaps being preserved somewhere else. For otherwise where would all the love go, where would the touch disappear to, when nobody is here anymore?

Often, when I was half-asleep, I would hear a slow trickle and the tinny sound of the bottom of the chamber pot, which was always kept under the bed; this was followed by slow shuffling steps creeping through the darkness; then the brass doorknob would surrender with a creak and the man, in a nightshirt and big woollen cap with a pom-pom, would walk through the little room where I lay dozing in the moonlight. I remained absolutely still. That little room served as a passageway between the big bedroom and the kitchen; here a maid had once slept, and now they made up the sofa for me. The old dry wooden floor trembled and squeaked beneath even the softest step. Usually, at the same time, the little goblets of thin glass would start to rattle. The jingling of the goblets and other mementos, all neatly arranged in the display cabinet, lasted for what seemed the longest time, certainly long after the man had emptied the chamber pot into the bucket that stood in the corridor. Then, in the yellowish glow of a bulb, which hung on a bare wire and every so often would flicker, he would fill his pipe and slowly smack his lips. The smell of cheap tobacco from that crumpled red packet was even sharper at night. The smoke would drift into every hidden corner of that big bourgeois house, which lay in apparent sleep and tranquility. Here I never truly dreamed. Everything was somehow real, big, and alive. Every wall and painting, every piece of furniture, had its own character, its own meaning, and most of all its own voice. I do not remember a single night or day when the house was not speaking, as if its walls had never entirely accepted the things that were carried into it from every direction with no rhyme or reason. People came and went in the rooms from season to season, too many in the winter and fewer in the summer. The house was always filled with subtenants, with occupants by socialist decree, with relatives, and with us, who were already quite a few. And every person would drag into the house whatever they had, and these same people later carried a lot away too. What remained were only things that had no value or use or were too large to be moved anywhere.

The handful of passengers who exited ahead of me instantly disappeared among the low houses. They all had somebody waiting for them, either at the station or at home. I remained alone. The first thought that came to me was clear and simple, as if I had read it in a book: when you have been away for a long time and come back only on occasion, nothing ever seems to change here.

And indeed, everything was the same as on that early morning when I left from this station. The pub with the garden facing the tracks, where I had hoped to quench my thirst and maybe ask a question, had obviously been closed a long time. There were only a few broken café chairs on the veranda, but the pigeons perched on the low wooden railing looked as if they had been there forever. Motionless, they were peering with tiny black eyes at the tracks, which disappeared into the distance. Since I was the only one left on the deserted platform, it felt like they were staring at me; everything else must have been unexciting for them, banal and empty, something they had long grown used to, the way people grow used to a painting that hangs in the bedroom.

That painting was again before me, the last large oil on canvas that hadn't been stolen, which used to hang in the big bedroom above the double bed. It had slipped long ago into the dark recesses of my memory; only its massive white frame seemed at times to still be glowing somewhere, but the image within its rounded sides I had until now considered lost to me. At that moment I again saw it in front of me.

A long brown table was standing in front of heavy dark-red velvet curtains tied back with bows on both sides. The large cut-glass bowl on the table was brimming with fruit. If I'm not mistaken, there were ripe peaches, apples, grapes, and a banana. The fruit had been painted with the flawless brushstroke of the realist; the colors and shadows, so far as they could be distinguished from the completely black wall in the background, were accurate, made with craftsmanlike precision — obviously, too much so, since the image did not in any way whet the appetite, let alone make you want to touch it. I am sure it was yet another of those many still lifes, those *natures mortes*, such as amateurs like to paint. But just when I thought the picture had dropped back into the depths of memory, probably to stay there forever, another detail came to me, one that often used to excite me, although as a child I was never able to interpret its meaning no matter how many times I went to look at it. Near the edge of the painting there was a disproportionately large knife. It rested on the rim of the table, in the darkest part of the picture, and had a sharp point and a black handle that melted into the dark background. I could never figure out why it was actually there; it seemed to have no purpose. The fruit was not for eating — it was on the table merely as decoration, far removed from the hungry or salivating mouths of children. Like any child, I thought the knife had been put there entirely by accident, that the painter had painted it because someone had left it on the table; or maybe it was added later, I thought, or was there for a reason I would never understand.

I was still standing at the deserted Sobota railway station; it felt like I had been there forever, and maybe I still am there today, like the princess in one of those beautiful fairy tales people tell themselves over and over, but always with a deep and inexplicable sense of unease that they might actually be speaking about themselves, about how they too have been waiting all their lives with their feet rooted to the ground, hoping that someday someone would come along and rescue them with the kiss that promises immortality.

So once upon a time at some forgotten railway station a pigeon lifted its round neck and flapped its wings, then flew up off the pub railing and for a few moments hovered in the air with its wings spread wide. I saw right away that it was the fattest of the group; its white, bloated belly was on full display, with its little claws hanging motionless below and its head held high toward the ceiling, so that the down beneath its neck ring was bristling. At that indeterminably long moment, with the animal still suspended somewhere between sky and earth, the old door of the pub creaked open. This excited even the birds, who moved a hand's width down the railing, which was covered in traces of their filth. A lady appeared in the doorway looking as if she had stepped out of a different time, a different world.

"That's the way, my dove, give it to them," she said lovingly, with a sort of mysterious candor, or maybe evil glee, to the fat bird; he had just now landed casually on the first female pigeon, who was gurgling and fighting him off with her wings. The other pigeons, all apparently female, were merely fluffing their feathers indifferently, or with a well-trained and mastered will, not voicing a single sound.

DUŠAN ŠAROTAR

The lady, I can't call her anything else, wearing a blousy pink dress that drooped from her bony frame like the curtain in the pub's open window, and paying no attention to me or, indeed, to anyone else in this world — maybe she only ever greeted those strange, meek, and filthy birds who spent all their time sitting around this forgotten railway station — now stepped into the daylight, beneath that mild late-afternoon sun without shadow or glare. The only thing shining, with a muted gleam, was her soft, wide-brimmed hat of white lace. Moving slowly — I now know it had been a long time since she had anywhere she needed to be — she walked onto the platform in a somewhat practiced manner and boarded the last evening train; no other transport would be passing through here for a while. Now it was just me and those dirty, self-absorbed birds.

My soul trembled with excitement when the whistle pierced the air, and the apparent peace and timelessness that watched over this deserted station were instantly broken, as if the old world was collapsing. The locomotive pulled the empty carriages forward with all its strength and, in the diesel engine stench, began rolling down the tracks. I stood for a moment as if rooted to the ground, watching the rumbling train dwindle into the distance, toward the plains of Hungary and on to Budapest. But then I realized I didn't have my suitcase with me, the only luggage I was carrying apart from the briefcase.

Without thinking, I ran onto the tracks and, like an idiot, started chasing the train, which was moving faster and faster as it receded into the horizon. What finally brought me to a halt was a second whistle blast. I was utterly exhausted and shaken to my bones. I don't know what shattered me more — the lost suitcase, my mad run, or the whistle. I felt myself falling, my knees buckling; somewhere a big eye opened, through which I saw something I will never be able to describe. I just lay there on the tracks. Above me, a wide, shallow sky hung across the boundless plain. It was as if I was already among the clouds, which were opening up like souls.

The only question: Am I, too, now one of them?

3

The same whistle that knocked me down — it may even have been a long, unbroken blast that penetrated my ears — had once, here, at this half-deserted and forgotten station, or *alomaš*, as people called it, echoed through the air one early April morning in 1944. It numbed people's bodies, so they more or less automatically, almost mechanically, with no real expression on their faces, started moving toward the platform; so their swollen, white eyes never closed again but only stared into a void filled with whistles and shouts, with wailing, weeping, and sobbing — which is to say, they were guided only by sounds and voices that became unbearably louder and louder until all that remained, above the world and in their memory, was a diluted, monotonous, and almost supernatural soundscape, filled with smoke escaping from the boiler of an overheated locomotive.

They had been herded here by Germans in pressed uniforms and polished boots, with Hungarians in hunting jackets trotting subserviently beside them. The train from Goričko was

DUŠAN ŠAROTAR

whistling and wheezing in the same lazy voice as it had now. As soon as the Hungarians, with an exaggerated, feigncd fury, got them out of the cold and soot-covered wagons, the Germans, with great meticulousness, divided them up. They stood the men in a line against the station wall, while the women and children were crammed into Černjavič's pub, which to this day is still there on the platform. The bar was shut down for that hour. The few patrons — mostly workers, who would usually be there nursing a cider or brandy first thing in the morning, but also travelers without luggage — were banished to the pub's garden, from where they had to watch what was happening at the station.

I see them now, as I stand again on this spot after so many years, surveying this quiet, almost forgotten station, with nothing but the poplar trees gazing into the sky and, hovering just above their tapering crowns, the white cumulous clouds. I see them now — whether in the sky or on earth, I don't know — these people holding on tightly to sleepy children, suitcases, and hastily wrapped packages, from which silk-embroidered tablecloths, big down pillows, fur collars, and books are protruding, with oil paintings cut from expensive frames hanging out of open handbags like long loaves of fresh bread. No one is speaking, everything is unfolding too quickly, with an inborn submissiveness and attention, such as might be expected of people who have been taught that order must always be maintained. They would complain later, of course, when they had a chance to speak to the higher-ups, to the men in charge, the ones who sit in quiet offices — no, now isn't the time, and anyway, what's the point of talking to these people whose uniforms aren't even of the proper rank; you can see they're just operatives, people with explicit orders from above; you won't get anywhere with them, they're just doing their job. It's all on paper, of course, but the paperwork seems all right, in order, signed and stamped; there must have been a mistake, a big mistake, which these people certainly won't understand, let alone resolve. Now they have to be patient, to make sure none of their precious luggage goes missing, and they have to watch the children, who are already restless and curious — they don't know this either, just as we don't understand it even today and in fact never will understand it.

The heavy doors on the freight wagons were shut one after the other, until the only thing left at the station was the wail of the couplers, just as now, when the train rolled off with my forgotten suitcase. Today I know that he, too, was among them — the man from the top of the stairs, who I had come here to look for, to sit one last time by his side, just as everyone must someday sit by somebody's side.

Back then, as he stood in front of the wagons with a yellow star on his sleeve, in that amorphous line, he did not yet know that he would one day be my grandfather. He was still just a nameless Jew, a particle without mass, something that would only ever be counted and subtracted. The only thing separating this man from all the other numbers was the painting, the simple still life he had hurriedly cut from its frame in the bedroom. It was hidden beneath his trousers, wrapped around his leg.

... *einunddreissig, zweiunddreissig, vierunddreissig*... he heard constantly pounding somewhere in the background. They were being counted, and this counting game seemed like it would never end. The voice he heard was clear; it was almost a school-boy's monotone voice, counting, as if during class. This was one of those boys who often had to stay after school and, as punishment, write out the numbers from one to a hundred on the blackboard with a small piece of chalk, while the other boys, who had already left, were running in the schoolyard or playing hide-and-seek with the girls. Something of the shame of ignorance combined with a suppressed desire for revenge was audible in this childish voice.

. . . *fünfunddreissig, sechsunddreissig.* . . he was pronouncing the numbers fearfully, with that distinctive hesitant pause, unable to hide the fact that they still gave him trouble.

At every railway station, or in larger open areas far enough away from the forest or houses where the deportees might hide, should they happen to escape, the endless counting was repeated. But in this sinister and, in a way, absurd activity of pronouncing the abstract names of those condemned to death — a fact that was still somewhere in the background like a mistake that would surely be corrected the next time he counted, just as this not-very-bright child had also corrected his mark in mathematics — in short, in this voice, these unknown quantities, humiliated, dispossessed, anonymous, and headed to certain death, who were a mere part of one of the most horrendous equations ever conceived by human reason — one million equals zero — were hearing something more, something left out of the initial calculation; namely, they were hearing a fool who could not be believed, let alone trusted with money. And it was this imbecile in the black uniform who was pronouncing this equation. The counting would begin even before the heavy bars on the cattle wagons creaked open and they were herded in no particular order onto narrow platforms or directly into naked fields.

The man saw a spiderweb stretching between the ploughed furrows, which had trapped heavy, sparkling drops of dew. This fragile image of a spiderweb swaying in the morning sun would never leave him. Although he didn't know why exactly, he saw unfathomable significance in it.

His body ached as they trudged over the soft earth, stumbling like frightened animals unaccustomed to human eyes and voices.

...*siebenunddreissig, achtunddreissig*... it continued as they were all pissing their shoes and trousers because they were forced to walk continuously in a circle and had to relieve themselves without stopping for a moment.

...*fünfzig*...

The bars shut. The wagon was full. The man, who was a little shorter than the others, was pressed between bodies. The tall shoulders, the bundles, the suitcases, the hats, all the things people had grabbed immediately off the floor as they crammed into the wagons, because otherwise it would have been impossible to stand, deprived him of light. He saw only lines, stripes, and shadows darting across the dark wooden ceiling. Then it started up again.

...*eins, zwei*...

The only question: How do you divide a person by a person, with no remainder?

4

The sky above the station was getting darker; the shadows of the poplars by the road were lengthening and slowly dissolving into evening, which glowed with that unmistakable sadness known only to those who are leaving or, after many years, again returning home. We are all wounded.

The town, too, was passing into silence, as if the birds, still hanging almost motionlessly in the air like souls above a graveyard, were speaking. I felt that the people here must still be able to hear it, that there was again, in this late-afternoon stillness, something of what remained. I knew I was home here. Everything the eye touched was passing — houses, streetlamps, the towering plane trees, but especially the people, who were slowly going somewhere unknown. It seemed like these were the same faces I had observed as a child, in the windows of the houses in our street. In these slow-moving, hunched figures there was still something of that light which the old masters had attempted to capture in hues of fiery red, dark blue, and, especially, black — that is, in an extreme palette. In these peculiar experiments with melancholy, it was still possible to detect something more, to see the trace that alone leads to the limitlessness, silence, and sadness of the people who live here. At the same time, these masters all knew how to convey, or as we say, had a feeling for, that interior world, which is the sole source of painterly light.

Again I smelled fruit; this, I felt, is the soft fragrance of the only painting I carry inside me, just as we all sometimes catch a glimpse of people who are no longer with us. We see them in a crowd, or crossing the street, or on a passing bus. But we never muster the courage to go after them.

I saw him shuffling down our street. He looked as if he, too, had just returned from a long journey. I followed him to our house, which in fact was long gone. I don't know if he knew I was here; maybe he didn't recognize me, although in some way, I know, I am becoming more like him every day. I set my briefcase on the ground and waved; I was about to call to him when he disappeared through the haustor that had once led into our courtyard.

Again I hear his slow steps as he climbs the twisting stone stairs; his gentle, bony hand, which all day long had been touching, smoothing, and folding cloth — wool, velvet, silk, linen, stylish polyester — in a small, dimly lit boutique that sold clothes and textiles, and those fingers, yellow from tobacco, which had countless times unfolded colorful printed fabrics for girls without money, ladies without taste, and, in particular, narrow-lipped gentlemen looking for something old-fashioned and cheap — these nimble fingers were now gently gliding and gripping the wooden handrail on the green, wrought-iron art nouveau banister; I see him — I am sitting again at the top of the stairs — first his hat, then his hand with the big gold signet ring, and finally his face, but only the thin, well-groomed moustache; his eyes are hidden by the brim of his hat; he is whistling, or humming, some unfamiliar light melody; we look at each other one more time, maybe for the last time, and then the man disappears into the big room — as

DUŠAN ŠAROTAR

we call it — which had once been a bourgeois family's sitting room at the top of the stairs; he sets down his briefcase, opens the window onto Lendava Street, and looks down at the road, at the spot I will keep coming back to ever more often, to listen again to that melody.

Much later, when the house was gone and only that melody somewhere still resonated, I would discover that there were actually two melodies echoing within those walls, but I was allowed to hear only one; the other remained forever hidden, wrapped in the silence of memory, as if there are two truths in the world, as a writer once wrote, one of which must forever stay hidden. The only thing that truly remains from the house is a violin, which now hangs in a corner of my study, without its strings or former luster and, most of all, without its sound. This violin once belonged to a different boy, who had forgotten it at home or perhaps left it with someone so that that melody wouldn't be lost. He had stood for the last time at the railway station, to which he never returned, with the man, my grandfather, who never said anything to me about this on the stairs. It was an April morning in 1944; the eyes of the boy, still in the first bloom of youth, were solemn, as if they had seen their own death, although no one yet knew the name for it. So now, when I touch the hollow, empty, dry violin as if hoping to awaken its soul, more and more often I say: *Shoah*.

This, I know, is that other, hidden melody, in which I hear a voice that is neither grief nor grandeur, but rather sadness and melancholy, the rustle of a forgotten wind, which says: write me a song.

There is an old beat-up piano in the big room. Its black lacquer has long since cracked; the fine veneer surface, separated in a few places from the wood, is peeling like suntanned skin at the end of a marvelous summer, but the melody of the forgotten piano is still the same.

My grandfather sits down at the piano, clenching a cigarette between his lips that hardly gives off any smoke, and his fingers, which shortly before had been smoothing cloth, now with the same elegance as if they were stroking the softest wool, or feeling black velvet pile, or tying a silk kerchief around the neck of a much-loved woman, are running, lifting and falling, over the black and white keys. . . . No, now as I stand on the street and look somewhere beneath that former sky, I hear only the wind bending the poplar trees, which line the road on which I myself will one day depart.

5

Whenever I return to the town, I always walk up and down our street, as I still call it. I still recognize it, although the squat houses with the dark kitchens are no longer there and all the people who once sat silently at their tables have long ago left. But I know without a doubt that somewhere still that haustor is there, leading to the other side, even if in its place they have put up an apartment building, in front of which I always stand for a few moments. The stairs are still here, too, on top of which the silent man sits day after day, alternating between pipe and cigarettes.

One day, without a doubt, I, too, will enter the haustor, just like the man in the worn black suit. Then I will walk for a long time. Maybe when I've gone about halfway, I'll stop, try to imagine what's ahead, and think to myself: if I turn around, I will never find out; if I keep going, I will never come back.

Translated by RAWLEY GRAU

Originally published in the short stories collection Nostalgija (*Franc-Franc,* 2010)

Sebastijan Pregelj

THE RABBIT, THE ELEPHANT, AND THE BLUE WHALE

I WAKE UP and open my eyes. I stare at the ceiling for a while. It's white and cracked. I don't understand. When did the cracks appear? When I painted the bedroom a few weeks ago, the ceiling didn't have a single crack in it. I close my eyes and remember the dream I just had. Somebody had been whispering to me not to get too excited. I think back a little further. I remember driving at night through the forest. I remember the fox by the side of the road and the lights blinding me; I remember the screech of the brakes, the crunch of crumpling metal, and glass shattering. I remember the airbag hitting me in the face and a thick, gooey darkness filling my eyes. I remember the sounds going quiet and the voices from far away that never came closer.

There was another person in the car. A woman. She got in when I was about halfway home. She was hitchhiking. She was standing by the side of the road and when she saw me she lifted her thumb. It's cold outside, I thought. All night and all day a fine snow had been coming down off and on. And there wasn't much traffic on the road. When would the next car come by? Would anybody stop for her, or would they all just keep driving? I let up on the gas and cautiously pressed the brake, since the road was icy in spots. I opened the door and told her to hop in. The hitchhiker climbed in and thanked me twice for stopping. Then for a few moments we were both silent. I was trying to think what to ask her. I wasn't really curious about anything. I just wanted to be polite. That's all. But before I could say anything, she told me she was headed back to Ljubljana. She said she was a student there, then added that she had classes the next day. Fourth-year pharmacy. I think.

I replied that pharmacists don't have any trouble finding jobs and they make good money. Or so I heard. The hitchhiker nodded and smiled at me. Then she told me she had been home over the weekend. She said she goes home every weekend. And always hitchhikes. It doesn't cost anything and you meet interesting people, she added. I looked at her and smiled. I suppose you do. She told me she was sharing a room with a friend in a flat where the woman who owned it also lived; the rent wasn't too bad but even so they wanted to move somewhere they didn't have to live with the owner. Her friend didn't go home on the weekends. She likes it that I do though. Her boyfriend sleeps over when I'm not there. We tell the owner he's her brother. The hitchhiker looked at me and smiled.

Our eyes met. I quickly looked back at the road, although at that moment I felt I could have looked straight at her and she wouldn't have minded. We could have looked at each other. I let up on the gas when the road began to curve, and when it went back to being straight, I didn't accelerate. I was waiting for her

SEBASTIJAN PREGELJ

to speak again. Her voice and the way she talked gave me goose-flesh. I was waiting for her to say something that would give me the chance to look at her. She didn't keep me waiting. Our eyes met again. We both smiled, then looked at each other some more. Then I looked back at the road and accelerated a little.

After the next curve, the road began to rise. When we got to the top of the hill we would first see a glow in the distance, then, a little later, thousands and thousands of lights, which gave you the deceptive feeling that the city never slept. I shot her a sidelong glance. She was looking out the window and saying that of all the seasons of the year summer was her favorite. Winter was her least favorite. Because she didn't like the cold. She got cold quickly. I thought of Katarina. She also got cold quickly. And of all the seasons summer was her favorite, too, and she didn't like the winter.

Before we reached the top of the hill, the hitchhiker asked me if I was on the road a lot. I shook my head. Not really. I spotted a fox by the side of the road. I stretched out my arm and pointed at the animal. It's so beautiful, the hitchhiker exclaimed. Yes, it is, I agreed and gripped the wheel with both hands because there was one more curve before the top. That's when I was blinded by lights shining from the opposite direction. A truck. Taking up both lanes. I turned the wheel, trying to avoid a collision, but the car was being carried directly toward the driver's cab, which was getting bigger every moment like some prehistoric monster that had managed to survive the long journey from the Triassic to the present simply by crushing everything in its path with its giant head.

Then time began to stop. Finally, I thought. Everything will still be okay. We'll make it. Nothing will happen to us. We got lucky. Relief filled my lungs and stretched my lips into a big smile. We got really lucky! And when time was almost standing still, there came the crunch of metal. I heard glass shattering and saw the airbag as it hit me in the face.

The sounds of crunching and breaking went quiet. From somewhere far away I heard a man's voice, but it never came closer because I was already leaving. The hitchhiker was next to me and I took her hand. The wind, which had been whirling snowflakes the night before, was now lifting us off the ground and spinning us faster and faster as if we were on some really big merry-go-round filled with flickering colored light bulbs and loudspeakers blaring every possible sound and noise. We just might make it, I thought, and at the same moment felt immense lightness. I didn't care anymore. In fact, maybe it was even better this way. I'm not sure.

I am lying in the bed looking at the white, cracked ceiling. As far as dreams go, the one I just woke up from was nothing special. I've dreamed plenty of stranger things and plenty of more ordinary things too. But unlike other dreams, this one was barely moving. It was motionless, like the motionless little figures and houses in a glass globe in which there are golden flakes swirling around that could easily be stardust.

In the dream I was standing in the middle of a green meadow. Spring was tipping into summer. It was a warm day. There was a girl there; she was standing a bit farther on. She had scratches on her face and arms. Blood was trickling from her left nostril. Her eyes were wide open and there was a smile on her lips. In the dream I didn't know who she was. Now I know she was the hitchhiker. She told me it was her birthday. I smiled and wished for her that she might find a prince on a white horse and a ladder leading up to the castles in the clouds; I wished for her that life might every day wash up a bottle bringing good news for her from across the seven seas; I wished a flower garden for her, and on every side of its white fence a green hill linked to a rainbow across which ladybirds are scurrying; I wished for her that she might watch the sunrise from one hill and the sunset from another; I wished for her that a chimney sweep might come by every day and calmly wait for her to grab his button and make a wish, and that a fat pink pig might suddenly appear out of nowhere with a four-leaf clover stuck between its yellow teeth; I wished for her that she might find a rabbit that brings good luck, and a white elephant that carries good health on its back, and a blue whale whose lungs are full of laughter. All these things you deserve, I said to her, and I felt incredibly happy, but then a voice from the other side of the glass dome whispered to me that I shouldn't get too excited.

Translated by RAWLEY GRAU

Originally published in the short stories collection
Prebujanja (*Beletrina*, 2011)

Arjan Pregl

LEGACY

THE RED BRICK walls of an abandoned factory. Tall windows looking out onto the bustling artists' quarter. A motorbike parked in front of the door. Silence inside. A leather jacket hanging from the coat hanger next to the industrial elevator, converted to domestic use. A record has just played to the end. Two empty glasses with remnants of wine. Red wine. Paintings on the walls. Paintings against the walls. Paintings on easels.

Red.

The door to the tall cupboard opens like some twilight portal. The streetlamp illuminates a naked male body. A leather belt is tied at one end to the metal rail, at the other end around the neck of the handsome youth with shiny thick hair, an athletic body, and semen smudged over his abdomen and legs.

Eleven hours later. The place is teeming with investigators. Gathering evidence, securing the scene of the alleged crime, taking photographs.

"It could be possible that the erection and ejaculation occurred spontaneously. There have been known cases of hanging where this has been reported. There is even a myth that a mandrake springs on the spot a hanged man's semen falls," Inspector Macdonald explains authoritatively.

A known eccentric with incredible intuition, he has dedicated his life to solving crimes by methods closer to obsessive artists rather than systematic criminal investigation. When he senses he can solve a crime, he doesn't sleep. He goes over all the possibilities, eliminates false leads, digs through evidence, checks all the statements over again, ponders, meditates, takes hallucinogenic drugs. Whatever it takes. He sees it as his duty. An obligation for life, ever since that psychopath he had been pursuing killed his... He has never spoken about this with words, instead it is expressed in the deep furrows on his face.

His opinion on painters is clear. Handsome, young, and beautiful, they drive motorbikes, wear leather jackets. Who doesn't know them, right, films are made about this, books written. Their apartments double up as nicely furnished studios in abandoned industrial buildings where they bring willing girls and women who are charmed by their youthful good looks and insubordination to the system. They are romantic, make love to them, then paint them.

"Even this is not enough for them," Macdonald sums up. "He probably had a different woman here every night, and yet, do you know what he did? In spite of all that, do you know what actually happened inside this wardrobe? Asphyxia erotica. Erotic asphyxiation. In this case autoerotic asphyxiation. You restrict the oxygen to the brain, become light-headed, ecstatic, your

ARJAN PREGL

body secretes endorphins, your orgasm is more intense. Much more intense! The problem is that you can pass out doing this, collapse and basically suffocate. Or your heart gives up. The autopsy will show which of these it was."

The following day at the police station. A roomful of police officers. "I wasn't correct. I was sloppy, missed an important detail," Macdonald says in a state of frenzy, unshaven, visibly exhausted. "Last night I went to celebrate the solved case. Like I always do. Alone. I ended up in the Zone Bar. The name was familiar. It was as if the signs were appearing to me but I didn't know how to link them. But I had it all right there in front of me, I could sense that. I walked past the lights. Red lights. Red. Red. I was sure there was something there but didn't know what. I needed to think about it. I ordered a pot of coffee. After the previous seven rounds of whisky, the barman looked at me as if I had ordered yak milk."

He laughs and beckons for one of the younger investigators. "Put the photographs on the table. Like that, yes. Did you notice that all the canvases in his studio were more or less red? It reminded me of another painter. Rothko. Large paintings with merely a few colored stains. Rectangular stains. But they are powerful, you see, primeval. There is something about them that needs no explanation, you just need to look at them. You stand before them and all of a sudden you feel small, as if these paintings were... making you face your own self. Then it depends on what you are like. To me they appeared as an abyss. You know, when you look into the abyss and the abyss looks back at you? And these paintings look at you. Well, in his later period Rothko painted more or less dark-red paintings, the color of blood, hard, dried blood. In the end he was found dead with his wrists slashed in a pool of red," Macdonald explains with excitement.

"That was one lead. But it was still unclear. I then went to check one more thing. Take a look at yesterday's corpse one more time. And I was right. Right! Our young painter had traces of lipstick on his penis. Red lipstick. Here, look." He lifts up a photograph. "I had it analyzed and it is Chanel's Rouge Allure," he adds, triumphantly, pulling a tube of the very same type of lipstick from his pocket.

"And then it finally all added up. The Zone, you remember, the bar I ended up in, the Zone? Have you ever seen *Stalker*? The film by Andrei Tarkovsky where three desperate men travel through a strange and highly dangerous landscape called the Zone? They travel and very slowly approach a mysterious room. A room that is said to grant the wishes of anyone who steps into it. But this is dangerous, as dangerous as Satan himself, you know. That your deepest wishes come true. One of the three travelers then tells the story of the Room. A person once entered it who wanted to see his dead brother one more time. Of course, the Room granted his wish. But instead of the one he expressed openly, the Room granted him a wish that was much deeper. Do you know what that was? He wanted to be rich! Fucking material well-being. He killed himself. He simply couldn't take it."

Macdonald is almost shaking.

"And here we have, I am convinced of this, the same thing! Our handsome young painter was looking for red, just the right red, the right tone of red. Everything around him was red, all the paintings, his brick-red apartment, even the lights in the neighborhood were red. And what happens? Along comes one of the women whose names he promptly forgets, and after a painting session she gives him a blowjob. She then leaves and he notices the wonderful hue of red on his dick that he clearly knew how to wield much better than he did the paintbrush. And that is when he realizes, it dawns on him, that he was never really in painting for the art but merely so he could get to screw the most beautiful women. All the time. Every day. Because we all know what young painters are like. That's their life. That's what they are like. But empty. And he decided to hang himself. It wasn't a painting that made him face his own self, but the lipstick on his dick!"

Macdonald is wheezing.

"But, and I need to stress this, in my eyes he has grown. His paintings were never, well, real, never deep. If you stand before them you never face your own self, there is, let's say, no abyss. The paintings don't go… beyond… life, death…. I find it hard to describe, I am no art critic, but surely you see what I am trying to say, don't you? His paintings aren't, aren't… fatal. Fatal, there, that's the word I was looking for. And this only became clear to him at that moment. So he decided to make the fatal move himself. He went across to the wardrobe, pulled the belt out of his trousers and… well, you know the rest."

Macdonald pushes aside the pile of photographs, collapses onto the chair, trying to catch his breath.

"Bravo. Wonderful. He's done it again," is heard around the room. There is even spontaneous applause. Whispering in the background, a young police officer addresses his colleague, "Should I tell him we found a suicide note?"

"Leave it," she tells him. "It won't change anything."

Translated by GREGOR TIMOTHY ČEH

Originally published in the short stories collection
Dolga zgodba (LUD *Literatura,* 2021)

ARJAN PREGL

Polona Glavan

NATTE

HER NAME IS Natte, and I'm imagining her so she can help me make sense of Berlin.

Natte is about thirty-five now. She was born on August 13, 1961, precisely the night the wall split Berlin apart. In the morning, her ten-year-older brother, Filip, completely forgot he had a sister. The wall was everything people spoke about. Natte didn't like it, the wall. At six she knew how to sign her name in the gravel behind the apartment block in Mitte, on the side of Alexanderplatz. She and the neighborhood kids played the wall game. They clambered all over the power transformer, the sentry kid had to run from around the corner and pull at your leg. Before pulling, they would yell bang, bang! Of course, nobody paid any mind. But if you were snatched off the box, you lost and you had to play as the sentry the next round. Natte though the Russians were shooting at the Czech because they were bad people. Soon afterward, her cousin was killed while climbing the wall. Natte started hating it then. The wall was her destiny. At fourteen her first boyfriend kissed her near Kreuz-berg, behind a tree right by the wall. She thought she was going to get pregnant; she cried. It felt like no use, but she still did. She told the boy she never wanted to see him again. In a year she was laughing at all this. She lost her virginity. By now the number of people who couldn't outpace bullets in their ascent to a better life was already past five hundred. There was just one time Natte felt like going over, when her classmate Ilse's sister did it. But she never admitted it. She started hanging out with the students, demanding the wall be torn down. At one demonstration she was almost arrested. Hand in hand with Robert, long-haired medical student, they fled to Lichtenberg. They were laughing. They smoked weed between the trees along the wall. Natte had never smoked weed before. She'd only been drunk twice too. They made love there, leaning against a trunk. Natte's eyes were open all the while, the lights from the west swaying into her lap. She'll never forget the streetlights of Charlottenburg, how she'd seen them years before her first visit. Next day she wrote some poems. She demanded people start calling her Renate. Robert called her Nats. When she got into university they broke up. She wasn't pregnant or anything, they just split. In college she wrote for the student bulletin. Her article "Follow Me, Sleeping Beauties" landed her at the police station. One time and never again, not even when she was drunk driving. She was lucky. She wanted to go to America all alone. She learned Polish. When the people rose up in Gdansk, she traveled there by herself. The city was gray and heavy with the sea. People pushed her away. Wojtyla was saying he supports the working class. She could barely understand them. There

POLONA GLAVAN

weren't ever any traitors in Poland. She felt lonely. She ran out of money, hitchhiking from Leipzig on. Laughing all the way. The wall should be made so tall that its shadow falls over Moscow, she wrote upon coming back. She barely slipped through. She accompanied her best friend, Christiana, to the clinic for her abortion. It was in Prenzlauer Berg, and ever since then, Potsdam was the last place she liked in her entire homeland. Two years later she graduated. She married. She stopped caring much. Her last name was still Schenkenberg. In the West they wrote graffiti on the walls and no one batted an eye. In the East they scribbled pale scrawls and got beaten up for it. Her father died, and her mother shrugged. She'd been acting funny like that for a few years already. Every day, the papers wrote about heroin taking down thirteen-year-olds in the West. Honecker said the wall would stand a hundred more years. The husband brought passivity and a Trabant car into their marriage. In 1988 they had their son, Kalle. Natte persisted he should be named after her cousin, who had laid beyond the wall for five hours before his dad finally pressed his eyes shut. Eventually, something changed in the people. They started just going over, in droves. Natte wasn't even thinking about that. People were talking. Natte's years were drifting away like she was scattering sand. Grandma and Grandpa came over from Leipzig, crumpled up eighty-year-olds crying with joy. It was November, crawling with folks. Come, daughter, crooned Mother, dragging her restlessly away from the screen, come let me take you to Ku'damm. It took them three days. With her husband, Natte went West every day after work. They explored it like a child, their own. By then eight hundred ninety-nine humans had perished, the last one nine months ago. None of them had a name, not anymore. Natte never consciously looked at the streetlights in Charlottenburg. She didn't remember them, ever, when she was there. Though she will never forget them, cascading over the zoo and spilling into Lichtenberg, falling straight into her lap as if they'd been waiting for this moment their entire life. A year later, she and her husband went to America. She didn't like it. Afterward she stayed put for five years. She had another child. Her grandmother died, followed by her mother. Filip moved to Munich. Natte has two kids now. She and her husband get along fine. She'd like to visit Oranienburger Tor since it's gotten so lively, but she knows she's too old for it. After work she likes to go for coffee before picking up her little daughter from day care. She's always alone. These are pretty much the only moments she's alone now, though she's getting familiar with everyone in there. Maybe it's time to change coffee shops. Sometimes, especially in the summer, a sweaty little figure stops her along the way, with a million shades of night sky in their voice, sporting all-stars and a backpack, saying excuse me, ma'am, can you tell me where the wall is, die Mauer ist, bitte? Natte smiles every time. She wants to say listen, aren't there enough walls around here already? But she plays nice, and she says she doesn't know. That she's not from around here, should the wanderer be especially puppy-eyed with their foreign accent. Sorry. Then, she picks up her kid at day care, or maybe she meanders around a while if it's a really nice day. Just don't tell hubby.

Maybe one of those with the Slavic accent was me. Holding David under the arm, I sat on the wrong subway train. Maybe I reminded her of Gdansk. And if not, I just made it all up.

POLONA GLAVAN

Translated by JEREMI SLAK

Originally published in the short stories collection
Gverilci (*Beletrina,* 2004)

Agata Tomažič

EGG

THE COFFEE CUP had a thick triple line along the edge, orange-brown, displaying the words Bellevue Liburnia. The waiter, approaching the table with his cart carrying seventeen metal coffee pots, wore a vest of similar color to that adorning the cups and trays and everything else on the hotel dining room table. Rajko was thinking about the pots, which were arranged in an asymmetric pattern, five, four, six, and two in a row. He nervously shifted around in his chair, almost lifting a hand as if, no, I don't want coffee, while the waiter was already grabbing the first pot in his reach. He lifted it in a wide arc and began majestically spouting the brownish liquid. It murmured in a midpower stream — poured from an altitude of twenty-three centimeters at least, imagined Rajko — frothing like a small waterfall. The demonstration of mastery acquired at a high-end hospitality school filled the gentleman of graying hair pressed sullenly against his skull with unease and anxiety, as he sat at the table set with a perfectly smooth, ironed, and starched tablecloth. Seizing up, he kept his eyes on the waiter, fully aware that something was about to go very wrong. Something he couldn't quite put into words, but which was unmistakeably announced by his deepest instincts as an absolute disaster. Something that always happens. To him, anyplace, anytime.

"Ow!" was the shriek coming out of Rajko's mouth as a splash of scalding coffee landed on his freshly pressed, though not quite starched, light-gray combed wool pants. It took less than a moment for the liquid to come in contact with the skin of his thigh, and then another split second for the nerve endings to communicate its temperature, dangerously close to the boiling point of water, to his brain. The stain, in the meantime, was growing and growing.

The waiter instantly slunk into another role — as if he'd just intercepted a hint from the stage manager lurking behind the heavy curtains next to the huge panoramic window overlooking the winter vista of the sea. The chap in the prime of his years, whose upper lip was bushy with a robust, firm, and thick black moustache, morphed into a servile trainee, neurotically wagging his cleaning cloth while stooping about.

As if fighting an invisible, pesky fly, Rajko waved him off with a scowl, lisping through his teeth that assistance would not be required, since he was about to independently wash out the stain. He stood up from the table with poise and headed for the lavatory — slowly, at a steady and dignified pace. The pain was wearing off, but the stain was still very much there. He'd be lying if he said he'd not been expecting something like this. If such an unfortunate event was to befall a single guest enjoying breakfast that

AGATA TOMAŽIČ

morning in that hotel, just a single symposium participant, he would have bet the house it would be him.

In the toilet he took off his pants and tried washing them under the tap, rubbing and kneading, finally conceding it had only made the thing worse. An expression of particular relief appeared on his face, as if, what had to happen, happened. Sometimes it's red wine, sometimes it's coffee, and sometimes — very awkward — it's a snotty egg stain dragging itself across his tie. Sometimes they're fresh out of a product he'd been waiting in line for. Or sometimes, the post office closes right in his nose. Or the red light comes up when he's already starting. Sometimes there's a mix-up, his name is confused with somebody else's and he's left without his seat on the train. Or flight. Sometimes his wife tells him she's leaving him over breakfast. No, wait, that only happened once.

Rajko pulled at his pants and slowly sat back at the table. The coffee in the cup wasn't entirely cold yet. He took it to his mouth, gazing through the glass panel at the tempestuous sea whipped by the wind. He knew when the spell of bad weather would end — the most radiant sun will emerge tomorrow afternoon, when the symposium is done and he'll be climbing aboard the bus taking him from the seaside resort. An expression of delight appeared on his face as he was thinking about it.

Relief had been familiar to him for quite a while now. It arrived suddenly, like a gentle breeze in the sultry summer heat, and he spread his arms in acceptance, surrendering to its bliss. It must have come on that day his wife announced she was leaving him. Without a warning, without any signs Rajko was able to observe or discern. Almost like in the movies: at a breakfast table just like this one, another notch tidier perhaps, with correctly arranged cutlery, cups, and plates. She wiped her mouth with a napkin, casting it at the table so that Rajko gave her a grumpy look from behind his reading glasses, its chain always limping around his neck, and she said, "I'm leaving." She got up and, with a gesture that unambiguously expressed a major level of entirely uncharacteristic violence, flipped over her cup of unfinished coffee. Right away, he knew she wasn't coming back.

It actually took quite a few minutes for Rajko to put what happened into perspective. He was rewinding the memory of that scene in his brain, into which everything that fluttered past even for a brief moment impressed itself indelibly, like it was pliable silt. Of all things, he was most amazed that the woman who so contemptuously told him she was gone was so old, with sunken cheeks and drooping lips. Only then did he realize she had, from the first moment he laid his eyes on her, been frozen into some kind of timeless image of eternal beauty and grace. Her skin was always so soft, her eyes gleaming sky blue, and her wheat-colored locks always so tenderly flowing around such an adorably snub nose that he failed to take in all the changes the passing of years had inflicted upon her. He noticed nothing. He was perceiving her like a precious statue, unchanging, immutable, a nonliving object whose only suitable treatment was the show of quiet respect and favor, by gently wiping dust from it every now and then.

For as long as he could remember — and Rajko actually remembered every moment of his waking days — meeting Magda was the single event that wasn't dominated by his negative disposition, his deeply entrenched conviction that sooner or

AGATA TOMAŽIČ

later, but most probably right away, everything was about to go bust. But if he were to scan the moving pictures of memory from any period of his life, something he was able to do at any time, and furnish them with a deeper insight, the directions to his emotions or thoughts, he would have realized it was not his decision but hers. Magda was the one who decided it was to be like it was to be. Magda was the one who, as their film unfolded, in all those decades since their paths had crossed and traveled the same rails together, time and again made sure to steer Rajko away from the mishaps and tribulations he'd be capitulating to, or was somehow manifesting, almost willingly, with his demure outlook. But her powers, too, weren't inexhaustible, and her benevolence had a shelf life. On it was written the date when she toppled the coffee mug and headed, suitcase in hand, into a new, bright future. Alone.

And yet, Rajko and his behavior, likewise, had a deeper dimension. He hadn't consciously decided for this so-called negativity Magda threw in his face at their parting, as if it were an acquired, nurtured behavioral pattern. His negativity was simply a defense mechanism protecting him against the savage violence of hope, the bloodthirsty aspirations that'll butcher a man's guts from within. Life is full of turning points and moments when things might be flipped on their head, when the spotlight might grace you with its favor, the cloak of fortune draping your shoulders for good. Or bad. These nodes in time are clearly set, each person may intuit them as they draw close. Then, the danger is greatest: should a person succumb to hope, risking the stinging pain of disappointment gnawing on their conscience for years upon years, or should they venture down the less breakneck, well-trodden path of quiet resignation, never leading into heights but also never, with broken wings, crashing into the depths of dejection?

Rajko could never muster the courage to rise up and tread a different path, the path of uncertain hope. His was safer and more predictable, as drab as it was it was straight and level, secure, one could find solid peace within stable and moderate misery. In fact, isn't stable misery a contradiction, since stability is a sign of happiness? Rajko knew in advance that his doctoral dissertation won't be receiving the Prešeren Award despite being nominated, knew that he'd never be named Head of the Institute, knew that his and Magda's child would never be born, though it had seemed it would be on several occasions. He didn't budge; he was jaded to the core. Content in his stability.

He was staring at the moist spot covering a good part of the fabric between his legs. Like a frail geriatric who unwittingly wet his pants. He didn't care. It didn't matter if it was still wet by the time he spoke at the symposium, it's not like anyone was going to be listening.

He heard the sound of wheels spinning. The waiter was again approaching with his tray, this time loaded with soft-boiled eggs in little ceramic bowls sporting orange-brown lines. There were twenty-three eggs. With apprehension he offered one to Rajko, who gratefully accepted, his downcast brown eyes as friendly as a spaniel's. He knew nothing could go wrong any longer. The tepid stain on his pants was his ally now. He reached for the spoon and cracked the shell, removing the shards, then sprinkled a few grains of pepper from the shaker onto the whiteness emerging amid the brownish cracks. He captured the white with a deft move, his mind already

AGATA TOMAŽIČ

embracing the juiciness of the yolk, the gently savory touch enriched by the pepper. Chewing at dry whiteness, he cast wry glances around the dining room. Most of the tables were occupied by pairs or trios, the professional colleagues were acquaintances sitting together. Only he was sitting alone. So what, it's not like he envisioned it any differently. He plunged the spoon back into his egg, painting on his sensory canvas the moment when the yolk would inevitably burst forth in all its flavorful smoothness. Alas, it was not yet to be, apparently the delectable yellow was farther below, at the bottom of this oddly particular egg. With slight aversion he swallowed another bite of plain white, reaching for the bread slice he was saving for the time he was to soak up the leftover yolk. He mixed around the shell with his spoon. Nothing happened. He reached into his vest pocket, retrieving his glasses. A repeat motion — removing some of the limestone husk, yet again tasting just white in his mouth. He made a sour face, his brain was certain to find yolk in there by now but there was none to enjoy.

Barely any egg left, and zero yolk. He rummaged for dregs at the bottom of the shell, bringing the plunder very close to his mouth, and squinted in disgust: white! There wasn't any yolk in his egg. They served him a yolkless egg. Not impossible, but a fantastically improbable phenomenon of nature. Bamboozled, he was fixing on the remains of the soft-boiled egg, feeling robbed. Twice: for receiving an egg without yolk, and for succumbing to the hope he was about to enjoy yummy yolk. He forgot: if just one among hundreds of thousands of guests passing through this vacation resort should receive a yolkless egg, it would be him. Actually, what are the chances of getting a soft-boiled egg with no yolk at breakfast? One in ten thousand? One in a hundred thousand? One in a million? Is this not an incredible feat, an outcome so outlandish as to exist beyond the most audacious plans, something only he could pull off, and with effortless ease? Magda would have been proud.

Translated by JEREMI SLAK

Originally published in the short stories collection
Nož v ustih (*Goga, 2020*)

Jedrt Maležič

MICHAEL JACKSON SIMPLY
LIKED CHILDREN

FUGAZI ON MY MP3 player while out on the balcony a discussion
rages about Michael Jackson and about this, that, and everything.
Sancho says he thinks Michael Jackson simply liked children,
that's it. He says that for him Zyprexa is a miraculous pill and that
he'll never get so fat you won't recognize him because he works
out all the time. *Sitting in a waiting room. . . I wait, I wait, I wait, I
wait.* To prove how nimble he is, Sancho, right there in front of
me, drops from a standing position onto the floor and starts doing push-ups, a hundred of them, out of pure mania.

Sancho has never heard of Don Quixote and Don's never heard
of him. In fact, his real name is Samir, and his parents' names are
Samir Sr. and Samira. He says they had no imagination. Sancho
has only just arrived but already he's the boss of this ward, because practically everyone is afraid of him and because he's so
strong he could crush anyone who isn't. He's respectful toward
the elderly, he says. He's respectful toward everyone, always and
everywhere, because that's how you earn respect for yourself, he

explained to us five minutes after he was brought up to us in his pajamas. When he wets his gangster hair and slicks it back, I notice that tattooed on his neck below the crew cut is some sort of letter, or maybe even an inscription, in Arabic. Hafez, he says, the Sufi poet. But he doesn't know what the line means and neither does he care, he says. He's supposedly arrived from Afghanistan, where it's not known how many people he's killed in the service of his homeland. Probably nobody.

Sweat is running down Sancho's cheeks. *I'm waiting, waiting, waiting, waiting.* He says it's because his body only cools itself down when he's upset and restless. I ask him whether now, among us, he is upset and restless, and he shakes his head anxiously and says that one has to differentiate between physical-effort sweat and psyche sweat. Michael Jackson was constantly sweating when he danced, he says, look at him, he swept away all the competition and yet there's no sign any of that fame went to his head. This statement makes me choke on the coffee I'm drinking, but I don't think it would be wise to break his authority and embarrass him in front of everybody, because it's still not known how many people he has killed.

I'm in line for a talk with the shrink. *I'm sitting in the waiting room. . . I wait, I wait, I wait, I wait,* so he can start with his questions. So long, Fugazi, because he's gesturing to me to turn off the private entertainment running through my headphones. Lately my world has been revolving around the people in the hospital, so it's only with difficulty that I can think when the doctor interrogates me about my family beyond these walls. I can easily occupy myself with what's inside, among these stumbling ones, and I've learned to love their sweat and tears. Sancho says things are similar in the army. You forget about the places and the people outside those confines, you get wrapped up in the drama inside. Gradually, that's how I explain it to myself, in this world in miniature you practice reality seriously enough that you're able to function along a similar pattern even after you go back home.

The shrink is not satisfied with my progress. Throughout the interrogation about my family situation, I respond with concrete examples from the hospital balcony. I've been spending my whole time talking about Sancho, the shrink remarks. Am I aware he has his own history and I have a completely different one? I am aware, I am, but histories are contagious, I say. In what sense? I don't know. I fall silent. It seems to me that I've caught something, I think, and pretty soon I'll have to pull myself together. And if he confided in me that Sancho is having trouble with the law? That sobers me up. So he really did kill some people down there, I say. No, no, no. Let's just say that you should keep an eye on your stuff, the doctor imparts. So he's a thief, nothing drastic about that, I think, and besides I haven't brought anything valuable with me into the hospital, some old clothes and a few diaries and pens.

When I put my headphones back on, I shuffle the songs back to the start and I *wait, I wait, I wait, I wait*, to clear up what kind of virus is spreading through my brain, making me feel more at home here than in my own home. I don't turn to the balcony, because Sancho is too loud as he awaits his conversation with the doctor and he's showing off, doing his push-ups. Instead, I think about how much I'd love to give him something, so he won't have to steal. But I don't have anything here. Maybe in my car, which is still parked in the nearby lot. It's worth checking. I just can't let myself be tempted into driving off, that's all.

So I go beyond these walls and the song changes the instant the automatic door opens. I go back to the beginning, I'm not sick of it yet. As if I'm waiting for someone to surprise me. I stare through the windshield for a bit and then it dawns on me. In the trunk I'm still hauling around my out-of-date collection of cassette tapes for which I don't have a deck. There are a few boxes of them, and hidden among them are some gems, which are slightly embarrassing to me, such as Michael Jackson's *Bad*. I'll give them to Sancho.

Heaped high with these precious objects, I take the elevator back up to the ward on which, it seems, they're in a state of emergency. The doctor is standing in the corridor in front of his office, the nurses are dancing around him, their arms raised in dismay. I can barely see over the boxes, so it's really not clear to me what's going on. When I put them down, I see Sancho, who is at the end of the hall, moving toward his room around the corner, and I can see he's cooked something up. I ask the first nurse what's going on. "They threw him out of the ward. He stole a car from the parking lot." No, no, that can't be true, I think, and run after Sancho, who's already at the door to his room. I've just come from the parking lot, and I didn't see anyone. They've either mixed something up or he really got on their nerves. "You were on the balcony the whole time! I'll vouch for you!" I call after him. Sancho shakes his head, while from behind me I hear a doctor: "He is well aware of the why and the how. We have zero tolerance for criminals here! That sort of stuff won't work here."

I grab Sancho by the shoulder and say, "Aren't you going to defend yourself? Stay and fight, you're a good fighter!"

He tells me there's no point and that the shrink has already decided because that's the way it always is, the poor get screwed over. Then he moves over to his hospital bed and starts stuffing things into plastic garbage bags. I run into my room, across from his, on the women's side, and I pull out *Bad*. The album will protect him from real criminals, since Sancho has no home, though he does have a dealer who's threatening to kill him because he can't pay for the horse he's already shot up.

I reappear at the door of Sancho's room and offer him the Michael Jackson tape. So he'll remember that, like Michael with children, he simply likes cars. So he'll know that he's not guilty because they're accusing him of theft, that even good people do bad things sometimes, which goes against logic. That the tape will remind him of the way back, which is always possible. He has tears in his eyes and he gives me a manly thanks, and we smack hands like some guys from the hood, and one minute later he's on the women's side of the ward asking me whether I'm really sure about giving him the tape.

"Is it really mine?" he asks.

"Yours and yours alone, but it's not like it's worth anything," I say with a shrug.

In his currency, it really isn't worth anything, since he can't smoke it or suck it up into his veins. After that Sancho doesn't say a word. He disappears into his room to pack.

A little while later, I receive a very small package from one of the hospital attendants. A "friend" has sent it. Inside there's a slightly bent and slightly bloodied earring for my unpierced belly button. At first I'm frightened because I'm sure, completely sure, that it's stolen, perhaps plucked right out of some local chick's navel, and I'm also afraid that he has hurt somebody on account of the jewelry. He doesn't know his own strength. But the hospital attendant tells me, "Don't overthink it, just accept it and tell him thanks." Right, I thank him, I think, and stow the earring into a pocket because they're calling me from the doctor's office.

The shrink wants to talk to me, for the second time today, to "clarify" something. We're wedged in right away when he mentions Sancho. It means a lot to me to uncover the real perpetrator, because I think of how awful it feels if you want to go home after getting healed and you realize some perfidious swine has taken away your means of transport. But I know Sancho can't have been the perpetrator. I had him in my sights the whole time, with the exception of when I popped out to the car, but even when I was gone I would have been the first one to see him, I explain.

How about if you worried a little more about *yourself*, the shrink points out, *about your life*? I don't answer. Right now the most important thing is not to send an innocent person to jail. If you must know, he didn't steal the car himself, he let his accomplices know the car was unlocked, says the geek on the other side of the table. I bet his mommy cooks him lunch on Sunday and proudly shows him off to all her friends, and, above all, he's not the one who supports her, like Sancho does. It would have been impossible, I claim, for him to move off the balcony while I was gone. These people have all kinds of maneuvers, whether you're aware of it or not. The doctor divides people between *these people* and us, I realize, and that really disgusts me, which is why I get up and slam the door behind me, and in front of the door of his office, indiscreetly bellow down the corridor: "Damn!"

The definitively departing Sancho, who is not ready to stand up for himself and who does not know what his own tattoo means, looks at me in the hallway, stunned, and asks me what in God's bloody name, what in God's bloody name just happened to him. Because that's not entirely his business, but between me and the doctor, I just mumble that the shrink labeled Michael Jackson a pedophile, whereupon Sancho simply shrugs his shoulders.

This is obviously not so important to him, even though he spent half an hour this morning defending the King of Pop's innocence. Actually, I feel like I'm the only one for miles around who is not indifferent to him, to Michael, or to the owner of the stolen car. Out of general protest and because it's not clear to me what it was that got into Michael Jackson to make him snap, I snatch the earring from my pocket and chuck it into the laundry hamper because today's the day they wash our pajamas. I hope it will rip holes in all of the bottoms and all of us will end up looking like *those people*. I go to my room so I can put my headphones back on and wait for something decisive, then I go smoke on the balcony and accompany the dull afternoon as it runs its course. I check my backpack. I check my cupboard. I check all my pockets but I can't find the headphones. Maybe I forget them in the psychiatrist's office.

I knock, but right as I'm knocking I realize where my most valued possession is or at least that it probably already departed, with that poor guy. I change my mind, and when the doctor opens the door to ask me what's up, I tell him I'd like to apologize for before and that maybe I'm ready for my therapy to finally commence.

He gives me an approving pat on the back, and right away I regret my self-humbling. I've found myself on the side of the privileged, of those who don't care if others creep knot-throated through the scorching sun to their dealers, debt collectors, and creditors. And, disgusted with myself, I suddenly feel relieved. I sit on the blue chair and hope that the doctor's joy will eventually dissipate, because I don't like to be docile. We're hanging in the air. For a moment.

Then I begin. "I broke up the family by myself, by my very own hand."

The doctor fights back a smile and listens.

Translated by JASON BLAKE

Originally published in the short stories collection Težkomentalci (LUD *Literatura, 2016*)

Sergej Curanović

THE SWIMMER

HE STANDS ON the shore, looking out at the sea. Both sons are asleep, she is reading a book. Nobody needs him and nothing needs doing. He thinks about swimming across the bay. It would be nice to exert himself. But he worries the distance will be too great. He has never swum that far before. He watches his wife and children. They look like a family from a catalog. Then he turns once more to the sea, glistening gold in the afternoon sun. Still apprehensive. He doesn't like this feeling.

He hears someone call out. His wife's friend has arrived. She has a child but clearly he isn't with her today. She looks good in her swimsuit and she's wearing makeup. Perhaps this is why his train of thought leads him to remember how, as far as he is aware, she is the only woman he knows personally who has cheated on her husband. As he has often done before, he wonders why it surprises him so much that women too can commit adultery. This rouses him. He makes up his mind that he will swim across the bay. He feels very thirsty but does not return to the women, wading straight into the water and setting off.

He swims. Trying to make his strokes look correct and graceful. He recalls that his wife's friend is an enthusiastic swimmer, she might congratulate him on his style. The realization that he wants her admiration disappoints him and he wonders why he is constantly seeking approval. This self-pity irritates him and he angrily dives under the surface. Having only just set off, he makes strong, long strokes and it is only when he runs out of breath that he notices he is deeper than he would normally be when diving like this. With an increasing sense of panic, he swims to the surface. When he calms down, he looks back toward the shore and sees that nobody is paying any attention to him. Swimming on, he stops again after a while to look around, establishing that he is the only person swimming.

Being alone in a giant body of water slowly overwhelms him, filling him with a sense of pleasure as well as fear. In his mind he tries to take in as much detail as possible. He tries to sense the sheer vastness of the water surrounding him and his own insignificance within it. To imagine the multitude of life in all its forms that lives within this environment. Random images from documentaries come to mind, he sees a shoal of fish, the large bodies of marine predators, fields of vegetation on the seabed, shots of microscopic organisms invisible to the naked eye. His sense of insignificance and helplessness grows. He will try to awaken feelings of elation and a mystical link with nature.

He attempts to get himself into the right mood. Turning onto his back, he opens his arms, making slow, lazy moves. Eyes closed, he faces the sky, observing the redness that slowly

SERGEJ CURANOVIĆ

appears beneath his eyelids. The muffled splutter of the sea is all he hears and his imagination draws an image of salt crystals crackling in his ears. Happy with these images, he persists for a while and is only woken from this reverie when the surface of the sea suddenly becomes wavy. He rubs his eyes and looks around. The other shore is still far away and he is still the only swimmer in the water. In a sudden flash of fear, it occurs to him that there may be some reason for this, and that perhaps he should return. But he can't be afraid all his life! How clichéd and ridiculous. His previous disappointment reappears.

To shed it, he once again makes a few strong strokes. The sensation that he is pushing the water behind him, driving his body onward, pleases him. In spite of the stinging sensation, he opens his eyes under the water. The light penetrating the surface turns from blue to yellowy green deeper down, but does not reach the bottom. Once again he is overcome by fear, forming the thought that he could die here in this water. As a child he had heard about someone getting a cramp and drowning. If it were to happen to him now, he, too, would probably drown; even if he shouted loud enough for anyone to hear him, it would most likely be too late for them to save him — he is too far from the shore.

He swims on, no longer opening his eyes as he dives under the surface. He imagines what would happen following his death: the children would wake up, it would be late, his wife would start to worry, and eventually they would call the police. They wouldn't search for him straightaway — it would already be quite dark by then. The following day divers would arrive. Visitors to the beach would see them and wonder what was going on. Someone would whisper they might be looking for someone who has drowned and others would feel unsettled. His wife would cry continuously, clinging to the hope that he might not have drowned, but perhaps also already thinking about how things would be from now on. Their mother's distress would upset the children and they would not want to be looked after by their mother's friend, the one who cheated on her husband. To calm them down, the friend would take them off to get ice cream.

Only then would everyone understand how much he meant to them. This thought, so often solacing and pleasing when he was growing up, now seems pathetic. He again despairs with himself. Why must he always end up thinking like this? In a bout of anger he swims even faster. But straightaway he feels tired and changes his stroke. His hands brush against each other in the water and he feels his wedding ring. What if it was to slip from his finger? The image appears before his eyes of the ring slowly sinking into the depths, lost in the darkness, with the bottom far below. He asks himself whether he would hire a diver to find it, whether his wife would expect him to do so. Trying to calculate whether the diver would cost more than a new ring, he decides that the chances of finding it would be minimal. He would feel depressed for a long time if he had to spend so much money over sentimental symbolism. A new scene appears in his mind, one where the ring slips off but he dives after it, clutching for it.

The darkness of the deep evokes an image of a monster. A creature of bloodthirsty if not evil intent, rising from the depths with swift and strong moves, opening its mighty jaws to grab

SERGEJ CURANOVIĆ

him. Its bite would reach from his chest to his knees, his bones cracking like dried branches, his blood creating a red cloud in the water. The monster would then once again vanish into the darkness covering the seabed and devour him down there. The scene disturbs though there is also some appeal to it. He thinks about how this imagery is borrowed from horror movies and that it could spontaneously spring up in the mind of anyone opening their eyes under the water to try and see the bottom. He ponders how his fear would have been different, had it not been for television, and about how people experienced fear before they had illustrations and books and stories.

The thought seems original and that cheers him up. Once again he stops swimming, turns onto his back. Closing his eyes, he tries to imagine ancient swimmers. He sees the first person who managed to stay on the surface and decided to move out of the shallows. If that person was as far from the shore as he is now, was his fear not like the fear of a sailor knocked off his boat out at sea? This too grows into an image and he now imagines himself to be the sailor. His satisfaction with his own imagination increases. Again he tries to envisage this new vastness of the water around him and sense his own smallness and insignificance within all the biodiversity of the oceans. Then he imagines the sky arching above him, the sheer power of the elements it contains. His thoughts return to the ancient swimmer and he is filled with admiration that he had been able to swim despite such fear. He realizes that, had he himself been one of his tribe, he would never have left the shallows. The only people who dared to swim then were those who felt a strong and pure internal desire to do so, whereas he isn't even sure whether his wish to swim across the bay was his own or whether it was inspired by some external impulse.

He flinches at the sound of a boat engine. Hurriedly he rolls over back into a swimming position. Someone has started the engine on a small yacht not far from him, probably in order to leave the bay. He looks around and sees that he is still the only person in the sea. The motor revs up, there is a sharp sound. The swimmer feels uncomfortable and smells petrol. He watches the man at the helm steering the boat out of the bay. It seems he hasn't noticed him. He swims on and another image arises before his eyes — he is swimming along and the sailboat approaches dangerously close to him. The helmsman doesn't see him and he himself becomes aware of the danger too late to escape. The image becomes a slow-motion scene of red blood spreading in the blue green of the sea, slowly fading away, while shredded pieces of skin and tissue float on the water in the sun. The vision comes to an abrupt end. He repulses the clichéd TV images again forcing their way into his mind. He wonders why his fears evoke the very images he hates seeing, and why he has to be afraid at all. To rid himself of this unpleasant feeling he once again starts swimming faster. He is getting tired. He feels the intense heat of the sun.

A short while later, he thinks he can hear a noise. He stops and looks around. Not far from him he spots someone who is clearly in trouble. He can make out that it is a man and that he is probably drowning. He quickly swims toward him, momentarily forgetting about any tiredness. When he gets closer, the drowning man is no longer making any noise. Late middle age, fat, and quite hairy with a gray beard. For a moment he reminds

SERGEJ CURANOVIĆ

him of his father. The man is desperately trying to keep his head above the surface, silently opening his mouth, flapping his hands with great effort, slowly like a sick bird. The swimmer realizes he needs to act quickly but hesitates for a moment. He raises himself to see whether there is anyone else close by who could help. Only the two of them in the entire bay. In panic, he tries to establish why the man is in trouble — clearly he must know how to swim, being this far from the shallows. He sees the man's hands are sticking out above the surface, so he swims closer. He follows the technique he must have once heard of or seen but it now comes to him by instinct — you need to approach a drowning person from the back. But as he swims toward him, the drowning man suddenly starts grabbing at him and manages to catch his hand.

The swimmer panics, trying to keep above the surface and get behind the back of the drowning man. He feels his strength is rapidly waning. It occurs to him that he will drown together with the person he is trying to save. To no avail, he repeatedly shouts at the man to calm down. The man has a steely grip and the swimmer is unable to free himself from him. He changes his position, turning his back toward the drowning man and starts kicking wildly. He can feel his kicks first hitting against a soft fatty layer, and finally against hard bone. The grip is suddenly released and in a surge of adrenalin the swimmer heads toward the shore. Before reaching the shallows, he stops and turns round, checking the surface. It is entirely smooth. He thinks about swimming back, trying to recall exactly where he had seen the drowning man. He isn't sure. Hesitantly he swims on the spot. Suddenly he is overcome by a fear that the drowned man will somehow drift toward him, and in a final dying reflex grab his leg and pull him down to the bottom. Despite this he continues to swim on the spot for a while, watching. The surface is entirely undisturbed. Apart from the barely noticeable rocking of the moored boats, there is no movement whatsoever. He turns toward the shore and, entirely exhausted, crawls onto the pebble beach.

Sitting on the hot stones, he scans the bay, squinting. There is nobody in the water and there is no movement on the decks of the moored boats. With a start, he turns around. To his relief the beach is empty. He stands up to check the edge of the forest. A few steps from the shore he still sees nobody around. Exhausted, he does what he had wanted to do as soon as he swam to the shore — sit down, rest his elbows on his bent knees with his head in his hands. He closes his eyes, listens to his deep breathing. Once again it hits him that he is recreating an impression exaggerated in movie scenes, the heavy breathing drowning out all other sounds. Thoughts frantically pile up in his mind. He returns to the moment of drowning and relives it. He sees himself handling it differently, with more strength and skill, calmly and in control, without panic and fear.

His momentary daydream is interrupted by a new dread. He thinks about the practical aspects of his predicament: a man has died; probably there is an obligation to report this; this means involving the police; he needs to go straight back and call them; he would probably have to wait for them on the beach so they might inspect the area; then he would have to go to the station where he will be questioned and a statement would be written up. He panics. He will have to explain why he kicked the man;

SERGEJ CURANOVIĆ

this is not something he could keep silent about because they would certainly conduct an autopsy. All of this could become fatefully and unhappily complicated. Swiftly he gets up. With a fear that brings a tingling sensation to his entire body. He looks around. Holding his head, his face twists into an expression of agony. It strikes him that this too is a response he knows from films, but he instantly sets aside the intrusive thought. He sits back down, taking deep breaths to try and calm down. He tries to pick up his previous thoughts. It seems very possible that the police would be suspicious of a foreigner who kicked a drowning man and perhaps broke his neck. You never know what kind of person the investigator might be and how they will see matters; perhaps they will qualify his behaviour as abandoning assistance or something like that, start a procedure and in the end put him on trial, even lock him up, perhaps for years.

His body is incredibly tense. Looking up, he observes the bay. There is no one around. The light is taking on its first evening hues. He makes a sudden decision. He will not report the drowning. His presence at the death of the drowning man did not in fact change anything, he keeps telling himself, he was merely a witness to an event, the course of which would have been exactly the same even if he hadn't been there. He clings to this thought and the sense of relief that an escape from this situation would bring. It makes him want to jump into the water and swim away as soon as possible. But he doesn't stand up. The thought that the investigators would somehow figure out that he was there when the man drowned burrows into his mind. He cannot rule this out. Even though he hadn't seen anyone himself, he could not be certain that nobody had seen him.

Fleeing the site of the accident would paint an even worse picture of him with the investigators.

He disintegrates into desperation. He tenses up again; he wants to cry. Trying to calm down, he lifts his head resting on his arms. He takes a deep breath and feels better when he sees there is still nobody in the entire bay. Surprised it can be so peaceful, it is almost like looking at a painting of the sea and not the sea itself. Then he sees himself, sitting still on the shore as part of this painting. He thinks about the details of the canvas and comes up with the idea that it also shows a drowning, but nobody else would realize that. The satisfaction at this train of thought dwindles gently from his mind.

When he finally snaps out of it, it occurs to him that he should get away now, before anyone else arrives. He hesitates and considers it. Perhaps he should report the event after all. The body is certain to float to the surface sooner or later. He wonders how long that takes. Of course, he should not ask anybody about this, or check it on the internet, because they might trace him. The vision of the body, probably bloated, upsets him. He sees how, swimming back, he accidentally touches the body of the drowned man as it rises from the depths. The grotesque image and his hesitation plunge him once more into desperation. Tears fill his eyes and this time he does not hold them back. Muttering to himself, he wonders why he even comes up with such absurd thoughts. He bangs his fist against his forehead, sobbing.

Then someone gently touches his shoulder. He flinches so strongly that he almost jumps away. Standing behind him are two young men. *Are you all right*, he is asked in English. *Yes*, he replies and wipes his cheeks. He realizes that his looks probably

SERGEJ CURANOVIĆ

indicate the exact opposite, so he affirms, *It's nothing, don't worry, thank you. Okay*, says the young man and moves away. It looks like he is about to leave but he hesitates, as if wanting to ask something else. For a few moments he observes the swimmer sitting on the shore, then he gives him an embarrassed smile and says, *Sorry to have bothered you, have a nice day*. The second man, who stayed a short distance away, lightly lifts his hand in greeting. He waits for his friend and they enter the water together, swimming away from the shore in an elegant crawl.

The swimmer watches them. It seems as if they are swimming directly toward the point of the drowning. He freezes, sensing the panic surging through him. Perhaps the body hasn't sunk to the bottom but is floating somewhere under the surface. He can see it happening, the young man with a downward stroke touching a hand floating upward. The vision is interrupted by voices coming from one of the boats nearby — *Idioten!* shouts an adult voice from below the deck of an expensive yacht on which two young men, probably brothers, are setting up a large electric barbecue. Something crashes onto the deck and breaks. The swimmer then hears other voices. He quickly gets up and looks behind him. Coming onto the beach are a young couple, the man weighed down with bags while the girl is trying to decide where to sit, glancing unhappily toward a family with a baby just settling not far from them. Then there is a scream. Someone must have discovered the body! He turns around in panic. But no, it was a cry of excitement. From the sailing boat moored not far from the drowning spot, a young boy with long hair has jumped into the water. He is shrieking with joy, inviting others to follow him. Realizing, however, that he has jumped in still wearing his sunglasses, he starts swearing. The others laugh while he dives under the surface to try and retrieve them. The swimmer watches, holding his breath. Two of the boy's friends then join him with a shriek and the boy stops looking for his glasses. They start playing around, dunking each other into the water.

Someone bumps into him from behind. A little girl carrying an inflatable crocodile apologizes to him and continues toward the water, her concerned father running after her. Inadvertently he follows them with his gaze which then slips to the far side of the bay.

All of a sudden it is full of people. Among the people on the beach he notices a female figure stepping out of the edge of the forest. He recognizes his wife's characteristic posture. She is shading her eyes, checking his side of the bay. She recognizes him and waves to him to come back.

Translated by GREGOR TIMOTHY ČEH

Originally published in the short stories collection
Plavalec (*Cankarjeva založba, 2019*)

SERGEJ CURANOVIĆ

Goran Vojnović

THE CITY WAS CELEBRATING

"I'M LATE."

"What do you mean, late?"

"Late."

"And?"

"Maybe it's nothing. But..."

"What?"

* * *

Walking past the Križanke Outdoor Theatre toward Congress Square, I still kept listening to her answer, trying to recall what had first crossed my mind on hearing it. The "Oh, craaap!" that had spontaneously shot out of me and was now pricking my conscience must have been based on a picture. It must have sprung from a clear image, which later simply evaporated from my head. What danced before my eyes instead was Manca's look. My "shit" had shocked her, and thanks to that shock I could observe how her anger was slowly, very slowly, being overwhelmed by an enormous disappointment.

I'm killing her with words
and watching how she bleeds,
I'm hurt by all her hurts,
we're dying by degrees.

I felt as if my night walk to the pharmacy in Prisojna Street was the beginning of life after our death. Absent-mindedly moving down the street, I was once again converting my feelings into poetry after an eternity of time. Like in my not-so-long-ago teenage years, I was murmuring while composing the burden of a melancholy love ballad. I was suffering for the sake of my nonexistent audience, proclaiming with an inaudible voice that, deep down, I was a gentle, feeling person rather than the crass asshole who had been stranded beside Manca on the couch, helplessly waiting for someone else to say the words she so desperately craved to hear.

"Can you at least go to the pharmacy?" she asked when she became resigned to me and my uselessness for a more serious conversation.

A split second, and I was at the door.

"Know which pharmacy is open?"

"No."

"Well, of all the. . ."

* * *

GORAN VOJNOVIĆ

Without a clue what she was expecting from me, I was surprised that I had disappointed her so badly. I couldn't fathom how she could have entertained the thought that I might be happy. She seemed to be even more aware than me of my idle running throughout the previous year, maybe even a year and a half. She must have noticed I was waking up later and later, and I was aimlessly wandering through the internet deeper and deeper into the night, merely pretending to look for useful information. She would have realized that sometimes I didn't leave the apartment for days and that I was growing tired of associating with anyone at all and of cracking jokes at my own expense, pretending that I was stoically bearing up.

I also knew that Manca had kept thinking of the job at the warehouse, which had driven us to loggerheads, and that our argument was the very reason why she had stopped asking me every day if I'd received an answer.

"Why shouldn't you work in storage?" she would scream even though she didn't want to hear my answer.

Or, better yet, she refused to understand what the feeling of being swindled, which I struggled to describe, really meant to me. Like many of our earlier fights, it turned into an activity game, in which I first describe my feelings with words that have no common roots with the concept and are not its synonyms, then I try pantomime, flailing my arms and writhing around the room, and finally put the complete picture in drawing, while she, far from articulating the looked-for entry, insists on shooting wide of the mark: "Stuck-up! Puffed up! Hoity-toity! Spoiled! Arrogant! Selfish! Proud! Narcissistic!"

But whatever Manca may have imagined was going on in my head, I didn't really feel that I was above forklifting containers around a neon-lit industry storage facility. Nor would I have been embarrassed to don gray-orange overalls and pin to my chest the name of the biggest social climber in the Logatec Municipality, who is about to finish building his villa with a swimming pool and Ionic columns at Kalce. I wouldn't even mind slaving away for a student's wage of a lousy six hundred euros a month.

No, the only issue was the swindle. The feeling of being swindled.

Behind my shadow, crawling
over my own body dead,
it's impotence I'm hawking
for the emperor undressed.

I was perfectly aware myself that my only problem would be the inability to shake off in that storage area the feeling of being double-crossed. I admitted to Manca that I had simply fallen for the fairy tale that I was going to enjoy all of my life. That I was going to do in my life only what I like to do and what I'm therefore good at. And that the Atlantis pool complex wouldn't be my sea, as the ad says, because my income would be high enough to warrant at least one holiday in Croatia every year.

So, I admitted to her I couldn't help being frustrated in a storage area because I would every day deliberately try and suppress the feeling of being different from the people satisfied with and enjoying forklifting, people whose only ambition

GORAN VOJNOVIĆ

in life would be to man the Linde H 80/900 forklift, which can lift eight tons of containers.

"Who do you think you are?" she snapped.

It was clear she hadn't understood me. Hadn't understood I was not like that but afraid of becoming like that.

"What do you think those five years at the Arts Fac make you? Slavoj fucking Žižek? You're nothing. A bloody high school grad! That's you in a nutshell. Fit to publish your jingles in a high school magazine. Only that."

Whenever she wanted to hurt me most, she went for my poetry. She knew it was a sore spot. Knew I was fully aware of my lack of poetic talent but couldn't come to terms with it.

"You should know."

That was my only answer, after which we didn't speak for three days. But we didn't mention warehouse workers or their forklifts either.

* * *

From a distance I noticed it was not an ordinary July evening in Congress Square, and my mind's eye began to project the recent newspaper headlines, one after the other. "The Greatest Mahler in the World." "A Symphony of Thousands." "A World-Scale Event in Congress Square."

A mere hundred meters before me were thousands of other, less self-absorbed Ljubljanians, witnessing the making of our city's history and celebrating, under the baton of the famous Valery Gergiev, the twentieth anniversary of our state and the hundredth anniversary of Gustav Mahler's death. A thousand musicians were performing his most intractable symphony for a bewildering crowd of enthusiastic listeners.

The city was celebrating.

I could have taken a turn at the National and University Library, headed down toward the Ljubljanica River, and thus elegantly evaded the parade of Ljubljana's pride at the solemn opening of the renovated square, but the urge to ignore such a huge crowd from up close was too strong. I wanted to be the only one to cross the square this evening without even glancing toward the stage for a single millisecond, the only one to ignore the magical, unique, and unforgettable. I wanted to be the weirdo looking at the ground and going his own way. I wanted, desperately wanted, to feel how utterly I didn't belong to the world of enthusiasts.

How could I have explained to Manca all of the feelings drawing me toward Congress Square? Or to anyone? The enormous lightness of drowning in my own pain?

I took pleasure in my lack of interest in the people who were overwhelmed by something happening outside themselves. Those people had ousted me from their world of continuous happenings, and I felt fully justified in enjoying my disdain. Fully justified in flaunting my own oustedness.

They love Valery Gergiev
and watch him, anxious
not to applaud between movements.
They love the wind howling in the loudspeakers
because they'll be able to talk
about how they knew it beforehand.

They love solemnity,
for to them it seems worth the money
they would not give for art.

This was my sweet little revenge for the hundreds of unanswered job applications and for the thirteen short replies that addressed me as "Mr. Jernej Demšar" and thanked me for my understanding, replies that I still kept in the "Job" folder in my email. Moreover, I was taking revenge for my three job interviews, for which I'd been forced by Manca to don my graduation suit, for all those polite phrases and sympathetic smiles. I was taking revenge for my completed MA thesis, on top of which I was now piling up mail, ads, and free sheets, trying to convince myself that this was my way of rebelling against the system.

The system, which was simply and patiently waiting for me to give it up.

For the first time that evening, I was feeling great. It was fabulous strolling behind the grand stage and pretending that nothing taking place on it was of the remotest concern to me. Instead, I was giving a huge finger to Maestro Gergiev, his symphonic orchestras and choirs, the presidents of the two friendly states, Slovenia and Croatia, and the rest of the mesmerized crowd in the square.

For a moment I even seemed to hear my own voice booming across half of Ljubljana from the loudspeakers together with Mahler's Tenth: "Fuck youuuuuuuu!"

* * *

On marching into Wolf Street, my feeling of domination over the community at large began to fade. The petty fears that used to fill my daily life began to return one by one. Again, I was alone with myself, uncertain and lost. Again, Manca and I were sitting side by side, and again I heard her say, "You've never given a damn about what I think, what I want."

"That's not true!" I countered, though I'd already surrendered in this fight and honorably admitted defeat.

"What's not true? You wouldn't know it even if I scrawled it across my tits."

She was waiting for me, perhaps even secretly wishing that I, too, would raise my voice. Instead, I dried up. Offended, she turned her face away from mine, then suddenly rose and started carrying dishes from the table to put them in the dishwasher. It was the first time I saw in her a frightened little child, pretending in front of me that everything was fine. I saw a curious little slip of a girl, finding it harder and harder to convince herself that she was satisfied in my monotonous life, which made her renounce her wishes, longings, and dreams.

> *Caught in our embraces*
> *she slips off unseen,*
> *turning, still and soundless,*
> *to a phantom dream.*
> *Beyond the illusions,*
> *what's hers is not mine,*
> *secretly, there she*
> *dreams not as do I.*

GORAN VOJNOVIĆ

"All right, tell me then what you want."

"I want to strangle you!" she said.

I dried up again.

* * *

Pharmacies have always given me the feeling that it's the healthiest people who whisper most conspiratorially across the counter. While nobody has ever tried to conceal a migraine or strep throat, people have always squirmed at admitting to hemorrhoids, herpes, dandruff, diarrhea, and other harmless ailments.

Or a girlfriend whose period is late.

"A Clearblue, please."

I whispered it so conspiratorially that I wasn't quite sure if the pharmacist heard me. But she must have learned to distinguish between diseases by the patients' volume, so she gave me a routine nod. She carried out her part of the task professionally, keeping a — probably professionally deformed — poker face, which cannot have betrayed my tribulations to the short queue waiting behind me.

I was enormously grateful to her, but I struggled to keep a poker face, too, to convince her that I was doing nothing I wouldn't be doing anyway on the second Saturday of every month.

Under all my pretended coolness, though, I was ruffled by the very sight of the little oblong box, ruffled so much that I was literally catapulted from the pharmacy back into the street, with my pace visibly quickened. Like a drowning man, I gasped for the fresh night air and all I could think about was how I wanted to get home as soon as possible and solve this night's mystery. The Clearblue, peeking from my trouser pocket in its green and white paper bag, was growing heavier with each step.

In my anxiety to be done with it, it even occurred to me on my way through Tabor Park that I might take a peek at it myself in the gloomy night shade of the park's plane trees.

You won't outplay destiny
if you play her game.
And no freedom will you see
if you're not a pain.

I hated gambling, I hated guessing, I hated possibilities expressed in percentiles. In all of it I could see nothing but an occasion for my defeat, and even in that particular magical gadget I could see only a Manca-like creature, chronically exhausted and wasted, glaring at me with a face turned into two giant circles under the eyes, hollering because I'd allowed our baby to throw up on the couch, and repeating that I should have foreseen it and been prepared.

I knew none of the things I should know and was on the brink of a classic panic attack. In fact, I had no idea about what every father should, according to the mother's opinion, know about babies, about children; all I knew was that the mysterious knowledge would be expected of me at some moment. And I knew at that moment any excuse, no matter how logical, would bring out a sentence beginning "You should have known. . ." and from that point on the decibels would soar to unimagined heights.

Everything would be easier if I had a job, I thought, and if I could fill a father's role by earning money, which would make me feel useful in a traditional and conservative way at least. Sadly, though, earning money was a feat just as unfathomable to me as had been, since time immemorial, the feat of making a baby burp. I simply couldn't envisage myself in a situation that might even hypothetically be described as "earning money."

I could do a translation, but I doubt anyone would be willing to pay for it. And if I were to write a general interest article, it would buy me a sandwich and tea at best. What's even more likely is that I wouldn't manage to get it published at all.

My social science expertise was impossible to cash in, and to this I had to resign myself. Even in happier times bursting with a future, when anyone could turn to profit even their own stupidity, Spanish-speaking sociologists of culture had hardly been in demand. Now, with the taps of transition turned off, a graduation thesis about how the movement of the Zapatistas, the last of the Mohicans of Latin American revolution, had influenced contemporary Mesoamerican culture was worth as much as a certificate in a water aerobics course for seniors.

In short, my thesis didn't increase my chances of employment, so I no longer saw any point to it. I had accepted it as an irrefutable fact that, such as I was, I could contribute to nothing really important. Society was getting along without my help, and to all appearances it wasn't going to need me in the future either. They had no idea what to do with me, and the feeling was slowly growing on me that they'd be pleased to shelve me somewhere like the dusty folders from the Social Accounting Service, which had once been stacked by my mum.

I was in a hole. In an infinitely deep abyss between childhood and adulthood, and what I might call my adult life was no
more than a distant point in a vague future, which was slipping
farther out of reach day by day. But the electricity bills kept arriving every month, and Mrs. Marinšek went on collecting a
bloodsucking rent.

*   *   *

In Trubar Street, I was slowed down and at the same time distracted by a drove of Italians sauntering in front of me and filling
the atmosphere with their cacophonous gibber. So I walked behind them for a while, watching their pageant of merry moods
and hoping those would rub off on me a little bit. Their ages
ranged from two girls who had recently turned teenagers to a
portly old man with a young man's laugh, but all seemed equally contented. At the genuine merriment of this checkered mix
of generations I thought, near as Italy was, those people were
in fact coming from a world very distant from mine.

I was downright disappointed when our ways parted and
when the intersection between the Ressel and Trubar streets
saw the frolicking Italians turn toward the Petkovšek Embank-
ment. I'd hoped they'd keep me amused for a while longer with
their loud and incomprehensible jokes. But as it was, at the moment they disappeared from my sight, my thoughts returned
to the little box in my pocket.

I desperately cast about for something positive in every possible outcome of my life's lottery. I ransacked my memory for
happy scenes from my childhood, looking for an image of family

idyll where I wished to insert Manca, myself, and our unborn child, and to force myself to sense in it something beautiful, something pleasant, something that would relieve my piled-up fears, at least for a moment. But I became more frightened at every scene featuring Manca and me as mother and father. The memories that began to surface more powerfully and distinctly than the others were the grayest ones, which I'd always wanted to drown in oblivion.

Like my father once upon a time, I was now sitting in the pantry, where I'd sneaked two hours ago in order to fix two chipboard shelves. In complete silence I was cowering on the floor, hoping my kid wouldn't catch me leaning against the wall, screwdriver in hand, hiding from him and his mom. And when he finally did open the door and was surprised to see me, I simply smiled at him as if everything were normal — I patted his head, hugged him close, and didn't answer any of his unpleasant questions.

And then I was again sitting absent-mindedly on the couch next to him, pretending an interest in the TV cartoon, though I didn't laugh a single time because I didn't understand English and couldn't make out which of the two dogs was talking. And because in fact I disliked cartoons and found them boring, but stuck there nonetheless and gave my kid a smile every few minutes so he'd know I was still there, that I hadn't disappeared.

And Manca, like my mother once upon a time, would peep into the nursery in the middle of the night, checking whether her baby had fallen asleep or was still waiting, despite the late hour, for her to return from her business dinner and read him a good-night story as she'd promised. She would stand there, looking at him and wondering how she could at that moment, in the middle of the night, make up for what she'd neglected, how she could make amends for another of her many broken promises: should she wake him up with a kiss to show him how glad she was to be with him, or let him sleep, the poor tired darling.

Resting her head on the table, Manca was staring at the birthday cake, slowly teasing out one sour cherry after another, even though she knew it was no use; her baby wouldn't touch that cake even if she picked from it every single crimson fruit. She knew, in spite of everything, a crimson trace would remain and her baby would know it wasn't the cake she'd promised, know she had again run out of time to bake his favorite chocolate cake, without fruit or nuts. Nevertheless, Manca went on picking the sour cherries from the cake and ate them all. And then she burst into tears.

* * *

Beating or not beating?
That is the question.
And if it's beating, then for whom?
For me? Or only for itself?
And if it is, whose is it?
Mine already?
Or still no one's?
Is it from God?
And if it comes, from where? Is it returning?
To whom? And why?
If to me, why me?

What will I be to it?
What will it be to me?

If it is at all. . .

* * *

The people in Congress Square were dispersing. Crowds dressed in their Sunday best were hurrying toward their cars, which would carry them back to their non-Sunday suburban world. But by that time I was no longer interested in those people, so I was able to raise my eyes and look around with curiosity. I could follow the perfect synchronization of the workers dismantling the stage and watch a young man routinely rolling up a long electric cable, as he must have done countless times in his life, while managing a relaxed conversation with his friend. All this I watched attentively and even glimpsed some familiar faces, but it was all a stage prop toward which I directed my empty glances.

Behind those glances I was bursting with the question: How can a total zero turn into a father in just one night?

From a poetaster who isn't even poet enough to dare play the martyr for the public and to sell his agony? From an unemployed almost graduate in sociology of culture, without any noteworthy work experience and without a single month of service to his name? From an unrealized mama's boy who's still chasing after her attention at twenty-five but dare not admit it? From a blockhead who doesn't even know if his girlfriend wants to have a baby? From a bungler with two left feet who speaks fluent Spanish? From a specious introvert who didn't catch on after high school that introversion was no longer in? From a poor teller of jokes and an abysmal teller of stories? From a decent skier who hates the cold, as well as snowball fights? From a lover about whom no girl has ever complained, but whom none has ever praised either? From a broke loser who borrows a pretty penny from his father every month and writes his debt down to feel better? From the owner of his grandpa's green Renault 9 and his mother's rusty Rog bike with a new basket? From a picky eater who doesn't like greens or funky cheeses? From an irregular smoker with a sensitive stomach? From a half-cured computer geek who still swears by Linux? From an unpromising fool obsessed with himself and his own vanity?

How can one become anything from all this?

*　*　*

"Won't you go at once?"

"I don't know."

Manca was sitting at the kitchen table, nervously fiddling with the little box.

"Better get it over with quickly."

"Let me be!"

I had a new chance finally to decipher the thoughts churning in her head, and this time I approached the arduous task like a detective. That is, I mobilized all the knowledge I'd garnered over the years from watching American crime series. I encouraged myself with my longtime thought that my obsessive TV watching was bound to prove fruitful someday, and that some folly or other I was committing in my life was bound to gain meaning in time. But the minutes of my detectivelike scrutiny of Manca's face revealed only a fear of what the pregnancy test might show.

I sat down next to her and took her hand. It occurred to me that she couldn't bear my closeness now and would try to wrench herself free, but once again I was wrong. Her palm was sweaty, and she clutched me as vigorously as if she were afraid I might slip out of it.

"I'm going."

"Okay."

I kissed her on the cheeks as if I were kissing a friend, as it seemed the only right thing to do at the moment. I topped it with a kindly smile, so botched that I was embarrassed by my own clumsiness. But Manca responded with a smile just as uncomfortable, and when the door closed after her the next moment, I finally had the feeling that we were in this together. And I was sorry that she was alone in there. It even crossed my mind that the Japanese might have invented pregnancy tests in which both partners could participate, thus deepening their bond.

Presently there came the sound of water draining from the tank and my thoughts were paralyzed. Motionless, I stood in the middle of the room and waited, with my eyes fixed on the toilet door, for Clearblue to determine the course of my life.

In there, all sounds subsided.

"Manca?"

I was ready to interpret the slightest rustle but could hear nothing except for the humming of the fridge and a distant city bus picking up speed.

"Manca?"

"Yes."

"Everything all right?"

"Yes."

And then again silence.

And forebodings.

They prey in deathly peace
beside your words unsaid.
I hear your silence, dead,
they mutely scream at me.

I should probably have said something but I could no longer trust my words. Instead I silently went on eyeing the little bronze boy on the door peeing into his chamber pot. I remembered how at a friend's birthday party Manca and I had rolled our eyes over a couple regaling the assembled company with an elated account of how their little boy had begun to pee standing up. Both of us earnestly wondered if they'd gone off their rocker after having the baby or if they'd always had rats in the attic, as my grandma used to say.

From inside the toilet, I presently heard a subdued snap and some other, indefinable sounds, followed by a distinct trickle of water.

The doorknob moved, and Manca hurried out and threw herself in my arms before I could register the expression on her face. She pressed close against me and I could feel the unusual commotion of her body, her ragged breathing in and out, which could only mean one thing. Concerned, I pulled out of her embrace and held her off to get a good look at her. There were tears running down her face. But Manca was laughing too. I thought it must be what we men confidently call female hysterics, though we never have the slightest inkling what is uppermost in that emotional cocktail: joy, sadness, anger, or something else entirely.

"Well? Are you pregnant?"

Manca went on crying and went on laughing. Jerking her head all the while in a way that couldn't be construed as any sort of answer to my question.

"You silly!"

I was lost. I wondered if I'd missed something, or perhaps lost consciousness for a moment. I was at sixes and sevens, and this I tried to relay to Manca with the most idiotic look I could muster.

"Do you think I'd be laughing if I were?"

* * *

When will shops begin
with happiness discounts?
For those under thirty,
will entry be allowed?
And may we there
expect a crowd,
such as we've seen
at faculties mill round?

* * *

Whenever I watched films with a happy ending, I wondered if a happy ending was happy forever. I wanted to know if Hugh Grant, too, remained happy to his dying day each time, like Snow White and her prince did. But now, watching Manca wipe away the remnants of her mascara under her eyes, gradually returning to her preearthquake state, I thought that every life consisted of countless little stories and that "happy" in fact meant being the one who lived to see the most happy endings.

And watching the smile on her face gradually fade away, I came to realize that no one was capable of remaining happy to their dying day because happiness and unhappiness are intertwined, unable to do without each other.

"Jernej!"

"What is it?"

"I'm sorry."

"What for?"

"For all of this. I panicked."

I was able to breathe more freely. Panic, nothing but a teeny-weeny panic. A welcome teeny panic, which had saved us for one evening from checking emails every fifteen minutes, from watching series like CSI: *Miami*, from Manca falling asleep on the couch, the TV set aglow, with me hanging on beside her and staring at the ceiling.

The teeny-weeny panic had saved us from all that for the evening, but as early as tomorrow we'd be free to resume our places in our story. Again, Manca would be a sophomore in architecture, preparing for the autumn exams, and I an

unemployed high school graduate wondering for whose benefit I should become a graduate from the Faculty of Arts.

Tonight, however, we were saved and all our problems blown
away for the evening.

All thirteen rejections, which I secretly reread every night
while Manca was sleeping in the next room, suddenly struck
me as funny. Funny was "Mr. Jernej Demšar," funny the re-
petitive sentences with which secretaries apologized on their
managers' behalf for their mistrust, funny the thirteen uniform opinions that I was incapable of performing thirteen
different jobs.

Funny were even the envelopes in which my father handed me the borrowed money which I in my turn handed to Mrs.
Marinšek for my monthly rent. Funny that I'd been trying for
months to scrape together the money for new car tires, which,
according to my mechanic, I urgently needed. Funny the delight with which I looked forward to my grandma's birthday
present of a hundred euros. Funny the bright boys in their expensive suits warning us, one after the other, that the years to
come would be even worse.

And funny was my joy because I wasn't going to become a
dad in those troubled times. Funny, everything was funny.

"What are you laughing at?"

"I don't know."

"How can you not know what you're laughing at?"

If I'd known, I would have told her.

Sadly, I had no idea which of all those funny things made me
laugh that evening.

Translated by NADA GROŠELJ

Originally published in the short stories collection
Dan zmage (*Beletrina, 2012*)

Vesna Lemaić

DEODORANT

IN THE STANDS next to us a homeless guy is sipping a beer. Azar, a girl from Iran, is sitting closest to him. She beckons toward him, pulls a face, and grabs hold of her nose. I look at the man. A very common case of a drunken Slovene minding his own business. I shrug, I just want to get on with watching the game. I move seats, so now I am sitting next to the man. In the heat he reeks of the alcohol he has ingested. I try to distract Azar, pointing at the pitch, overdoing the cheering. But the stench is more tangible, stronger than my exaggerated gesturing. The reality is that the homeless man has not had a shower. Azar probably uses the deodorant she was given in the toiletries packet at the asylum. I don't use deodorant but had a shower at home before I came.

The migrant team Persian Cats scores a goal. I clap with my hands extended but next to me sense that Azar is sitting quite still. I turn to her with an enthusiastic expression, as if to say, look, your team is winning.

She grimaces again and gestures toward the man next to me. His presence bothers her. She is still distracted and all I want is for everyone to have a good time. The situation is getting to me. I only wanted to watch the football match but the real match is now taking place in the stands.

I am here, hanging around with my political convictions like the net on a goalpost. I don't want them to shatter. I somehow like Azar and want her to feel good when we hang out beyond the fence of the asylum. But I don't know how to fit all this together. So I choose an own goal. I lean toward the homeless man and ask him whether he can move. I don't tell him he stinks. My armpits are sweaty — you can't cover up reality with deodorant.

Translated by GREGOR TIMOTHY ČEH

Originally published in the short stories collection Dobrodošli (*Cankarjeva založba, 2018*)

Andraž Rožman

THE STORY OF A MAN WHO
STAYED ON HIS FEET

GRAVEL CRUNCHED BENEATH Joc Podlesnik's feet as he walked toward history. Opening before him were the Ljubljana Marshes. Brown patches of grass revealed that winter had barely given way to spring. Not, however, the intensity of the sun. It was beating down on the wooden building that was once a double hayrack and now a proper little house. Running past the field in which it stood was the local road, right behind it, the railway line.

"It's been thirty-eight years," Joc sighed when we reached the hayrack that no longer served its original purpose.

"It's all different. But look, the support is the same, and the laths too."

He touched the rough wood, running his hand across it. We walked all the way around the building that was like a simple weekend house, noticing the lighter-colored, freshly treated wood, raising our gazes to the new balcony on the top level.

"They've brought in some gravel. They must have raised the floor slightly," he commented insightfully.

We peeked through the door and could feel the coolness of the empty, dark space. We didn't, however, go up to the top where Joc used to sleep on the hay. Private property is private property, after all. Especially in these days.

"It is the first time I am here in all these years. I wonder what would have been if I had jumped onto that truck back then and gone off to Macedonia."

He had changed his mind at the last minute but also didn't want to go back home to Litija. In the third year of the technical school in the capital where he was training to be a milling machine operator, he found himself incapable of facing the difficult thoughts that seemed to be taking hold inside his head. At the hayrack he had thought about what to do with his life and decided he wouldn't go back to school. He slept on the hay, stayed low whenever he heard the farm workers out in the fields, licked the sweet dew from the grass every morning. For three days that was all he had.

After his third night in the hayrack in Lavrica, a village just beyond the outskirts of town, he crossed the main road in the morning and asked for some water at one of the houses. He drank a glass of water, got on the bus, and a little while later marched into the police station at the center of town. It was September 10, 1981.

"I remember well the sports commentator Mladem Delić on TV shouting *Boruuut! Boruuut!* just as I came home."

On that day, the swimmer Borut Petrič beat the Russian Vladimir Salnikov in Split to become the European 400 meter Freestyle Champion, and Joc set off on a path that he later often called his "career of madness."

Although he was running away because of school, he in fact liked it. He wanted to study history and geography. Countries, towns, different worlds, all attracted him. But school was also what made his problems worse. Only a few days into his third year, he felt that things were not going well. It was almost as if he had forgotten everything over the summer break, even though it was only the start of the school year and they had yet to be given any grades.

"I didn't want Mother to have to come to school because of my problems," he said in a soft voice.

Standing next to the former hayrack, looking toward the Alps, basking in the sun, he said, "Look, from here you can see the summit of Triglav, and Grintovec, Storžič, Stol, Begunjšči-ca. How I love the mountains."

We ascertained that it was probably mostly to do with fear, on which he was incapable of setting limits. After what happened at Lavrica, he went to the Center for Mental Health for the first time and spent a whole month there. He was taken there by this Slovene language teacher.

This was Joc's first contact with psychiatry.

* * *

We stopped outside the football stadium in Litija. The door leading through to the locker rooms, the bar, and the pitch was locked. We went to the other side, up the road, and in the shade of the trees of the nearby forest continued along the path to the practice pitch where a few young men and women were sitting in the grass, though, due to the heat, nobody was even thinking about kicking around a ball. With his thin, sunburned legs Joc waded into the tall grass that separated the practice pitch from the road. It almost reached his bare knees. He straightened his glasses on his pointed nose, turned his curly head on which gray had almost entirely masked his black hair, looked around, and showed me where he used to play football. He had been captain of the youth team.

Even as a boy he was devoted to football. He followed his home team of Litija in the 1970s when it reached the Slovenian top league and when the club was supported to success by hundreds, sometimes thousands of people. In the boy's dreams there was space only for football. He would pick up balls at members' matches and trained enthusiastically in the youth sections. All until 1982 when he turned eighteen.

It was soon after what happened at Lavrica. He felt unwell. Inside his head he could feel a kind of pressure, he could not concentrate on the exercises during training, overcome instead by feelings that he didn't know and still finds hard to describe.

"I'm not really sure I know what it was about. At the time I didn't yet believe I was Tito's son, but I became more and more scared. I realized there must be something wrong with me. I asked the coach to call my mother."

Word got out that Joc had emotional distress. When he wanted to return to training, he was told he was no longer desired at the club.

"They had decided I was a disruptive factor." His world collapsed. "I don't know what to say. I felt betrayed."

Later, when they invited him to join again, he didn't want to return. For a number of years he didn't play proper football but merely futsal, then he was invited by the club from the neighboring settlement of Kresnice.

Not too long after being thrown out of his first club, he began perceiving himself as Tito's son. He corresponded with a girl he fancied and in the end fell in love with. One night he decided that his crush was dancing at a disco in nearby Ribče. He set off on foot. As he walked along the Sava, the moon reflected in the river.

"I imagined I was being protected by Tito's security guys, sending secret messages to each other through the flashes of reflected moonlight on the water."

When he reached the club, he initially watched the dance floor from afar. Of course, his crush wasn't there and in his frustration he tipped over a portable toilet outside the joint. The police were called, they took him home, and he ended up at the Polje Psychiatric Clinic for the first time.

"When I'm in such a state, I don't think about anything, I also don't feel any pain, I just look for any object that I can throw somewhere. But I quickly come to and see I am doing myself harm with such behavior. That is what saves me. And the fact that I am always an optimist. It never even crossed my mind that I would raise my hand against myself, not even when things were at their worst."

And what is it like when he "comes to," as he calls it?

"I am always a little embarrassed, especially when I'm taken to the Clinic in Polje. There I am dehumanized. If you ever see me in a state like that, just tell me firmly, 'Joc, you'll get sectioned again.'"

He cringed his bony face, quickly turning serious as the skin on his thin, slightly hollow cheeks and around his mouth convulsed.

"The worst thing is when you have to get undressed. Two huge guys, medical technicians, escort you into the changing room. If you're too slow you can get knocked around the head. You are given some pajamas and sent to the closed ward. There used to be thirty or so people there, now there are far fewer. When I was first locked up in 1982, they washed me with cold water from a black pipe as if I was a pig."

And they still tie people to their beds. According to the law, a person can be tied to their bed without a break for up to four hours and then the doctor has to decide whether the bodily restraint with belts, as it is called in medical jargon, can continue. A number of people have reported being tied up continuously for much longer than is allowed. One of them described how even as recently as the summer of 2020, he had been tied to a bed for around 17 hours. Social workers are pointing out that in view of respecting every individual's human rights, this kind of forced restraint and incarceration need to be abandoned.

Joc later had numerous encounters with institutionalization. These taught him the best ways to act whenever he was locked up. You are released soonest if you do your best to accept the regime at the psychiatric hospital. The system likes obedient patients. If you are not obedient and resist the regime of rules and medication, you are in for a bad time. You might be tied up, given a larger dose of drugs, or punished in some other way. Many people have confirmed this. Joc was often tied up, but over time he developed patterns of behavior that got him released sooner.

Decades ago, when he first came across psychiatry, the methods used were even crueler than they are today. He was one of the last patients to be put through insulin shock therapy. People were injected with insulin until they fell into a coma. The effects were salivation, fatigue, irritation, lividity, and sometimes also brain damage, even death. While some psychiatrists insisted the damage to the brain represented an improvement because those subjected to insulin shock were no longer as "tense" and "hostile," the risk of death was 5 percent, and according to some research even as high as 7 percent. Therapy using insulin shock was mostly abandoned throughout the world in the 1960s but Joc was still receiving it two decades later, in the mid-1980s. Psychiatrists chose candidates for insulin shock therapy based on their physical characteristics. They chose those that were strong and fit who could withstand the shock. And Joc had a sporty physique.

For sixty days they injected him with insulin for around an hour every day apart from Sundays, sometimes keeping him in a coma for an hour and a half.

"They reset me then," he would say.

In two months he was given five successive injections of insulin seventy-three times; sixty shocks were successful, thirteen were not.

"You can't imagine what I was like here," he said, pressing his finger on the vein near his elbow joint. He opened his arms and pointed to the button on the pen. "That was how thick the needles were. I had dark patches on my skin for twenty-five years."

Tied to the bed where he would have an epileptic fit, he would toss about as if wanting to fly off, but the straps were stronger than his body. Every time he woke up he was brought an apple, a sandwich on a white plate, and a metal cup full of Jell-O.

"I never felt anything during the therapy and I can't remember anything about it. It was painful later when I was sent to my room. I could barely get there."

He showed me how he used to feel his way along the corridor, leaning onto the wall as if he were drunk.

After a while they stopped pumping him with insulin but that was not the end of injections. He would have liked more conversations for the soul and fewer substances for the body.

"Some years ago I attended group therapy sessions where I learned how to talk about myself and the world. But I never had one-to-one sessions. They aren't covered by the health system and I don't have the money to arrange for them privately."

With a psychotherapist he could have tried to get to the reasons that brought him into conflict with social norms, could delve into his past, perhaps discover something surprising, inspiring, or painful. Thinking about it now, on his own, he concluded that the divergence from social norms was linked to his upbringing. Especially with the absence of his father.

*   *   *

When he was living in Litija, his inner tensions led to a traumatic experience that he has still not entirely left behind.

From the football pitch, we turned toward the neighborhood where he used to live. We parked in front of a park where there was a playground, a basketball court, and a small football pitch.

"Look over there, there used to be a rope suspended between those hills and we would climb down it," he said in a weak voice.

ANDRAŽ ROŽMAN

He had been rather tired all day and wasn't feeling well anyway. He wasn't sure whether it was due to the heat or because he had been given an injection two days ago, perhaps what also contributed to this was him reviving what were for him important but also difficult memories.

His former home was only around the corner.

"I feel a little uneasy."

We walked on.

"Just turning this corner makes me feel dizzy."

We continued anyway. He led me around the six-story building. It was clear from the exterior that the building had been renovated at least once since when Joc lived here. He noted that the three silver birches had grown a great deal since he had last seen them and he looked up toward the top-floor apartments.

"I lived in that bedsit on the left."

During one of his episodes, there was a fire.

"All the walls were black. Everything went up in flames, my degrees, trophies, information about my father...."

For a long time he blamed himself.

"It was a dark November day and I was trying to find my thermal socks to go to football practice. I couldn't turn on the light because the electricity had been cut off. I made a roll out of a newspaper and lit it on the gas stove. The paper burned, I put it out with water. Then I lit another roll, walked up and down the apartment, found the socks, and went off. But this time I had not put the burning paper in the sink, I just dropped it to the floor and trampled on it to extinguish the flames. A few hours later the fire began."

It happened about a year after his mother's death and around half a year after he had been rejected by the family of one of the girls he liked. For months before the fire he had not been feeling his best. He had ups and downs.

"A few times I once again imagined that Tito's security guards were keeping an eye over things. Normally these periods wouldn't last long, but then it went on for months, though I didn't tell anyone that anything was wrong."

It was hardest when his mother died. She loved him and tried to provide everything she could.

"She deprived herself of many things so she could buy us this place."

When Joc was a child she had worked in Nuremberg for seven years, had a job at the Siemens electric motor production line. He saw his mother a few times a year whenever she came home for a visit and sometimes went to see her in Germany. While she was away, he lived with his aunt and her two children. Life in a miners' settlement was tough. He was made to work out in the fields, was sometimes given a few slaps, and never felt he was like the other two children in the house, even though this was his home for seven years.

"I recall once asking my aunt why I was not supposed to call her Mother, if we all lived together and that was what my two cousins called her. From then on she became Mother and I started referring to my real mother as Mummy."

After the fire, he felt as if everyone in town was pointing their finger at him. And then he got himself into financial trouble.

"I accumulated a debt of a hundred thousand euros," he said, surprising me.

ANDRAŽ ROŽMAN

I doubted his claim, just as I had often wondered whether everything else that Joc talked about was true. It was as if there was a warning printed on his forehead, a fading warning, one less visible with every meeting, nevertheless, still there. And the best medicine for doubt is facts. Joc's words were confirmed by a statement from Litija Municipality, which gave a sum of the amounts for maintenance and other costs for his address between 1995 and 2013.

The municipality had subsidized his mother's costs at the old people's home, and his costs for staying at the residential community of the NGO Šent. At the time there was a rule in place that you should reimburse any contributions if you sold property. Until 2017, the law stipulated that an owner of an apartment was liable to reimburse any contributions by social services up to the value of the property.

Just before the fire, Joc was trying to sell the apartment and had also received the deposit for it. He dreamed of renting a bedsit in Ljubljana and getting a stall at the market where he would sell products from Turkey. When the apartment burned down, its market value was of course drastically reduced and he needed to return the deposit, which he had in the meantime already spent. He was left with around 800 deutsche marks, some of which he used for clothes. The rest of the money somehow vanished.

"When I got the money, I felt almost drunk. I remember putting the banknotes on the table and telling a friend to take as much as he wants. Some of the money was taken by the buyer of the apartment, claiming he would keep it for me because I would just spend it. But I never saw that money again."

This was just one of the many instances of people taking advantage of him when he was having a crisis. So he stayed without any money, a huge debt, and eventually, after many years, filed for bankruptcy.

After the fire, when he had nowhere to go, some local addicts gave him a space in one of the spinning mill blocks. Then he was found accommodation by the NGO Šent, which in the early nineties began organizing residential groups for people with emotional distress. Joc was among the first to live in such a community. He stayed with Šent for almost two decades, moving about during this time, especially to locations in and around Ljubljana where these residential groups operated.

* * *

People like Joc fall through the system, both on a personal or family level, and on a social level. While on the personal side it left him with questions that nobody, let alone a child, can answer themselves, from the social aspect he was treated like just another number. Of course, the system could have written off his pointless debt that would never be paid off. But this is not in tune with modern times. Pointlessly inflexible paragraphs of the law need to be strictly followed and often it seems as if interpreting the law in favor of the individual, especially a vulnerable one, is simply not tolerated. He was also let down by the health system. Instead of ensuring he could discuss his problems with a professional and provide appropriate care in the community for his development, they simply injected him with medication, locked him up, and tied him to the bed.

ANDRAŽ ROŽMAN

In Italy these methods were moved away from four decades ago when, in Trieste, under the leadership of the pioneer of the modern concept of metal health, Franco Basaglia, the system was revolutionized. This movement managed to achieve the closing of institutions and moving the residents into care in the community where now various supporting services and cooperatives offer people with mental anxieties both education and work. In 2000, Italy closed down the last long-term psychiatric care institution, similar to the Social Care Institution Hrastovec in Slovenia, while Trieste also no longer has a university psychiatric clinic such as the clinic in Polje near Ljubljana. The process of deinstitutionalization has long been in place in many other countries. In Slovenia institutions are still robust. A total of around 2,700 people live in special institutions, 700 of these in closed wards, though some estimates put the number of people in institutions at over 20,000. And current legislation allows for an increase in the number of beds even though this is in conflict with European Union guidelines and the International Convention on the Rights of People with Disabilities. Upon signing it, Slovenia committed not to build new institutions or increase the capacities of old ones, but to dismantle them and convert them into services that will offer people care in their home environment. Our social security system is still far from this goal, and it is not surprising that Slovenia is one of the most institutionalized countries in Europe.

Joc never had the kind of support introduced by Franco Basaglia and prescribed by the Convention on the Rights of People with Disabilities. Because Joc didn't have a safe environment in which he could develop his undeniably rich potential, he has been through much that he never wanted to go through.

"I have been beaten so many times that nothing gets to me anymore. I get on with things, try to have a good time and keep a positive outlook on life," he said in one of our conversations as he explained by association how acquaintances would persuade him in periods of severe mental distress to take out loans for them that they would pay the installments for but in the end merely took the money. And how he felt discriminated against in Litostroj where he worked in the eighties, everyone seeing him as the "court jester," and how once, upon his return from the psychiatric hospital, everyone at his favorite bar in Litija fell silent as he walked in and stared at him.

"I went with my best friend to the joint we regularly visited. Everyone knew where I had been. Before I entered it was all noisy, people talked, making a racket. When I stepped through the door, they all fell silent. Then my friend said, *What is it? It's only Joc!* Well, then they began coming up to me, asking me how I was, and so on."

Such experiences made him feel that people avoided his company and that he was not "normal."

"Ten years after I burned down the apartment I still didn't have any contact with anyone. I thought they would blame me. It was all my imagination. But they didn't make the first move either. I have thirteen cousins and keep in touch with only two of them — the two I lived with when I was a child."

* * *

　　　　　　　　　ANDRAŽ ROŽMAN

Joc looked like a skinny football player who has just finished a game and, cleaned up, was leaving the locker rooms, walking past enthusiastic fans into the night. He was wearing bright red shorts, trainers, a black polo shirt with a pattern of crocus leaves, a fashionable ring, and around his neck a pendant shaped like a football. He wouldn't give up on football, even less so on keeping neat and tidy. His mother used to say that he liked nice clothes, just like his father.

We arrived at a village in Lower Carniola. The road took us up a steep hill and when we reached the top Joc instantly recognized the villages of Črmošnjice and Gače on the other side. In the afternoon sun a few women were tending to the graves of their dead as we walked across the white gravel. Joc was initially a little worried that he might not find the grave, but he pointed it out instantly.

"Look, over there, by the wall."

On a black gravestone there was a black-and-white framed photograph next to the name. In it a young man in a white shirt and tie, a dark jacket, and a mole on his left cheek. His short haircut doesn't hide the fact his hair is curly. All his life, Joc has been trying to find traces of this man. And from these traces complete his father's story of which he knows very little.

"I was thirteen when he died. I first saw this photograph ten years later."

He urged me to look at the date of death for his father: 1977. He only saw him in person once in his life, but it probably doesn't count.

"I was six months old when mother took me to court with her, so he would officially acknowledge me. She told me I didn't take my eyes off him."

He spoke in a focused and calm way. I realized how much like his father he looks, not only due to the curly hair, but the mouth and his slightly pointed ears. He picked up a burnt-out candle and kept his hands busy fiddling with it. He wished that he and his mother hadn't been visiting relatives the day his father allegedly came looking for them. The neighbors told them he had rung the doorbell.

For a few minutes we continued to stand there, talking a little, staying silent a little. Then Joc had had enough. He walked away, still holding the candle, which he threw into the bin on the way to the car. Driving away from the cemetery we went for a drink in Novo Mesto. We talked about a wide range of things, without concentrating on any specific issue, nonlinear, in a way inspiring, the conversations through which I had gotten to know Joc. Like drawing zigzags with a pencil on a page, a single word could send Joc to an entirely different theme that he then pondered about long and wide, so I occasionally had difficulty following him. I thought Joc could probably be good at many jobs. He could have been a journalist. He read any newspapers he came across every day and there was no important news that he didn't know about, from politics and economics to culture and sports. He remembered so much information that some of his acquaintances jokingly called him Google. He could also be tour guide, a historian, or geographer, and with his melodic voice even a radio presenter.

It was getting dark in the center of Novo Mesto. We sipped our drinks and had ice cream, watching the world go by. I tried to get Joc to talk about our visit to the cemetery.

ANDRAŽ ROŽMAN

"It feels good here in this renovated square. It makes me think that Father might have driven through here sometimes with his family."

What about before, when we went to see his grave?

"He's my father, half of me. . . . I regret that we weren't at home when he came. Or that I didn't establish contact with him. Finding out more about my roots is a dream on the one hand, on the other hand it is probably best to leave things alone."

What about his photo?

"Looked like a nice man."

He had a spot on his face.

"I didn't look at the photo close enough to notice it."

And it has been a long time since you last saw it.

"I think it was 2011. First, I drove at three in the morning to visit Mother's grave, then a few days later, I came out here to see Father's."

During his crises he liked going on night trips to places and people important to him.

He liked traveling anyway, it gave him a sense of independence. He enjoyed these trips, even though he only went to places a few tens of kilometers away. His disability pension didn't allow him longer trips, places one reaches by plane.

"When I had a car and could drive around, I felt free, as if the entire world was before me. When I hit the clutch and put the car into gear, the car sets off. . . . I wish I could have a car."

He got a similar feeling taking the train to Trieste to buy a lottery ticket. Although he has often spoken about it with all seriousness like a business plan, explaining how he will share the winnings and also buy me an apartment, these trips were for him mostly an outing. He'd have an espresso in the Piazza Unità and then return to Ljubljana.

"I am happy with what I have. It gives me a little joy."

But it was not about joy. The lottery ticket was possibly the only exit to independence, to personal choice. Nobody wants to be dependent on social payments, everyone prefers to take care of their own affairs. Joc also, who over and over again began the process of becoming independent, tried very hard to build a life for himself, though something always came between and ruined it all. He lacked any support that would prevent his fall in times of crisis. Some support could be offered by auxiliary services in the community, if they existed in Slovenia.

We continued our discussions about this, that, and the other, then Joc suddenly stopped. Our attention was drawn to two women walking across the square. Joc noticed the girl in the blue dress. His face was shining. I recalled him telling me about a friend with a similar diagnosis, a similar label that followed Joc wherever he went, but ever since this friend started a family, for years now, he has forgotten all about any diagnosis.

"When you start talking with a woman you like, you soon get to the question about what you do. This is where the first problem appears. Now that my hair is turning gray, I can get away with saying I am retired. But a girl of around thirty-five won't be interested," he said with a smile.

What about meeting a slightly older woman, I asked, trying to be encouraging.

"With a couple of kids? Yes, I could get into that. Then I would most certainly work, even though I am not supposed to. Look

ANDRAŽ ROŽMAN

after the family. Hope that I would get on with her children, who would probably be older, more grown-up. It is not good when kids reject you or let you know that you are not part of the family. Family life would be full. I would need to fight, but it would be nice," he stated, rather like when planning how to share his lottery winnings, though with a different, ever-weaker voice, as if this tone was the scar of unhappy endings. "In the end, they all run away or I get chased away by their parents. With all my bad experiences, I don't even try now. I prefer to wait for a sign from the woman. I don't want to appear intrusive. Clearly, I have my mother's gentle side as well. Otherwise, I have lived more like a hermit in recent years."

Being alone is a conundrum that many people try to deal with.

"I don't feel lonely, if that is what you mean. I like solitude. Or I like company, but I prefer being alone. Being alone is an art."

And where is the key to this art?

"You need to be self-confident. And make sure you are never bored."

* * *

From Joc's story we could gather that he was through the worst, but nobody knew whether he would have other crises. So far, they have always returned, sometimes milder, other times worse. He would often say that he now enjoys his days, especially since he left the Šent residential group. He says he spent too long there. It was supposed to be a transition into an independent life but he stayed with them for eighteen years.

"Šent did a great deal for moving people from psychiatric institutions but then became an institution itself."

While he lived in the residential group, he would receive forty euros in pocket money a month and coupons for buying food at the local supermarket. This was the only thing he had to go on in making decisions about personal needs.

"If you want to learn how to work with money you need to have money in your hands. If I want, for example, to buy half a kilo of prosciutto, then that is my problem. Making decisions about these things gives a person their independence, which I didn't have, caught up in a kind of mold, becoming miserable. Now the system has been improved with independent residential units," he said, adding that becoming independent wasn't helped by the constant admonition from the social worker as to when and how they should cook and tidy up. His desire to make his own decisions about himself and his everyday tasks is probably more important than it first seems.

He now lives in one of the municipal housing units, intended as short-term solutions to the housing problems of socially disadvantaged people but, with a lack of any other solution, Joc and many of his neighbors stay on for years. Although he would prefer to live elsewhere if he had a choice, he had more of a sense of independence here than he had had in the residential community. He is only reminded of his medical condition by his monthly injection and the occasionally not-so-stable mood, the occasional crisis, and every few years perhaps a hospitalization. He lives more freely, but not entirely. Of course he wants to live in a place of his own, have active employment. The notion of deinstitutionalization also includes the fact that Joc should be the one to decide where and how he lives, is educated, works.

Joc is someone with experience and a great deal of knowledge of the mental health system. He has talked about his experiences at various faculties, to the media, even abroad. Adept at public speaking, he is regularly invited to various events where he explains the course of rehabilitation and emancipation from institutions. He usually explains it by saying that even though psychosocial rehabilitation can last for the rest of a person's life, one can live a full life if they have support within their social environment and have as little contact with institutions as possible, only as much as is absolutely essential at the most critical moments. He also sees the solution in a greater role for individuals with experience of mental trauma.

This is also why he is a member of the Svizci society, led exclusively by users. They promote the development of peer groups and ways of rehabilitation that is based on a multidisciplinary approach that does not only include psychiatrists but also people with experiences of mental trauma, their relatives, social workers, and psychotherapists. One such method is an open dialogue that has in some European countries led to a decrease in hospitalizations, less medication, and a friendlier environment for people in need.

Some years ago, Joc was also a member of a group of activists who helped a friend, Mijo Poslek. Mijo's situation was even worse. While Joc had never lived in a special institution, Mijo had been locked up in one from the age of four until he was forty-eight, for most of the time in the inhumane conditions at the Hrastovec social care institution. In 2010, he was freed by members of the Iz-hod movement who organized a 700 kilometer walk from Hrastovec to Ljubljana, visiting psychiatric clinics and special institutions on the way. They arranged for Mijo to join them. And he never returned to Hrastovec. Once outside, he needed help with integration into society — help that was not forthcoming from the state. Joc was one of the key members in the group that helped Mijo enter his new life. He spent a lot of time with him, helped him shower, took him for walks, prepared him food, helped him solve many problems. After just over seven years of freedom, Mijo's body shriveled away, apparently due to the side effects of the medication he had been receiving for decades. Joc was able to help him because he has become an expert through his own experiences. In a developed system of care in the community, this work of his would have been paid.

"Mijo and I also argued sometimes, but we were friends. He had such an extraordinarily hard life, harder even than me. If nothing else, we got him seven years of freedom."

While he talked about Mijo, and other stories, my thoughts returned to the hayrack in Lavrica. It is still standing, just as Joc is still standing. It is not as it was, but Joc, too, has changed. Perhaps neither the hayrack nor Joc has ever been as strong, as restored as they are now. And the hayrack is not merely a hayrack.

"On the one hand I was sorry to see it rebuilt, I would have liked to have seen it as I remember it. But I am happy it is still standing, like me. It symbolizes that I have stayed on my feet. That I didn't find an escape in drugs or anything like that. That

ANDRAŽ ROŽMAN

I am a person people can rely on, that I am neither corrupt nor evil. I think I have at least reached that, if nothing else."

That in itself is plenty, I cried out.

"I know. But I didn't take advantage of my own potential. I didn't write a book, build a house, plant a tree, create a family."

Perhaps it isn't too late for all that?

"It isn't. I have decided to throw myself into the battle of life. Let the future bring what it has to bring. I hope that by sharing my story with you, I will be able to help someone not to give up."

Translated by GREGOR TIMOTHY ČEH

Adapted from the publication in the short stories collection
Tu sem; zgodbe, ki jih ne želimo slišati
(*Cankarjeva založba, 2021*)

Anja Mugerli

THE LINDEN TREE

THE NIGHT IS peaceful. Janez is resting the rifle on his shoulder, I'm clutching the axe in my right hand. With the left I feel for my hair, remembering it's now barely covering my ears. We're leaning on the slender trunk of the young linden I planted one year ago. They say planting a tree is a symbolic act, and this linden was my new beginning. I'd tried many things before it, even a visit to the hypnotist, which had left me drifting for months between reality and childhood memories, but it was all no use. Then, I remembered something I'd read in a magazine as I was waiting at the clinic. Under a photograph of a tree, smooth trunk and top perfectly circular, it said *Planting a tree = a new life.*

It's pitch-black around us; there's thousands of stars in the sky. I can't remember the last time I saw this many stars. I want to tell Janez about it, but I keep quiet so as not to make noise. When I came home with the linden last year, it couldn't have been more than a meter tall, its roots safely tucked in a plastic bag. I went outside and stuck a shovel in the midst of the meadow. I was breathing heavily, I was digging. Autumn had begun,

the faraway hilltops were already changing color. The wind ruffled my hair, I was feeling better from one minute to another.
Janez arrived when the linden was already fast in the ground,
he found us together. I sat there blissfully, watching the fragile branches quiver in the temperate breeze.

I'm discovering ever-new stars up there. Next to me, Janez
sighs.

"No luck," he says.

I'm a little angry at him but still silent. Nocturnal winds are
howling by. I'm listening for the distant grunting of boars but
there's nothing. Janez puts the rifle butt against the ground.

"Best if we go sleep now."

I need to say something, I'm scared he's about to really leave
me all by myself under the linden tree.

"Have you ever seen this many stars?" I ask.

Janez doesn't look up. "I'm off to bed," he states with annoyance, trying to prop himself up on his rifle.

I'm riled up now. "I'm staying here," I insist.

Janez shoots me a rebellious look. I know this is going to
work, just as it has so many times before, and so I'm holding
my ground. I can feel something inside him going softer. He
leans back on the trunk, we're not talking. I'm eavesdropping
for squeals in the distance, but all I hear is the call of a night
bird somewhere off in the forest.

Before the pigs showed up, I'd finally started doing better. I
cleared out the weeds in the garden, planting tomatoes, beans,
and lettuce. I cleaned the house properly, wiping all the windows, dusting the wardrobe tops. I started doing my nails again,

ANJA MUGERLI

and I'm taking a Pilates class. Janez says I look really good too. Three days ago, though, I was left utterly brutalized by the linden. The sun hadn't even peeked from behind the hill, and in the gray dawn I was staring at half-naked branches, shredded remnants of heart-shaped leaves barely hanging on. I felt as if someone had pulled a noose around my neck and I was blacking out. Janez tried making it better, he went to the hardware store and came back with a protective net we ran around the linden trunk. That night I went to bed slightly relieved, but the next morning was a disaster. The net was all chomped up, drooping pathetically to the ground, and the linden was badly chewed up. I cried myself helpless then started googling, mad with reckoning. Only three strategies against boars: netting, which had already failed, human hair, and bullets. I thought about it for a minute then stood fast before the mirror. Ever since I'd had my linden, lush locks were once again growing in the place of wispy colorless tangles. I grabbed them in my left hand, snapping the scissors right at the crown. I hung my hair on the linden branch stuffed in a cloth bag, hoping its scent would be potent enough. Nope, that was another failure. Since I wasn't going to just give up my linden, I was left with one final option. The next day, I shoved the rifle into Janez's hands, grabbing an axe for myself from the basement, though I didn't really know what to do with it.

As we sat under the tree, Janez turned to face me, asking, just as countless times before, "You sure about this?"

Finally I can hear something out there. Straightening up earns me a glance from Janez. I'm holding my breath, waiting for the sound to return.

"You hear that?" I whisper.

The air around us turns still, as if there's a storm brewing. Certainly I'm about to catch wind of animal noises. I'm conjuring shapes in the distance, motion in the dark sneaking closer. I can feel it's about to happen, I'm tightly grasping the axe. The blade glimmers.

Janez cuts through the silence. "Sorry, but I've had enough of all this."

His voice surprises me. There's something stiff about it now.

"I'm positive I've heard squealing this time!"

Leaning on his rifle, Janez gets to his feet, saying, "You're always positive about something." He hesitates for a moment, then adds, "Your optimism is killing me, all right? You always find that impossible sliver of motivation to try just this *one more thing*."

I can feel the pounding in my chest getting faster, I'm expecting grunting any moment now. A single clear sound will do.

"Me, I just *can't do it* anymore, get it?"

The rifle falls to the ground with a thud. Janez is standing over me, there's thousands of stars behind him. I've never seen him like this before.

"Why can't you ever be happy with what we have?" Now his voice is turning alien. "Why always keep drilling for more?"

Still no hog noises — I'm starting to lose hope, but I rally, announcing, "I just wanted us to be happy."

Janez drops to his knees, his face is right next to mine. "Can't you see we *were* happy?"

"All this time, I thought you wanted it too," I say in a trembling voice.

ANJA MUGERLI

The hope is draining out of me, the linden above me is disappearing. The axe is all I'm holding on to now.

Janez breathes out, "All I wanted was you."

I close my eyes.

We tried everything. The examinations and hours spent at the clinic were torture. And worst of it all was the waiting, which never brought what we'd been so hungry for. If I think about it from a distance, it feels like I'd spent years of my life on a sadistic ride that ended in a horrid crash. When the gynecologist told us there was next to no chance I could get pregnant, that we should be considering other options, the shock cut so deep I was reeling for weeks. That was when the anxiety attacks started. The first time it happened we were on vacation. In the square before the cathedral I collapsed to the ground, feeling like I was choking to death. I was clutching my throat, wheezing, "I'm dying, I'm dying. . . ." while tourists with cameras around their necks walked past us, staring. Someone aimed the lens at me and took a photo. Coming back, I no longer wanted to get out of bed. I spent my days sleeping, my nights staring at the ceiling. I stopped taking care of myself, my looks, even my hygiene. Janez brought a doctor home, he prescribed antidepressants.

Janez puts his hand on mine. "When I realized we could never have a family I was shattered, but I was also relieved. I thought you'd finally stop torturing us. I thought we could go back to being happy, like before."

His voice has regained that relenting tone, the one so familiar whenever I was being stubborn that we should just *try it*, just another therapy, just another medication. I'm suddenly disgusted by his voice, I'm glad it's dark so I can't see his face.

"It all happened exactly because of this, what you're doing right now," I hiss. The axe blade glitters, as I go on. "This negativity, it's a cancer on everything you do!"

Janez moves his hand away.

"Everything I did, I was doing for us!" I shout, piercing the night with my war cry.

"And what exactly was it you did? Lie on a medical table with your legs spread while I jacked off to porn magazines in a room? Waste away in bed for months without talking to me while I'm worried out of my mind?"

I want to say something, something like fuck off, get out of my life, but the rage splashes over me like scalding water. I can't manage a sound.

"You're so blinded by what you *want* you can't ever see what you *have*," says Janez.

The tears in my eyes are so hot I need to squint. I clench the axe handle and get up. Facing the linden tree, I take my swing. The blade cuts the trunk more easily than I would have imagined. Another chop. Janez tries stopping me. My swings are fierce, each impact shaking the linden to its roots. In the daybreak I can see it giving in. I push my body against the trunk, panting as the ragged leaves softly hit the earth. Light is flickering on the horizon; the morning sun exposes the ravished linden bare. Its eaten-up branches resemble toothless gums. The rootless trunk looks like an amputated limb. The bark is deathly gray. Lying there in the grass, it looks like an old woman, exhausted and frail. Like it's never even been in the ground. Like it was never my linden to begin with.

ANJA MUGERLI

Translated by JEREMI SLAK

Originally published in the short stories collection
Zelen fotelj (*Litera*, 2015)

Nejc Gazvoda

THE CALL

SHE WAS SITTING about three feet away from me, leaning against the bar, her eyes running up and down the muscled waiter who was drying glasses and probably waiting for better times. She was drinking a martini. I wished I were a sugar crystal on her lips. She knew I was watching her. She didn't react. She crossed her legs a little more. A gorgeous knee, with a tiny scar by the joint. She'd covered it with powder. What was going through her head? Was she single? I was looking for signs. Hickeys on her neck. The way she was sending looks around, since it wasn't only me who had noticed her. Those weren't the looks of a single woman. Her eyes flitted over us like we were little doggies that would always come back to her. And we did keep on looking back. It's just that she swung her gaze so fast we froze. And sank back into our glasses.

She stood up and went to the toilet. The waiter blatantly checked out her ass.

"Why don't you add a catcall, buddy?" I said.

"If I see you when I'm not working, I'll fuck you up, you and your mother," he said, making a rattling sound by rapping his massive signet ring against the bar.

She still hadn't returned. The seconds were ticking by very slowly. It felt like the place had turned still. Like everyone was waiting for her. Then the bar top shook slightly. Her phone was vibrating. It was small and had a bright-pink custom case. The waiter wasn't around. No one was watching. I grabbed the phone. Adrenaline was whistling through my veins and I felt somewhat aroused. The screen was flashing: SWEETIE. My hand was already stretched out to put it back. But the waiter still wasn't there. And maybe that last beer really was for courage. Too much courage. I picked up.

"Hello," I said.

"Katarina? Hello? Who is this?" said a man's voice.

"Her boyfriend," I answered, a bit hoarsely, shaking from the excitement.

"I don't have time to fuck around. Really. Her dad's been taken to hospital. Heart attack. He might die. Tell her to call her mom right away."

The line cut out. I looked up. The waiter was watching me. His ring shone bright under the bar's neon lights. I slowly reached out my hand and put the phone back where it had been, staring the waiter in the eye while he stared fixedly into mine and washed some glasses. Then she returned. Even before looking her way, I could hear the clicking of her high heels. She sat down and crossed her arms. This time she didn't stare at anyone. Her eyes were half-closed. I could feel droplets of sweat collecting on my forehead.

The waiter turned off the tap and wiped his hands. He went over to her. At first, she withdrew her head a little, but then he bent down and murmured something into her ear. She turned to look at me. She also told him something, a little agitatedly. I stared into my beer. I heard her get up and take two steps. I felt her standing right next to me. I looked at the waiter. He was standing there with crossed arms, taut biceps, smirking at me.

"Your dad's dying. He's in the hospital. Call your mother," I said, staring ahead.

The waiter's smile disappeared. He dropped his arms to his sides. He was shaking slightly. A few seconds passed. I could hear her taking deep breaths.

"Thank you," she said, after a moment and honestly.

Her voice was slightly tremulous. She put the phone into her purse and walked with quick steps out of the bar.

The waiter and I drank some beer, first on me. Then on him. Then me again. We were still in the bar after all the others had left and the waiter had turned off almost all the lights. We sat in the dark. It was easier to drink if we didn't have to look each other in the eye.

Translated by JASON BLAKE

Originally published in the short stories collection
Vevericam nič ne uide (*Goga, 2004*)

Ana Schnabl

ANA

WHEN WE WERE little, my sister was always stronger and faster. While I spent my evenings reading in the recliner, an early gift from Grandpa hoping one of us should develop a broad spirit, she was out there adventuring. At the neighbors', in the ravines, under hayracks, amid the ruins of the old factory. I envied how she never got tired, I envied the pink luster of her cheeks when she returned home from her wanderings. At bedtime, when she was combing her long, heavy brown hair, sprawled out in front of me on the mattress, if the day was especially hard I wished all of it would just fall off. I was hoping she'd wake up like me, with a sensitive scalp, dandruff, with problematic skin that contorts into a nasty red with greasy white patches during exertion. I envied how Father lifted her up like a cheerleader each time she ran into his lap, whirling around till they were both dizzy. One afternoon, coming home from the store, she jumped on his back when he wasn't ready for it but he still held her, staggering, losing balance. He fell backward on top of the radiator, onto the little girl, and she hit her crown just behind the sharp metal edge, just enough so that the fall wasn't deadly, only very painful. The scar was overgrown by hair, the memory of peril by the laughter.

Her laughter. Graceful, bubbly. The kind that doesn't put you down but heals. A laughter to which I, too, was invited, though I repeatedly decided to keep away.

Naturally, she was the first to grow breasts. She wore them proudly, like she used to wear those girly necklaces Father brought home from his travels. While my own chest produced nothing but fatty small buttons I liked to press with my thumb to see if they'd pop out again, Mom was already shopping for my sister's first bra. "75B," she liked to boast. With her boobs covered in playful hair, slender waist hinting at feminine hips, her witty character buoyant with an awakening sex drive and flirty glances, she was an instant favorite with the boys. That was a time when I thought terrible things about her, but my anger had no place to lean on. Her actions, her replies, her challenges, her jokes — they were all normal and standard, adolescent and silly. Only here and there, a glimpse of adulthood would flicker up in her demeanor. Like when I was coming down with salmonella and she took me to the doctor, staying with me long after our parents had gone to bed. Or when she stood up to our Slovenian teacher for calling an immigrant child slow in front of the whole class because they were too scared to ever open their mouth. When she realized her vanity could hurt me, comforting me with kisses and hugs.

And so, my anger could only rail against her beauty. I tried dressing it up, I was telling myself I was bigger than that, bigger than superficial impulses. Efforts like these are always in

ANA SCHNABL

vain though. Beauty has no force of its own, it damages with another, each time reflecting what it receives. Receiving hatred, it returns injury. Receiving love, it returns the illusion of immortality.

In the final August days before high school, her body was once again quicker than mine. While shopping around for new clothes to impress on our first school week, she got her first period. She reported that it arrived without burning or cramping, drifting into a whimsical mood only after the pad was already rustling between her thighs. She demanded ice cream. Staring at the motley bowls, our mother announced, "From now on, everything will be different. You'll be serious and responsible. I hope." I was resentful again. Her rise to a new level of womanhood made me feel so inadequate. Like life would never pull me from the bottom of the closet. Like I'll always be miserably misplaced.

That was her body's final triumph.

I often wondered if I'd even be able to notice, toward the end of our freshman year, her looks warping to woes if she weren't so beautiful. I studied her meticulously, like a precious rare insect under the magnifying glass. The flinching of wings, the trepidation of the antennae, the twitching motions, the quiet, pattering voice — I responded to it all. I discerned the details. I tracked the slight sag in the magisterial arch of her eyebrows. In the span of a few months the skin around her eye sockets turned gray, as if her velvet-green eyes were resting in gossamer. Her hair shone with a greasy, no longer fairylike sheen. It was shedding, the way an animal sheds its winter fur, in tufts I encountered in the strangest places. Along the fridge shelf, between the pages of a fashion magazine, in the kitchen sink. Her toned figure was being scraped by an unknown wind, the muscles were sliding from her skeleton, from her arms, from her shoulders. Her hands were comically elongated, her joints were protruding. One evening, just before she wrapped herself in a towel in panic, I caught sight of her naked: over the still-round breasts, ribs were reaching like metal rods. As if her boobs were hanging from a grate, falling out of a prison window. Her torso looked thirsty. Dry. In the screen of my memory, I can still see the sharp bend of her pelvic arch, faded skin sinking in.

I experienced these changes as an innocent decomposition, I witnessed them with satisfaction. They were just details after all, minute deteriorations, dusty flakes of ugliness. Indeed, I hoped my moment would finally come. A spotlight for the sister who leaped ahead into the world, and in turn received less. The first child. The child for granted.

She started hiding from us, even from me. She knew that the density of her body was my intimate interest, and so she yelled at me I was crazy. "And if you're not, you will be," she cried out, banging the bathroom door. That spring I recall first hearing her screaming at Father, who was first to express his worries aloud. His dearest daughter was no longer his ally. Any time he would hug her or put his firm hand on her shoulder she went stiff. Terror crawled across her face, her sternum shot up at the ceiling as if the heart underneath wanted to launch into space. She didn't talk about school. She never spoke about her friends. One evening as they crossed paths in the hallway she was stuffed in a thick bathrobe. I heard our dad ask, "Finally relaxing, are we?"

She tossed around in her bed all night, sobbing. I didn't console her. I couldn't understand what perfection was crying about.

The color of her voice turned dull, coffeebitter. She wore baggy clothes. Leaving her lace bras and panties in the drawer, she made Mom buy her a pack of cheap cotton ones. They got in a fight at the store because she wanted them a whole size bigger, so they would cover the crease where the thighs meet the buttocks. Mom was resolute, she told her that this weird phase of hers would pass and she'd be sorry for getting stuck with a dozen knickers the size of a tent canvas. To avoid new conflict, my sister always left home the way Mother wanted her to. She changed in the school bathroom, untangling her bun and scattering hair around so that it was almost covering her entire face.

It wasn't a phase; it wrinkled into years. Mom wasn't yet able to distinguish adolescent mulishness and pose from a desperate threat. From the paving of the end.

She started smoking. At sixteen she was smoking a pack of the strongest cigarettes a day. If I bumped into her in the schoolyard I avoided her, disgusted by her nervous sucking on the filter tip, a mannerism schoolmates began teasing her with, half in jest, half seriously. Under the corrosive curtain, stage front was the sister who renounced her beauty. Her persistent flagellation, her commitment to an inexplicable mission instilled in me the most dreadfully vicious rage, a livid disorder by which everything she was doing was performed to ridicule me, to gloat over my insufficiency. Only the haves may squander. The havenots cannot patch the hole with suitable matter. Whatever is shoved in there doesn't fit, falling short, overflowing.

I can still see her, jittery with nicotine, slender as a stalk, leaning against the frame of the metal bike rack behind the school: she steps on the cigarette, digs a water bottle from her bag, and drinks it up, then, hunching ghoulishly, turns away from the audience, reaches into her pocket, and puts her fist to her face. Maybe she sucks at it, maybe she swallows. The secret ritual, my maddening trigger.

She stopped running too. Mom only found out she was skipping practice from the team captain. At home, her rebellion sparked lightning. "Leave me alone, all of you! And I'm never going back there!" In a gesture of defiance, she lit a cigarette in front of our mom, blowing smoke in her face. Mother was petrified. Her eyes darted around, she was opening her mouth like a panicky bird, taking shallow breaths. When her daughter hit her with the second cloud, she gave her a powerful slap. Her face revealed a bleeding, ruptured dent, the imprint of a wedding ring. That left a small scar. It made her just a little uglier.

The sister was moving away, and Mom and Dad were moving closer to me. Mother kept saying how she always knew I'd grow up into a sensible person. She didn't ask me about my sister, she could probably sense the tangled bond between us. Her conscience must have been torn by the knowledge of hypocrisy, the knowledge of a discarded relationship with her strange and unlovely daughter, the knowledge that she, birth mother, doled out her love so that the greater part fell on the beautiful child. Dad was following me around like an insulted dog. He was expecting the same kind of warmth from me he'd been receiving from my sister, the radiant ease she was once so indiscriminately beaming. Up until then I was starved for connection, but once it was starting to form, it formed under perverted conditions. I was still just a surrogate, and she was still the one they wanted. I wrapped myself in a shroud of hatred. I fantasized that she'd never been born, how all the beauty that was imparted to her dissolved within me, absorbed by the single daughter, all the sweetness and grace of the accepted, beloved one settling within myself. My hatred burned persistently, wickedly.

It was only quenched by coincidence, on the last Tuesday before summer break. I was finishing my third year. When afternoon classes were done I went to the gym lockers; I'd left my sports gear behind. The hallways were empty, sparse chatter emerging from the classrooms here and there. To get to the locker rooms I went through the semibasement stairway, a dank tunnel where every breath made an echo. Descending, the surrounding sound was overpowered by the reverberating boom of my heavy steps. As it faded out I discerned a male bass, recognizing it as our gym teacher's. I swerved toward his room to explain why I was there. His commanding voice was gradually merging into words and sentences that I wasn't really registering. I was only startled by the coarse "Do you understand?" overlaid with the scene where our teacher's shovel-shaped hand was gripping the thin nape of my pallid sister, bent over at the waist from the hunger and angst. She let out a resigned, obedient "yes." She slowly turned around in my direction. Her eyes were blank like the eyes of dead cattle. Frozen with terminal horror. I couldn't tell if she recognized me, it seemed as if her entire life force was spent on the word she'd just uttered, leaving behind nothing but a worn-out husk.

The teacher said something but I kept staring at my sister. As she drifted past me I managed to squeeze out, "Ana, what's going on?" I backpedaled from the study without hearing what the giant man was telling me. In a torrent of unstructured panic, enveloping, constricting, I sprinted back upstairs. I didn't find Ana there.

Before sleep I asked her about it again. She murmured into the wall, "Forget it, it's not your business."

All my wishes came true. My sister's beauty and zest rotted away. People were opening up to me as if they'd just discovered me. A new continent, gnarly yet unexplored, with so much to offer. So much that had always been there. As my sister sank into darkness, a landscape of new potential for bliss opened up before me. With each layer evaporating from her body, I received new will and new power. That night, though, my chest was inexplicably heavy. That night, the magma of my rage stilled unexpectedly, though I hadn't vomited it all out, and it hadn't yet charred all in its path. Perhaps my sister really was suffering. Maybe her body, all porous by now, wasn't taking it out on me after all. That night I listened to her breathing, trying to meld through, to inhabit her mind, her memories, experiences, sensations. I got nowhere. I had no knowledge of my sister. In my jealousy and insidious glee I had never seen her as a person. The distance between us couldn't be bridged by compassion, there wasn't enough substance to it. The events of that afternoon festered in my imagination into dreadful forms from which I extracted all the reasons for my sister's torment. Its outlines were growing increasingly blurry in a hallucinatory undulation, as my insides were burning with intuition. With the earthquake came the worry. The worry of a person trying to atone for being witness to violence. A selfish worry. The summer that followed was a game of pretense and avoidance. I was convinced Ana's silence was exactly that — *a game*. She was about to drop her bulwark, her might was nearly spent by now, it must be. She was only dragging the heavy metal around, protecting herself, to punish me for the spite I inflicted on her in my mind. It was a penance I was willing to serve. I never told our parents about my inklings of my sister's gloom. There was no way I'd waste the chance to be the first to bond with her after the fall. I also didn't know what I was really suspecting. If I had named that which I'd been weaving in my sleepless nights with its true name, perhaps it would have manifested, appeared among us, and then the responsibility of brand-new injustice would have been upon me. I was barely able to carry the one. I was terrified. I was keeping quiet before our parents to protect. Primarily myself. After all, Ana would spill the contents sooner or later. She had to.

I said nothing as she was transported to the hospital, dehydrated and delirious, to be tube fed for a week on fluids containing raw butter, sugary cocoa, and milk. As the pale brown liquid pushed its way inside her, tears of disgust were streaking down her face. I was silent as mother pulled balls of cotton from her bag on the bedpost and burst into tears. Father soundlessly pressed her against his chest, staring at his daughter who no longer lay on the bed but was stretched across it, like frayed fabric. I observed the despair they were parading up and down the floors of our house with the patience of the humiliated. I was silent when she spat in the face of the nurse who'd brought her a caloric shake, scratching and clawing at her. Even when she could no longer walk and refused any food whatsoever, my faith in Ana was unshakeable. I told the doctor her condition was about to change any moment now. There was no reason to panic, my sister was good, down to her very foundations. She will do the right thing. She will absolve us from the suffering, she will release me. I was counting on her goodness long after she stopped being human. I firmly held her hand, scanning the fuzz-covered face, the grotesque knots of purple-blue veins on her vertex and back of the hand, the rising and sinking of the pointed collarbone. Her exuberant, moist body had decomposed into paper. I caressed her absent-eyed face and put my hand on her belly. In the warm pulse of my tissue, I wanted her to feel that we can start over. My feminine hand won't break her, it won't be finishing what was started in hatred of life. I held on to inexhaustible hope, I concealed my guilt into faith that she would illuminate what I'd seen on that June afternoon, that she would explain how innocent it all was. I was silent when her eyes turned to glass. I stood by with such committed silence that the room was still enough for me to hear the end of her heartbeat. I stood by the corpse of my twin sister. Mute.

Translated by JEREMI SLAK

Originally published in the short stories collection Razvezani (*Beletrina, 2017*)

Eva Markun

NO MERCY

THE DOCTOR'S OFFICE is cold — the health center is keeping its heating costs low and the lino bites at the toes, quietly consuming the skin. The smell of disinfectants hangs heavily in the room as she practically collapses onto a chair covered in that rough sheet the foul color of which reminds her of human excrement. Rubbing against her, chafing her because she has to move, lift her blouse, and place her legs so her exposed intimate parts don't jump straight at the gynecologist's face after the examination. The doctor straightens her glasses and smiles encouragingly, as if she is about to begin some standard chat about the weather and prenatal bleeding but after a brief pause decides it really is not necessary, turns around and routinely grabs the plastic bottle of gel.

Lidija shuts her eyes tight — though she should be used to it by now — and her whole body shudders at the first touch of the cold liquid being stickily spread across her entire belly. It is as if she has suddenly found herself in a morgue where her body will be cooled in order not to degenerate and decompose alive. And she continues to keep her eyes firmly shut as she feels the instrument moving up and down her hard belly with brutish harshness, knowing very well what it will reveal. After so many consecutive pregnancies, she didn't even need to spend money on unnecessary tests at the corner pharmacy from where the *on-dit* would spread to the entire village. Matevž would be quite happy with that. One less expenditure.

And while she kept her eyes closed, despite her oversensitive sense of smell and despite her feeling as if her gall bladder was being pushed up into her throat, and despite her forever sensitive nipples, despite her vanished remnants of libido, and despite her hardened belly, the torturous instrument, as well as entirely freezing her abdomen, also informs her of a fetus implanted in her uterus.

"Mm," she says, placing her hand on her forehead. "That I already know. Does everything look all right?"

God knows how at every pregnancy she half hoped for an ectopic embryo, anencephaly, or the worst form of spina bifida, any kind of complication that would justifiably wash this unfortunate aggregate of fish cells and human DNA into the common collection point of human fates. But what God knew stayed between the two of them, unlike the village grapevine that wondered every time they saw her whether Matevž had knocked her up again and what the hell was wrong with her self-respect, allowing herself to have more children than the inaugural and venerated average of two.

"Everything seems just fine, Lidija," the doctor says with a smile.

When she was having her first child and the doctor had only just taken up her post, she would, hand almost shaking, check every parameter in order not to miss anything. Now, after so many pregnancies, both felt like they were old acquaintances, as they had, since that first meeting, seen each other more often than Lidija's mother came to visit her.

"Should I check the gender?"

"No! No, no need. I really don't want to know. After five girls in a row, I really don't want to know the child's gender."

"Perhaps it will be another healthy girl?" the doctor cheerfully replies, once again pressing the instrument firmly against Lidija's abdomen.

Lidija twitches and tries to breathe deeply to calm the uncomfortable tension in her belly as the probe pokes at her, pushing too deep into her body. The doctor glances at the screen, which is turned in a way that Lidija would have to turn her head entirely to see the miniature beating heart it displayed, so instead she stares uneasily out of the window at the falling snow behind the frozen panes of glass, wondering when she will finally wake up and all this will seem like an unfortunate nightmare of the Jungian subconscious.

"Everything is as usual," the gynecologist says meaningfully. "A healthy baby. Would you like a picture?"

Lidija shakes her head, reaching for the paper towels, fighting off the instrument and the sticky gel from her hardened belly, then pulling her blouse back over her freezing stomach. If this bunch of fish cells ever hatches, it will probably be the most chilled creature in the world.

"As usual, then?" she repeats the doctor's words with a slight disappointment and goes off to find her trousers that she had casually left somewhere on the way to the torture chair.

"Mhm," says the doctor with an indifferent nod as she prints off a black-and-white, stripy image from the old-fashioned machine. "If you want, I can refer you for a morphology scan at the hospital. They have a better ultrasound there. Just in case."

"What on earth for?" Lidija sighs and pulls her coat over her shoulders. "It's not as if I will have it aborted if its heart valve doesn't function properly or if it has six fingers. You know that."

The two women look at each other, one from above her glasses, the other lowering her gaze, Lidija already reaching for the door handle. She doesn't care anyway. The gynecologist stuffs the printout into her pocket and escorts her to reception, waves a prescription for iron supplements at her, waits for the nurse to hand back to Lidija the little girl sleeping in the car seat, and politely closes the door behind her.

Number six. Lidija looks at sleeping number five in the seat she places on the bench, stroking her eyelashes, so the child in her sleep restlessly turns her eyeballs. She sits next to her in the empty waiting room, swinging her legs, as if needing to convince herself of something, then looking at the seat and her belly, and the empty, cold, Socialist-era benches. In the Arab world, six daughters would probably be some kind of blessing. Six daughters, six dowries brought to the house. Camels, cows, goats, sheep — a reward for the fecundity and fertility of the female body, being given away in recognition of the forever insatiable male nature. Perhaps not in the Arab world. Nigeria perhaps? Senegal? Not, however, in some remote village in a

EVA MARKUN

remote country in a remote part of Europe where every child is an expense — an expense for the parents, but belongs to the state, and her body with its forever bloating belly is an ineffable perversion that everyone simply shakes their head over, as if it was something totally abnormal. Six children. Six girls. Six proofs that her uterus is incapable of producing a male heir whose mythical penis was all that Matevž and her mother-in-law wanted, as if it was the only proof of human greatness.

Lidija slowly lifts her hand and strokes her young daughter's cheek, then picks up the girl in her car seat and blanket, carefully resting it on her thigh with a sigh of someone who has done this countless times, and slowly waddles off toward the car. She has six children. Six girls. For God's sake!

* * *

"Just as well you're home," says Matevž without even looking at her — he had heard the roar of the car before she reached the corner, and at the same time ignoring what the vehicle was trying to tell him. He was stuffing the rubbish from the back seat of his van into a large cardboard box that will end up in the yard, where the cats and dogs will disperse its contents across her flower beds.

"Can you feed the pigs for me?"

That is all. No "how was it" or "is everything all right," such miniscule sentimental phrases have long been obsolete, now all that matters are the pigs and the five hundred kilos of scabby potatoes they have to feed them until they roll about in their own fat.

"Mhm," says Lidija and unbuckles kicking number five from the car seat. "So, can't you do it, or what?"

Incomprehensible mumbling comes from the vehicle and two pairs of trousers and a worn-out jumper come flying out, then Matevž slams the door shut and pushes the cardboard box to the edge of the yard. The bags under his eyes are so big that number one and number two, who loved the snow, could ski down them — well, provided they could afford the filthily expensive ski gear. Instead, they were left only with filthy pigs.

"I need to take Mother to A&E," he sighs. "Again."

The youngest daughter sticks a lock of Lidija's hair into her mouth. Lidija lowers her voice to speak to her husband but Matevž immediately silences her, keeping his voice at the same low frequency.

"Not now, please," he responds tiredly, stroking number five on that pile of hair on the top of her head. "Sort out the pigs, right? I'll be back when I'm back."

Just great: back, when I'm back — what an absolute tautology! And although in the language of all kinds of queues and her mother-in-law's fictitious symptoms this once meant the far end of eternity, Lidija forces a smile and a deficient kiss on the cheeks, before placing number five on her hip and dragging herself up the stairs to their apartment so she wouldn't have to watch the drama unfolding in the yard between the mentioned protagonists of the main act. The pigs will have to wait for the stage to clear, though Lidija couldn't imagine how she was supposed to carry fifteen-kilo buckets to the pigsty that was moved to the far end of the farm so that her mother-in-law didn't have to put up with the smell, aware that there were many things at the beginning of every pregnancy she hadn't imagined she would be doing but in the end still had to get on with.

"Hi, pumpkins," she greets the other numbers who are still diligently doing their homework at the kitchen table even though she left over an hour ago and they should have long finished. The computer in the corner suspiciously switches off, and the girls innocently flutter their eyelids. "Are you hungry?"

Of course, they are not — they are and they aren't, but they will never reach a compromise, so Lidija steps into the bathroom to change out of the clothes that still stink of gel, turning away from the annoying mirror that reflects the red lines and cracked skin of her previous five pregnancies. But this time she glances toward her reflection and briefly holds her blouse above her belly, wondering whether there is even room for another set of stretch marks on her zebralike abdomen; for now, it still looks innocently flat, with an inconspicuous bulge in its lower part, and an extruding navel that her hand rests on. Is there anything in there or not? On the one hand she regrets not having inquired as to the child's gender, on the other hand she is so resigned to this unfortunate cavalcade of successive girls that it seems almost impossible her uterus would even recognize any other gender than phallic absence. But what are they to do with six girls on this farm?

Before she is able to conclude her communication with this annoying hardened belly, the door handle moves and number three quietly slips into the bathroom, widening those large brown eyes of hers with far too much insight for her age.

"Are we going to have another baby?"

Lidija gulps, trying sourly to smile but merely managing to pull a face. Do even her children now only see her as a birthing machine? But she doesn't need to answer because the child comes up with her own response.

"But we don't have anywhere left to put it!"

"Don't we?" Lidija responds as she pulls her blouse back over her belly and tries to find the brush and hairpins in the drawer. "Isn't there some space still left in your room?"

Number three shakes her head as she drops onto the toilet, the only sound that follows being her peeing. "There are three of us already. And Maya keeps kicking me. When will I be able to have a bed of my own?"

The eternal question. Just as well she is not asking for a room of her own — this ongoing and unobtainable wish that girls on their way toward puberty want more than chocolate, which she could use to bribe them when they were younger. Or, God forbid, a house of her own, something Lidija would also gladly sign up for, but the reality of the ground she is standing on soon became clear.

"Perhaps soon," Lidija says, trying to be positive. "In a month's time or so when Daddy will get another support payment."

"Seriously?"

The kid climbs off the toilet with a ridiculous grin but then past experience catches up with her and her mouth turns downward.

"You already said that last year," she sighs almost inaudibly and stands on tiptoes to pull the chain before offendedly pushing her way past a numbed Lidija and returning to the kitchen.

Seriously? Lidija leans against the cold bathroom wall, near the window Matevž had left open. Outside she can hear her mother-in-law getting into the front seat of the car and Lidija has to close the window in order for her voice not to drift up toward her. *Not a single son! The farm must stay in the family, Matevž. I will not leave it to you when you have only daughters.* Lidija closes her eyes and feels her hardened belly that with its silence refuses to say anything to her. There have been words enough anyway.

* * *

It takes almost the whole afternoon before Lidija, between trips to the cauldron and back, and this, that, and the other, manages to make sure that all the numbers have something to do and that everything is under control so she can spend fifteen minutes out in the freezing cold carrying bucketfuls of pig swill, the foul-smelling slop in which castaway pieces of potato float in their own misery, splashing over her hand every time she tilts one too far forward or backward.

Almost too cautiously, with the automatic precaution of a woman who has been pregnant too many times to allow her brain and her blood cells not to absorb the mantra about the maximum ten-kilo load allowed together with toxoplasmosis, undercooked meat, not to mention syphilis, she lifts the bucket into the wheelbarrow. She almost falls into it when the scent of overcooked slop invades her nostrils, causing a mini Nagasaki in her stomach. Dizzily she leans backward, her hands holding on to the cauldron, waiting for the nausea to settle, gritting her teeth, despite the bad enamel and calcium loss, and pushes the wheelbarrow toward the pigsty. The things people would do for a pork chop.

Despite the bad weather, the pigs had not yet moved into the half-constructed sty, which looked as if it might collapse due to the snow on its roof. They preferred to nuzzle through the snow and mud, turning the field in front of the sty into a brown-and-white slurry. Normally the pigs started staying indoors after the first November frosts, rolling their huge bloated bodies around the straw, looking from afar very much like corpses. This year, however, Matevž had found somewhere a crossbreed with some wild pigs and they appeared more like huge, well-built sheep rather than pigs and they loved nuzzling around, mud flying in all directions. The winter cold didn't seem to affect them and as soon as they heard the wheelbarrow on the gravel path from the farm, their grunting and growling echoed through the tree-tops, dripping onto Lidija who had to wipe her wet nose with her gloves, otherwise it would freeze in the cold.

She stared at the pigs. They were pushing around the trough, all but filling it with mud, jumping into it and toward the fence. Lidija thought, They are going to push it over! She had never felt this uncomfortable close to the pigs. The hogs stared at her through those dark, intelligent eyes ringed by bristly eyelashes, so piercingly that she could see in them the coldness and cruel realization about the inevitably of fate. It was almost as if they knew very well what their purpose was and for a brief moment she felt sorry for them — they were so alike, she and them — trapped in an enclosure, the only path out was slaughter. The growling boar, the loudest of them all, dripping saliva from his half-open mouth, flanked by two of the largest tusks she had ever seen on a pig, stared at her as if knowing very well what is to happen in a few months' time. Well, he might even survive all the others, considering the fact that they forgot to castrate him — he'd been hiding somewhere under the sty when the vet under the direction of her mother-in-law snipped away at those testicles. But all the others would be slaughtered in order to generously satisfy the infinite need for pork under which Matevž's wider family was raised.

Still staring at the pigs staring right back at her, Lidija grabbed the bucket handle. She had poured in too much of the slush, now looking alternately at the pigs, the bucket, and her belly. Suddenly she lifted the handle, painfully and slowly raised the fifteen or twenty kilos of stinking slop, staggered under the weight, gritted her teeth, and tipped the feed over the fence so it splashed into the muddy trough, all over her boots. It was instantly clear what was happening around the trough and why it was so hard to get closer because the pigs were jostling around it with such violence, stamping all over each other, that she had no choice but to empty the second bucket all over their heads. They would probably not move out of the way even if she shot cannonballs at them. Exhausted, she sat down on an upturned pot, rubbing her cold hands in the slightly wet, stinking gloves. Her belly stiffened again and, almost freezing, she reached for it. Does it really matter? She tried to breathe out.

By the time she had finished transporting the slop from the house to the pigsty, she was muddy and filthy from head to toe and her belly hurt so much that all she wanted to do was fall onto the sofa — but she needed to stay awake, there was homework waiting for her, spread across the table and the kitchen counter, and the pile of dishes in the sink, catching the last rays of the halogen lamp from under the cupboards. She was unusually absent and when she was finally able to roll into bed in order to calm the unbearable beating in her hardened belly, coiling around her like a constricting armor, she closed her eyes and fell straight asleep before she even managed to cover herself with the blanket.

*   *   *

She dreamed about pigs — not any pigs, these very pigs, their pigs, these hairy pigs that trampled the mud until they squeezed every last drop of dampness from the field. She stood at the edge of their swamp, their mud bath, holding a grindstone and a knife on some kind of woolen cushion that felt prickly in her hands. The large boar stared at her for a moment then, swinging his snout sideways, growled fiercely and stood there, as if wanting to communicate with her. She did not understand what — she was afraid of his teeth sticking out of his dribbling mouth like elephant tusks, pointing straight at her.

Then the boar stood up on his hind legs and, like an awkward child trying to take its first steps, with an almost comic walk, approached her, his hoofs sinking deep into the chocolate cream mud. She wanted to take a step backward but her dream body instead took a step forward, her bare feet plunging through the soft mud in front of her, sinking down to her ankles. It was strangely warm — soft as life as it squished around her toes, almost gluing itself to her as she stepped into it with her other foot, eventually getting stuck in the slimy substance.

She had almost forgotten about the boar, and when she looked up again, he was standing right in front of her. His eyes, dark as onyx, blinked casually, his mouth half-open, saliva dribbling onto her feet, trickling through the mud between her toes.

EVA MARKUN

But the boar didn't hurt her, he took the knife and the grinder and went back to the pigsty, leaned the grindstone against one of the collapsed beams to begin sharpening the knife with such skill as if he was in fact a professional butcher caught inside the body of the four-hundred-kilo curly-haired pig.

First he slaughtered the sow, skillfully and lovingly cutting its jugular so she bled to death softly onto the floor, then he sliced her in half as if she was butter — stripped the skin, then the bones, and chopped up the head, as if preparing the carcass for the butcher's shop — all the internal organs separately, the muscles, the bones, neatly dividing it all right in front of Lidija. The sow's large organs throbbed warmly before her, red and pink scarlet they sat there, looking at her. Eventually the boar rummaged through the offal and pulled out something large, dark, blackish red, and elongated, and placed the organ in front of her. He took the knife, ripped it open like a fruit. Throbbing inside were small piglet fetuses, each wrapped in its own placenta, their umbilical cords still pulsating. Then the cord stopped throbbing and the twitching, jostling spasms of the tiny fish like embryonic freaks made her close her eyes. It was as if they were silently screaming, gasping for the air they would never taste. It was something she could not endure, not even in her dreams. A moment later her hand felt something horribly slimy, wriggling, and she opened her eyes, silently glancing at the boar. Lying in her hand was a pig's fetus, twisting and turning rapidly. The boar nodded, and in the language of her dream she suddenly understood him.

She felt sick — her dream body raised the hand with the fetus, opening her mouth so that the tiny piglet slipped down her throat, an engulfing soft organic mass, almost entirely blocking her airway until she gulped. The fetus began to convulse, moving down the esophagus to the stomach, circling around for a while, then boring a narrow channel, entering straight into her uterus. She shuddered. Her abdomen, hardening even in her dreams, suddenly relaxed and she exhaled, not even realizing that she had been holding her breath.

The exchange was not yet complete. Nonchalantly the boar stepped toward the dead sow, took the knife, and wiped it on his curly bristles, one of his hoofs then reaching into a secret sac, pulling out its long curly penis that began to swell and pulsate before her eyes. A brief tug, and the organ fell off, just like that, as it would in a dream, without any pain.

She stared at the boar, it grinned as if they had just closed a deal. Then her dream body bent over, almost devoutly picked up the still-throbbing phallus from the ground and swallowed it effortlessly, despite its size. It slipped into her womb with such ease as if this was its sole purpose. She closed her eyes and felt the pig's embryo and phallus fusing within her womb, replacing the useless fetus she had been carrying along with her through so many pregnancies — the empty, unnecessary female chromosome deficit.

* * *

She woke up sweating at six, got number one and number two off to school, then went back to bed and pulled the covers over her head. Matevž's side of the bed was empty and cold. Nobody had slept in it, and she had clearly gone through last night's nightmare alone. The tension in her belly had eased and even though she ought to be entirely shaken up by her dream, she was unusually calm and set about her daily tasks as if on autopilot. Matevž only appeared after lunch, pulling out of the car a wheelchair for his mother who seemed almost triumphant when Lidija noticed her from the window as she was washing the dishes. How could she not be — a few minutes before Matevž a whole array of other relatives had driven into the yard, even some they never saw, which must mean that her mother-in-law was dying again and organizing one of her *ante mortem* funeral processions.

Lidija felt like drawing the curtains and hiding in the increasing darkness of the winter evening, ignoring the costume parade and drama into which such effort was being put on the stage below her. She imagined them all, sitting on benches next to the tiled stove, wooden chairs in the kitchen and the old sagging sofa in the living room that was made for a large family, waiting around for the lights to go out. Behind her numbers one, two, four, and five were playing cards, without paying much attention to what was happening all around them, sensing the tense and gloomy atmosphere descending upon the house. Only number three, sitting on the kitchen sideboard, dangling her legs, rushed across to her card-playing sisters as soon as she saw Matevž's sister's Volkswagen, shouting, "Nives has come! Mummy, Mummy, can I go and see Gran?"

A cold silence prevailed at the table, especially between Lidija and her eldest daughters who gulped, knowing only too well what this sentence meant, and also why they didn't hear it often. Lidija nodded silently. A weary-looking Matevž burst into the kitchen with a wave of cold, announcing that everyone was gathered in the lower floor.

Nobody seemed bothered that they had been hanging around for a whole hour without anyone even coming to greet them, Lidija thought to herself bitterly, then untied her apron and pulled her loose tunic lower over her belly with the conscious mass of cells swimming inside, knowing very well what the first lines of today's drama were going to be.

"Hello, Lidija, you're not pregnant *again*, are you?"

Matevž's family and relations boasted the double-edged attribute of saying everything out loud and so, before the entire room could start speculating and things got out of hand, Lidija nodded apologetically and withdrew into the shadows of the kitchen, even though she knew that escaping Nives, who had taken on the role of hostess for the evening, would bring no relief — if anything, it might have the opposite effect.

Number three hopped around Matevž's sister's feet — "Can I help, can I help?" — generally obstructing her task of piling cheese and salami onto platters while her son sat on a chair next to her, stuffing himself with chocolate.

As soon as she had arrived she had commented to Lidija, "Wow, I really don't know how you can bear this, such lively children. She's so full of energy."

Lidija had to force herself to stare at some undefined spot on the kitchen wall not to look away, then she sent number three into the living room to play with the other children, among whom her daughters were still the majority.

"I couldn't put up with that many children," Nives said, vehemently grabbing some platters piled up with what looked like ready-made food and carrying them off into the living room.

EVA MARKUN

Lidija sat number five down on the bench. The girl promptly reached for a piece of cheese. In the silence interrupted only by the sound of scoffing chocolate, Lidija began setting out the next platter, waiting for the chance to use a headache or a dirty diaper as an excuse to go back to her bedroom. She kept being interrupted by various uncles, calling out, "Another girl! I didn't even know you were pregnant again! Which number are we on now? Third, fourth? Are you planning on continuing turning them out until you get a son? It's stale sperm, I tell you, you're not having enough sex!" Until her mother-in-law silenced them by banging her stick on the wooden floor, demanding they pay attention to her and her alone. A cue to exit the scene, Lidija beckoned to Matevž and took numbers five and four upstairs to sleep.

As they all lay stretched across the bed, Lidija stared at the ceiling, listening to the sound of her two youngest daughters' breathing, holding her hand on her belly, thinking about the pigs. She wondered what they in fact wanted from her with those intelligent gazes from the depths of their black eyes, as if they were aware that in a month's time or so, they will be hanging, skinned and bled in the cellar next to the barn, dripping into the sewer. For no other purpose than for Matevž being able to buy his next sow and next boar, then put all the rest of the money into the farm that will in the end go to Nives anyway, Nives with that large munching son of hers. As if we are living in the fourteenth century, damn it, and patriarchal society with its huge clubs and armor is once again at the height of power, only waiting to yet again smash upon someone's head.

But her hand on her belly was in a way calming. Isn't it funny? The chance that this time, for a change, she might have hit that Y chromosome was ridiculously small and nothing had helped over the years, neither finding the date of ovulation, nor changing the pH of her vaginal mucosa, nor drinking god-knows-what tea that helped Matevž's aunt give birth to three sons in succession. All these years of living with the false conviction that it might all be better, that perhaps an xy instead of an xx will bring some change into this tragedy! Still, a small part of her held on to those phallic dreams and the unspoken arrangement with the pig — as if the mud-rolling beast could see deep inside her and tried to give her that missing part, something that was totally meaningless and could not help her, but that continuously kept sacrificing her on the altar of traditional ideology, to which nobody was openly purporting to adhere but everyone partook in with their well-intentioned advice.

* * *

At the next episode of her dear mother-in-law's death throes, when it was once again her turn to carry buckets of slop to the pigsty, she counted the pigs for fun. At first, she paid no attention to the dreams that had ruined her night, but this time something troubled her. She tried to pick out the sows in among the other curly-haired pigs, while the boar stood almost calmly by the fence, watching her. There should have been three sows, but even though she counted all the pigs at least six times, she could only find two. Both of them gazed at her with the same look — a mix of annoyance and curiosity as to why, after they had eaten all the slops in the trough, she was still standing there, staring at them. Lidija shook her head, put the empty buckets back into the wheelbarrow, all dirty with mud, though this time the dirt and the stench didn't bother her. She opened the gate and in a surprising surge of boldness, stepped in among the pigs and went right up to the sty.

The pigs gathered around her, sniffing her jacket pockets where there was still some dried bread. Her hands shaking, Lidija offered them the crusts. The barrows almost jumped at them and then totally forgot about her. The sows and the boar that had been watching what was going on from the corner of the pen, standing up to their knees in mud, came closer to her, extending their snouts. It was only then that Lidija noticed that the sows were pregnant and that, at least judging by their swollen teats, they were not far off farrowing.

"Would it be a problem if this time you left the sows?" she asked Matevž once they got all the kids off to bed and it looked as if Matevž would have to go off to look after his mother again. "I think they are pregnant."

Wiping his face on his sleeve, Matevž gave her a bemused look. "What now, thinking of breeding pigs are you? Look, I don't know. They are hard to sell, nobody knows this breed, you see. . . . I thought we would slaughter them and get some ordinary pigs next year, it's bad enough that everyone is already complaining that the meat this year will be different."

She raised her eyebrows.

"Well, if you want to? But you will tend to them, I have plenty of other shit."

Yes, Lidija thought bitterly to herself once he left, shit is the right word. Shit and mud, and we're all up to our knees in it, not only the pigs. And she placed her hand on her belly, on number six, closing her eyes, sensing that growing inside her was something else, not merely a mass of cells, something incomprehensible, some duty, a kind of debt, as if she had to atone for the dreams, as if she was indebted for something — and to whom? The pigs! She couldn't get it out of her mind.

She never talked to anyone about her growing belly — she didn't dare to, nor had the time. Despite the continuing cold, she took along with her waddling number five and hopping number four, so they all had frozen noses as they pushed the wheelbarrow stacked with wood and nails, trying to repair the sty as best they could. Sod the Y chromosome, Lidija rolled her eyes at the comments of Matevž's relatives who looked upon her with pity, as if she had gone mad — it was not encoded in their nature that a woman might know how to wield a hammer or a battery-powered drill, let alone a handsaw; and she found it convenient that she had an excuse not to have to hang around the stage following the tragicomic drama of the dying mother-in-law in three acts and an epilogue.

She did have to, after a long time, occasionally call her father and listen to ten minutes of ranting about her useless husband before she could ask him how to look after a pregnant sow, but in the end it was worth something. The ramshackle pigsty was temporarily patched up — though, with everyone's rude comments about it, it was astonishing it did not collapse — and the sows were, somewhat to their surprise, moved into it. Matevž just shrugged his shoulders and allowed her to get on with it.

EVA MARKUN

"Do you know what?" number thee eventually muttered at her. "If you can build a pigsty, you could also make me a bed."

Lidija glanced at her sideways. "And the mattress? Where am I supposed to find one?"

"If you get her out of my bed, we'll think of a way," said number two hopefully. "She peed in bed the other night."

Lidija had to smile. "Well, only if I find the right wood. I know that Grandpa saved some somewhere. But you will have to help me with the pigs, right?"

It was funny how they undertook their tasks without any objection when she explained the mathematics: number three counted the piglets that had yet to be born and converted them into notional sums of money, then into notional lists of things she needed — shoes, blankets, bedclothes for her new bed — so they cooked, mixed, and carried buckets of slops almost without complaint, and the pigs got fatter and fatter. Lidija didn't want to tell the girls how soon they would be ready for slaughter. Despite the announcement of the imminent visit of the Death Reaper, her mother-in-law was sharpening the knives and preparing the slaughter tubs as if this was the last thing she had to do in this world before departing for a better one, her last act *par excellence* in life, her ceremonial sacrifice of Matevž's pigs for the welfare of the entire wider family.

"You did tell her about the sows, didn't you?" Lidija asked him one day, sick of listening to the sound of knives being ground. "You did explain that we won't slaughter the sows?"

Matevž raised his head from the paperwork he was engrossed in and looked at her, his eyes at about the level of her belly, so she shifted uncomfortably and hid it under the blanket.

"Yes, I did," he muttered and returned to concentrating on the numbers.

"But did she hear you?"

The only answer she got was the shuffling of papers and the scratching of his pencil.

*　*　*

For a moment the grinding ceased and in the dead silence Lidija drove off to her gynecologist with number five in the car seat next to her and number four in the back seat. She then drove back without being any better informed about the purpose of it all or the gender of her child, but despite this, loaded up with prenatal vitamins and a bunch of bottles of iron supplements, as if it would help her. On their way back she tried to figure out whether the potatoes were already cooked enough so she might carry the swill off to the sty as soon as the girls fell asleep, as they were half-asleep in the car anyway, both nibbling on a bread roll.

She could smell the blood even before she drove into the yard. Knots in her stomach and her bile somewhere close to the upper part of her esophagus, she unbuckled the girls from their seats and carefully placed them on the frozen ground. They plodded off like storks, holding on to the weathered walls of the barn to the ramp below it. They had almost reached the corner when a subhuman scream so full of pain cut through the air that they all stopped and held their breath.

Lidija would normally send the girls back into the apartment and switch on a marathon of cartoons at full volume, but this time a single thought echoed through her mind: not my sows, please, not my sows. She left number five and number six, petrified and holding hands, at the corner of the barn and ran to the ramp, trying to keep her gallbladder inside her body with her hand. She reached the building, stepped over a stream of blood that was trickling through the half-open gate to the pen, and looked straight into the eyes of the dying pig, rasping and wheezing asthmatically, catching the last gulps of oxygen that were escaping through the gaping slash in its neck. She sensed that it wanted to move, deep inside her feeling the pain that was overcoming its entire existence, as if it was part of her, and she gasped for air herself, feeling the same numbness as the pig that was being held firmly by Matevž and his uncle, so it couldn't move.

Matevž looked up and in his gaze she could sense a shadow of guilt, then he saw the girls making their way through the junk on the ramp toward the dying animal.

"Get them inside," he growled, still holding on to the wheezing pig. "They don't need to see this."

And Lidija numbly obeyed. She didn't think the girls had even seen anything and they went to bed, forgetting entirely about their usual groaning, probably sensing how upset she was, how nervy. Her hands shook so much she could barely hold up the good-night story which kept moving about as if sailing on a rough sea instead of a warm blanket. The moment they finally closed their eyes and their breathing calmed, she leaped outside — in such a hurry that she even forgot her coat and the baby monitor they normally used for the two younger daughters.

The men below the barn were just tidying up as the pig carcasses hung on hooks in the cellar, bleeding onto the dung heap.

It was so cold her fingers hurt and when she pushed open the heavy door and was hit by the smell of boiling water and excrement, she stared sadly at the men and the pigs dangling from the hooks behind them. She didn't need to count them — there were six — to know what had happened.

And inside her, amidst all that cleaning of intestines and scraping at skin, an emptiness grew, a kind of endless cosmic hole threatening to devour her. Her hands trembling, she ignored their remarks. "Lidija, are you pregnant again? You look a little rounded again! Will it be another girl? Will you wash the intestines, Lidija?" She went straight to Matevž, who was leaning against the wall with a bottle of brandy, pouring himself another shot.

"You promised," she said, voice shaking in the low tone they had adopted for conversations in the house where there was not a millimeter of private space and where everyone knew everything, even the frequency and duration of your average crap.

Matevž looked at her with the glazed look he always had when they slaughtered pigs. He didn't dare place a knife on the pig's neck when sober, he really didn't.

"Are you pregnant?" he asked in the same low voice.

Lidija turned on her heel, stomping out of the barn past the kilos upon kilos of hanging meat to satisfy his relations, past the kilos and kilos of his relations that only came whenever there was something to take away with them, and they took a lot — apples, potatoes, pork.

As she scrambled into the yard she realized she was shaking. All the muscles in her body were trembling — she wasn't sure whether it was from the cold or her rage. Apart from this she didn't feel anything, just spasms going through her limbs. Standing at the far end of the yard were Nives and Matevž's mother, next to them in the thick cold of the winter's day, spread out on the plastic tablecloth were various porcine organs and a meat grinder.

"Nives, where's the uterus?" asked her mother-in-law, feeling her way through the meat in front of her, unable to find it. "We could cook it for dinner tonight."

"It's here somewhere," muttered Nives, rummaging through the mess of internal organs. "No, that's the liver. . . . I must have misplaced it in one of these piles."

For a moment Lidija felt like leaping out into the yard, dipping her hands into the still-warm, pulsating meat, grabbing it, sticky with mucus and muscle membranes, ramming it right down Nives's and her mother-in-law's throats until it piled up in their stomachs. Their endless demand for offal, fried liver and kidneys, boiled pig's snouts and trotters, floating in broth like boats going out to sea! She wanted to pour these internal organs all over them until they suffocated in their endless greed for every single piece of pork! She closed her eyes and almost cried out, seeing before her a very vivid scene of her mother-in-law, a plate in front of her with a baked pig embryo neatly presented with sprigs of parsley and some of Lidija's vegetables from the garden arranged around it. Crunching as she sticks her fork into it, seeing her carve out of the roast the blind unborn eye, popping it into her toothless mouth with a sigh of otherworldly pleasure.

Before she could no longer hide it, Lidija, despite the emptiness she felt inside, turned and hurried round the corner toward the pigsty so they would not see and make fun of the expression on her face or the hours and hours of pointless work, her daughters' thousand hopes, which were all swallowed up by the universal fundamental need for pork: fried, boiled, roasted. She buried her hands in her armpits to warm them up and went across to the pigsty, almost automatically, as if needing a place where she could scream all the curses that had been building up inside her for years. She just wanted to pass by, see the empty pen, the entirely emptied pigsty, but suddenly her foot stalled and then she slipped. The path was so frozen that she simply lost her balance, fell on the icy surface, crashing straight onto her pelvis. The fall punched the air out of her lungs.

Crying out in pain, she held her belly. She had the feeling something had ripped apart within and crashed to the ground with a scream and the clatter of cracked porcelain. The pain was so intense she could not move for a moment. She was totally paralyzed, overwhelmed by the scattering of matter inside her, wrapping her into an icy cold that surged through her bosom to her eyes, forcing her to close them. The very next moment she began fighting, as if in doing so, in getting up again, she might save the being inside her, prevent it from aborting. She put all her effort into sliding farther down the ice so she could straighten herself and hold on to the fence next to the road. Her hands shook and she grabbed on to the post but could not raise herself up. The cramp in her uterus was so terrible she bit her lip until it bled. Gasping for air, she tried to bend over to at least slightly alleviate the pain but her body wouldn't allow her to — stiffened, her legs twitched painfully, trying to find at least some support, until the pain stopped just as suddenly as it had begun and she felt a fluid warmth in her groin.

EVA MARKUN

She stood up weakly, felt the oozing liquid between her thighs, though she knew very well what she would find. Then came a deluge from her lacrimal glands through which she barely managed to feel her way across to the pigsty.

It was over. Goodbye number six.

She managed to crawl across to the wooden sty; burning with pain, she no longer felt the cold and pushed herself through the door where the only survivor, the huge boar, looked at her with those cold eyes that knew precisely what this was about. Lidija collapsed onto the straw which looked just as clean as on the day she and the girls carefully spread it there — pigs are surprisingly extremely clean animals, at least to the point where they don't defecate in the same place they sleep. She curled up. The boar lay motionless at the far end, its breath creating clouds inside the makeshift refuge. He didn't move, mourning the devoured promise, staring into the unuttered emptiness of his continued existence.

The first contractions came sooner than she expected — or she had simply lost her sense of time. As she bled over her only decent pair of trousers until her lost child soaked them totally, the sun set, though the moon had yet to rise. Through the gap in her eyelashes as she closed her eyes to endure the pain in her lower back, she silently counted the stars that were lazily moving across the sky.

She faintly wondered whether it should have lasted longer when another jolt shook her so she couldn't help herself crying out and her body pushed the redundant child out, as far away as it could. She felt it on the skin in her groin. She tore her trousers off and immediately the fluid, blood, and the tiny embryo with the placenta trickled out with one last push into the cold winter night.

Then her body stopped, stopped and numbed in the emptiness that overwhelmed her, just like after giving birth. She rubbed her almost frozen eyelashes and felt around with her hand until she found the tiny body among the straw. Shaking, she managed to place it in the palm of her hand and move it toward the weak light coming through the window.

The cluster of cells was already defined — it had a kind of fish-human shape, tiny feet and hands, and still-closed eyes. The head looked abnormally large for its tiny body — the entire thing, together with its gray-pink skin and blueish veins, was no bigger than a lemon or a sour measly apple. Her child. In the bad light she could barely make out its gender before she gently let go.

She looked at the boar in the corner who only now totally disinterestedly raised his head.

"I'm sorry," she said, voice rasping before taking a step forward, her legs in the soggy and cold socks shaking like a newborn lamb.

"I am returning this to you," she added, bending over, carefully placing the tiny corpse in front of the creature, as if sacrificing a long-owed offering to some unidentified entity whose surrogate was lying in front of her.

The huge boar stared silently at her across the mass of his curly white hair, then he peered at the carcass lying in front of him. He sniffed it with his enormous snout, not once but a number of times, as if trying to figure out what had been placed before him. Then he produced a long squeal similar to those that had been coming all morning from the cellar, opened his

EVA MARKUN

mouth and gobbled up the tiny body in a single sway of his huge jaw. The cluster of cells disappeared in between his giant tusks and down his gullet.

Translated by GREGOR TIMOTHY ČEH

Originally published in the short stories collection
Menažerija (JSKD, 2017)

Contributor Biographies

ANDREJ BLATNIK (1963) is a writer, editor, and university professor. He writes mainly short stories and novels. In his work he explores the various aspects of especially romantic relationships, their misunderstandings, reconciliations, and the impossibility of completely understanding each other, depicting them with humor, irony, and a bit of melancholy. His style is laconic and minimalistic in expression, intertwined with metatextual elements. He received the Prešeren Foundation Award in 2002, was nominated for the Cankarjeva Award (2021), and was shortlisted for the Kresnik Award (2009) and the Novo Mesto Short Award (2019).

SERGEJ CURANOVIĆ (1980) works as a translator and lives abroad. His stories, collected under the title *Plavalec* (The Swimmer), differ in length, character, and atmosphere. They are written in a concise and precise style and range from an intense dialogue-driven detective story about a series of mysterious kidnappings to a report on a mystical event in a sea turned desert to an ambitious prehistoric road-trip story on memory and human universals to a piece about two writers dueling for their essence by writing a story about each other. He was awarded the 2020 Novo Mesto Award.

DUŠAN ČATER (1968) is a writer, translator, screenwriter, and editor. He has worked as a columnist for several Slovenian newspapers and magazines, and has been a freelance writer since 1995. He has written scripts for television programs and several original plays. The typical narrator of his novels and short stories is a bohemian writer who writes tongue-in-cheek accounts of his everyday adventures, spiced with eroticism and intoxicating substances. He was nominated for the Kresnik Award in 2003 and won the Fabula Award in 2012.

NEJC GAZVODA (1985) started his career as a writer with *Vevericam nič ne uide* (Nothing Escapes the Squirrels, 2004; winner of the Fabula Award for short stories collection) when he was still in high school, and became recognized as a voice of a generation. The feeling of alienation in his work is often portrayed as verging on the absurd. He has finished his study as a film and TV director and is also a scriptwriter, a playwright, and a theater director. He was nominated three times for the Kresnik Award (2007, 2008, 2010).

POLONA GLAVAN (1974) is a novelist, short story writer, and translator. She is renowned as a keen traveler, and it was her travel experiences that first inspired her to write. This inspiration is discernible in her short story collection *Gverilci* (Guerillas, 2004), where she prioritizes the sharing of deeply intimate human experiences. Her typical protagonists are everyday, mostly lower-class people fighting their personal battles in the background of the contemporary social situation. She was shortlisted for the Kresnik Award in 2002 and again in 2015.

TADEJ GOLOB (1967) has a thematically very diverse scope of works. Being an avid alpine climber, he appeared among the writers with the book *Z Everesta* (From Everest), where he describes Dave Karničar skiing from the highest mountain of the world, a mountain that the writer also ascended. He continued his career by writing biographies and novels, until redefining his style by writing a successful series of crime novels that were also turned into a television series. He received the 2010 Kresnik Award and was nominated again in 2014, 2017, and 2019.

DRAGO JANČAR (1948) is the best-known Slovenian writer, playwright, and essayist both at home and abroad, and one of the most translated Slovenian authors. He worked as a journalist, freelance writer, and movie script editor and writer. During his long career he received multiple awards and nominations, at home and abroad. He was awarded the Kresnik Award four times (1999, 2001, 2011, 2018), the Prešeren Foundation Award (1979), and the Prešeren Award for his opus in 1993. Jančar's novels, essays, and short stories have been translated into twenty-one languages.

BORIS KOLAR (1960) is an ecologist, ecotoxicologist, and an international expert on environmental risks. These are also the themes he explores through his short stories, which often depict the consequences of human actions on their environment. He is known for his humorous novels and short stories that feature mostly animal protagonists. His writings are in touch with nature, bright, and, above all, humorous. His debut novel, *Iqball Hotel*, was shortlisted for the Kresnik Award in 2009.

TOMAŽ KOSMAČ (1965) started publishing his literary texts in 1987. The protagonists of his short stories, which are his speciality, with their feet in the mud but their heads in the sky, mock everything they have turned their backs on of their own volition, including the world they would least like to be rescued from. He has a distinctive theme that could be paraphrased as "alcohol and people from the margins of society", but described with (self)irony and humor. He was nominated for the Fabula Award for best short stories collection in 2010.

MOJCA KUMERDEJ (1964) is a writer, philosopher, and publicist. She has also published critical pieces on contemporary dance, performance, theater, film, and intermedia art. In her stories, through the perspectives of a rich cast of characters, the inner frays and stitches of the human individual and the contemporary society are revealed with scintillating sharpness and witty interplay. Her protagonists are people living in the grip of desire, which determines and at the same time overwhelms them. She was the winner of the Prešeren Foundation Award and was shortlisted for the Kresnik Award, both in 2017.

VESNA LEMAIĆ (1981) has published three short story collections and two novels. In her writing, she explores life complexities, rooted in a social reality where even ordinary situations can reveal layers of unexpected meaning. Her books are populated by a variety of characters, from young activist to a retired officer of Yugoslav army. The narrative of her prose is playful, defined by metaphors and twists. She received the Slovenian Book Fair Award for Best Literary Debut (2009), the Fabula Award (2010), and the Novo Mesto Short Award (2019).

MIRANA LIKAR (1961) works as a writer and teacher. She writes short stories and novels, often centered around multiple generations. In her work she tries to describe how big historical events, such as wars, as well as small ones, often seen as insignificant, have an impact not only on the life of the individual but also that of their descendants. Her stories seldom rely on coincidences but result from the inexplicable paths of destiny. She has been shortlisted for the Fabula Award (2011), the Kresnik Award (2021), and the Cankarjeva Award (2021).

JEDRT MALEŽIČ (1979) is a writer and literary translator. Through her work she demystifies the topic of staying in a psychiatric hospital as a totalitarian institution in the twenty-first century and discusses diverse LGBT communities and their existence in a closed or hostile society. She has also written three novels, tackling respectively the New Age mentality, historic refugees, and lesbian divorce with a child. She has received nominations for the Kresnik Award (2022) and Novo Mesto Short Award (2017).

EVA MARKUN (1990) is the youngest writer in this anthology. The open endings of her stories often leave the narration in suspense at the moment of resolution or thickening of tension. The events in the stories are linked by a subtle thread that revolves around the relationship between nature and man, the position of women in contemporary societies, and the incoherence of individual perspectives that fail to find a common language. Her short story collection *Menažerija* (The Menagerie) received the 2018 Novo Mesto Award.

MIHA MAZZINI (1961) has published more than thirty books in Slovenia, which have been translated into twelve languages. He is also a screenwriter and a filmmaker of award-winning short and feature films. One of his short stories won the Pushcart Prize in 2012. His novels and movies deal with the themes people would rather not speak about, from the bizarre musical craze of Mexican music under Yugoslav Communism to the tragic fate of the citizens that the Slovenian government erased from the files. He received the Kresnik Award (2016) and was shortlisted for the Fabula Award (2011) and the Novo Mesto Award (2019).

VINKO MÖDERNDORFER (1958) studied at the Academy of Theatre, Radio, Film and Television (AGRFT) in Ljubljana and worked in numerous theater companies around Slovenia. To date, he has directed over one hundred productions. He is also active as a film, television, and radio director. He started writing in the late 1970s and his complete works total over ninety published books of poetry, prose fiction (for adults and children), plays, and essays. He is the recipient of the 2000 Prešeren Foundation Award and was nominated for the Cankarjeva Award in 2020.

DESA MUCK (1955) works as a freelance artist and writer and is also known as a film and TV personality. Her literary oeuvre consists mainly of works for young people and children, but she also writes for adults. She is known for her humorously colored fictional works in which she skillfully combines tension, humor, and the problems of young (and not-so-young) adults. Some of her books were made into movies and TV series. She also writes comics, movie scripts, radio plays, and texts for the theater. Her work has been translated into thirteen languages.

ANJA MUGERLI'S (1984) writing is subtle, with deep psychological insights into the protagonists of her stories, who are often faced with the impossibility of real closeness even with those who are, emotionally or through family ties, supposed to be the closest. The inner anxiety of the characters is often represented in the form of objects, elevated to the level of symbols. She was shortlisted for the Kresnik Award (2018) and the Novo Mesto Award (2020). In 2021, her short prose collection *Čebelja družina* (Bee Family) won the European Union Prize for Literature.

MAJA NOVAK (1960) is a writer, translator, and journalist. She studied business law at the University of Ljubljana and worked as a business secretary in Jordan. She started publishing short stories in the early 1990s. They were later published in the collection *Zverjad* (Wild Beasts, 1996), where she redefines and twists the structure of different literary genres through the use of irony and elements of the grotesque. For *Zverjad* and the novel *Cimre* she received the 1997 Prešeren Foundation Award; *Cimre* was also shortlisted for the Kresnik Award.

SEBASTIJAN PREGELJ (1970) has been publishing stories in literary publications since 1992. His literary world is inhabited by dreamlike sequences and archetypal figures connected by the same recognizable narrative voice that interlaces inner perspectives with outside observations, creating a feeling of "distant proximity". In his newer works the blurring line between fantasy and reality was replaced by an interest in a more realistic, historically based storytelling. He also writes children's literature. He received the Cankarjeva Award in 2020 and has been nominated multiple times for the Kresnik Award (2005, 2009, 2011, 2015, 2020).

ARJAN PREGL (1973) studied fine art. Besides writing prose, he also works as a visual and conceptual artist. He says for himself that he "paints with words and writes with images". His visual work responds to everyday sociopolitical events, but also to the history of painting. His writing can also emerge in dialogue with visual art, often verging on experimental visual prose. He uses a variety of techniques and tries to tackle problematic situations in a humorous and ironic way, using wordplays, and intertextual references.

CONTRIBUTOR BIOGRAPHIES

ANDRAŽ ROŽMAN (1983) usually writes about marginalized people. He worked as a journalist for more than fifteen years. He published his first literary nonfiction book in 2019; *Three Memories – between Haifa, Aleppo and Ljubljana*, a story about a Syrian-Palestinian poet and publisher, was nominated for the Kresnik Award. In 2022 he published a the novel *Tito's Son*, a story of mental health, psychiatric institutions, deinstitutionalization, hearing voices, psychoanalysis, and homelessness. He is strongly connected to the alternative public spaces of Ljubljana.

ANA SCHNABL (1985) is a writer and translator who used to work as a journalist. In her work she depicts her protagonists through a stream of consciousness like narrative that most often reveals unresolvable tensions, disclosed in the form of almost imperceptible language slips that underline the discrepancy between what is said, what is meant and everything that stays unspoken or alluded to. She received the award for Best Literary Debut in 2017 and was nominated for the Novo Mesto Award in 2018.

VERONIKA SIMONITI (1967) started writing as a storyteller for Radio Slovenia. In her precise, eruptive, and nuanced language, she tackles various projections of social and personal fears. The protagonists find themselves in a world that has abandoned them or with which they can no longer make genuine contact, and so they flee elsewhere, most often into memories or imagination or deep into their unconscious. The stories are crafted in a carefully ambiguous language and often presented with an unexpected twist. She was nominated for the Kresnik Award in

2015 and later won it in 2020. The same year she was also nominated for the Novo Mesto Award.

ANDREJ E. SKUBIC (1967) is a novelist, playwright, and translator. His novels range in style from realistic stories — sometimes focusing on intimate human relationships, sometimes on contemporary social conflicts — to satires and dystopias. His unreliable narrators, often at odds with a world that they do not entirely understand, often sway between hilarity and tragedy, reason and absurdity. He has received the Kresnik Award three times (2000, 2012, 2015), the award for Best Literary Debut (2000), and the 2012 Prešeren Foundation Award.

DUŠAN ŠAROTAR (1968) is a writer, poet, screenwriter, and photographer. Since 2012, he has been actively developing and exhibiting his photography cycle entitled *Souls*. His photographs are also part of the permanent collection of the Murska Sobota Gallery. The focal themes in his most recent writing are the fate of the Jewish community and the Holocaust in Murska Sobota and Prekmurje. He has been shortlisted for the Kresnik Award three times (2008, 2015, 2022).

AGATA TOMAŽIČ (1977) is a writer and columnist. She currently works at the Research Centre of the Slovenian Academy of Sciences and Arts and keeps in touch with her audience as an avid tweeter. Her prose is witty, with linguistic and stylistic sophistication and content that intrigues with its unpredictability and the bizarreness of everyday life, intertwining horror and humor. Her characters often hide their contempt and loneliness behind a socially acceptable mask, thus revealing what can lie beneath the surface of correctness. In 2021 she was nominated for the Novo Mesto Award.

SUZANA TRATNIK (1963) is a writer, translator, activist, and sociologist. She has been a lesbian activist since 1987, and is a cofounder of Škuc-Lezbična sekcija LL, the first lesbian group in Eastern Europe, and much of her work continues to focus upon LGBT activism and scholarship. The two main themes in her fiction are the marginal destinies in contemporary urban life and presentations of childhood in 1960s and 1970s Yugoslavia. She received the Novo Mesto Short Award for best short stories collection in 2017 and the Prešeren Foundation Award in 2007. She has also been shortlisted twice for the Kresnik Award (2008 and 2020).

JANI VIRK (1962) writes novels, short stories, poetry, essays, and scripts. He works at the national television RTV Slovenia as Editor of the Drama Department. In his texts he deals with solitary individuals devoured by feelings of inadequacy and loneliness, who see m unfit for the role society has attributed to them. In the search for meaning (and, sometimes, love) they often find themselves walking on the edge of an existential void. He is also the author of many documentary and travel films.

GORAN VOJNOVIĆ (1980) is a writer and columnist, as well as a film and theater director. He is best known for his 2008 novel Čefurji raus! (Southern Scum Go Home), which won him numerous awards, including the 2009 Prešeren Foundation

Award. This novel was also the basis for a theater and film adaptation. In his novels he often tackles the themes of childhood, family, the past, nostalgia, and the world of short memories and long delusions. He is the author of four feature films and several theater plays. He has won the Kresnik Award three times (2009, 2013, 2017) and was nominated again in 2022.

Translator Biographies

JASON BLAKE teaches in the English Department at the University of Ljubljana. His translations from German and Slovenian have appeared in Dalkey Archive Press's *Best European Fiction*, and his translation of Jasmin Frelih's novel *In/Half* was published by Oneworld Publications. Blake is also the author of *Slovenia: Culture Smart!*

HUGH BROWN was born in Andover in 1968. Educated at Downside School in Somerset, he went on to read Classics at Merton College, Oxford. He moved to Ljubljana in 1994 and later lived in Verona, Barcelona and Alghero (Sardinia) before settling in Trieste in 2014. He is a freelance translator, translating from Slovenian and Italian.

GREGOR TIMOTHY ČEH

Gregor Timothy Čeh was brought up in a bilingual family in Slovenia. He studied Archaeology and History of Art at UCL, taught English in Greece, returned to England to complete a Master's degree at Kent, and now lives in Cyprus. He translates contemporary Slovene literature for publishing houses and authors in Slovenia, with translations published in both the UK and US.

RAWLEY GRAU has translated numerous works from Slovenian, including novels by Dušan Šarotar, Mojca Kumerdej, and Sebastijan Pregelj. Two of his prose translations were shortlisted for the Oxford-Weidenfeld Prize, and in 2021, he received the Lavrin Diploma for excellence in translation from the Association of Slovenian Literary Translators. Originally from Baltimore, Maryland, he has lived in Ljubljana since the early 2000s.

NADA MARIJA GROŠELJ received a joint BA degree in English and Latin from the University of Ljubljana and obtained a PhD in linguistics in 2005. Since 2005, she has been registered as a freelance translator. She mainly translates from English, Latin, and Swedish into Slovene, and from Slovene into English. Her book-length translations include the fields of literature, literary theory, philosophy, theology, and mythology. Her translations into Slovene have been recognized with several awards.

JEREMI SLAK graduated from the Faculty of Arts in Ljubljana. He has been translating scholarly texts, poetry, and prose for two decades. His noted translations include *Of Freedom and God*, a contemplation on liberty by the essayist Marjan Rožanc; the poetry of Vilenica Award-winner Antonella Bukovaz; *Soul of Slovenia*, an anthology of literary classics; and the monograph *Vipavska*.

About Sandorf Passage

SANDORF PASSAGE publishes work that creates a prismatic perspective on what it means to live in a globalized world. It is a home to writing inspired by both conflict zones and the dangers of complacency. All Sandorf Passage titles share in common how the biggest and most important ideas are best explored in the most personal and intimate of spaces.